Also by Cathleen Schine

Fin & Lady

The Three Weissmanns of Westport

The New Yorkers

She Is Me

The Evolution of Jane

The Love Letter

Rameau's Niece

To the Birdhouse

Alice in Bed

They May Not Mean To, But They Do

They May Not Mean To, But They Do

Cathleen Schine

Sarah Crichton Books Farrar, Straus and Giroux New York

Sarah Crichton Books
Farrar, Straus and Giroux
18 West 18th Street, New York 10011

Grateful acknowledgment is made for permission to reprint lines from
"This Be The Verse" from *The Complete Poems of Philip Larkin* by Philip Larkin,
edited by Archie Burnett. Copyright © 2012 by The Estate of Philip Larkin.
Reprinted by permission of Farrar, Straus and Giroux, LLC.

Library of Congress Cataloging-in-Publication Data
Names: Schine, Cathleen, author.
Title: They may not mean to, but they do : a novel / Cathleen Schine.
Description: First edition. | New York : Sarah Crichton Books/Farrar,
   Straus and Giroux, 2016.
Identifiers: LCCN 2015036418 | ISBN 9780374280130 (hardcover)
   | ISBN 9780374712204 (ebook)
Subjects: LCSH: Families—Fiction. | Domestic fiction. | BISAC: FICTION /
   Literary. | FICTION / Contemporary Women. | FICTION / Family Life.
Classification: LCC PS3569.C497 T46 2016 | DDC 813/.54—dc23
LC record available at http://lccn.loc.gov/2015036418

Designed by Abby Kagan

Our books may be purchased in bulk for promotional, educational, or business use.
Please contact your local bookseller or the Macmillan Corporate and Premium
Sales Department at 1-800-221-7945, extension 5442, or by e-mail at
MacmillanSpecialMarkets@macmillan.com.

www.fsgbooks.com
www.twitter.com/fsgbooks • www.facebook.com/fsgbooks

1 3 5 7 9 10 8 6 4 2

To my mother,
from whom and to whom
everything, always

They fuck you up, your mum and dad.
They may not mean to, but they do.

—from Philip Larkin,
    "This Be The Verse"

They May Not Mean To, But They Do

—— 1 ——

Molly Bergman moved to California, and it broke her mother's heart. There are daughters who spend their lives trying to escape their mothers, who move to their particular California the minute they're able to, who never stop moving to California. Molly was decidedly not one of those daughters. It was a painful move even before her parents got, so suddenly, so old.

Molly's mother was named Joy, and people said, Oh, they broke the mold when they made that one. People who loved her said it, people who did not love her said it, too, for the same reason. They found Joy disconcerting, and they were right. She was so intimate and so remote, as remote as a faraway, nameless planet sometimes; sometimes soft and sympathetic. She was talkative, yet she heard everything you said or thought you might say. She was wise and she was deep, intuitive, the kind of person to whom people confided their darkest secrets; she was scatterbrained and easily distractible and often forgot people's darkest secrets, which, she always said, was just as well.

She seemed to Molly, growing up, to be the busiest and most

important mother in New York City. Joy's work was her vocation, that's what Joy said when she was happy. When she was frustrated and tired, she said it was a velvet coffin without the velvet.

She was also beautiful, radiantly beautiful. Like a doe, fragile and supple and quick. She was blond, but her eyes were as brown as a doe's. When she smiled, everyone around her smiled, and she smiled a great deal, though it was often from abstraction rather than any particular moment of happiness. She loved New York because, she liked to say, she fit in with all the misfits.

Molly and her brother, Daniel, began their lives with Joy and their father, Aaron, in a two-bedroom apartment with dinette on the West Side of Manhattan, the dinette converted into a third bedroom. Their neighbors were immigrants from Eastern Europe, émigrés from Brooklyn, teachers and violinists and opera singers. You could hear the opera singers as you walked down Broadway, arias amid the car horns. There were mom-and-pop dress shops and dairy restaurants and bakeries, and Molly remembered the square rooms, the high ceilings, the shutters that folded in on themselves, the deep windowsills on which she used to sit and look out at the street. But when Molly was eight and her brother six, their father inherited his family's manufacturing business, and the Bergmans left West Eighty-ninth Street. Aaron said the West Side was becoming seedy.

There were fewer Eastern European immigrants and Brooklyn escapees on Park Avenue, no dairy restaurants, more gentiles. It was a quiet, civilized neighborhood, at least until late afternoon, when the private schools let out. Molly and Daniel still went to their progressive private school on the West Side, but when Molly got off the bus, she could already hear the commotion of the East Side children at the corner store. She always waited for them to leave the store before buying her own candy and secretly envied them their noisy cabal and, even more secretly, their school uniforms.

"Across the park is as far as we go," Joy declared. "No farther, Aaron."

Daniel did go a bit farther when he grew up. He and his wife, Coco, and their two little girls lived on the Lower East Side. That was inexplicable to Joy and Aaron, moving to the tenements their grandparents had left behind. Inexplicable, yes, but *accessible by subway*, Joy said to Molly. The Bergmans were New Yorkers, she said, had always been New Yorkers. This was a fact, in a way that Molly's move to Los Angeles could never be.

Each time Molly left New York after a visit, Joy felt the air go out of the city.

"You're too attached," one of her friends said. "My daughter lives in Australia."

Joy shuddered. A daughter in Australia might as well be a dead daughter. Divorce was a terrible thing, and she was sorry Molly had given up a perfectly reasonable husband so she could be a lesbian in California. It was peculiar, having a lesbian daughter, though plenty of her friends did, too, it turned out. But many things were peculiar in this world, and Joy had overcome her discomfort with Freddie. She even called her "my daughter-in-law" now. Freddie was a lot of fun, warm, kind, gainfully employed, and low-maintenance, everything a mother-in-law could ask for. Joy did not blame her for being a woman, or tried not to. Molly was happy, Joy could see that, and it warmed her heart.

But what good is a warmed heart if it is also broken? Joy's heart was broken. By California.

"California"—even the name had become ugly to Joy, like "Lee Harvey Oswald" or "Sirhan Sirhan."

Joy's parents had moved several times during the Depression, first to places where someone could take them in, then to places where they took others in. Each move was a shock to Joy, an almost physical jolt. So many people left behind—shopkeepers, neighbors, the policeman on the corner, the ladies sitting on their stoops. They were what made a place a home. There were so many things one had to give up in this world. Why would you choose to give up your home? For California?

Perhaps she should move to California, too. Aaron might not know the difference.

"Would you like to move to California, Aaron?"

"*Come if you dare, our trumpets sound,*" he sang. "*Come if you dare, the foes rebound . . .*"

He could not tell you what day it was, but he remembered his Purcell.

It was Sunday and she had ordered him a dinner of French toast from the coffee shop. New York was good for the elderly in that way, the deliveries. She had come to include Aaron in the category of "the elderly," she realized with a pang. And where does that leave me, she wondered vaguely. At any rate, it was too difficult sometimes to herd Aaron and his walker out of the apartment and down the street to the coffee shop. She could have made French toast, she supposed. If there had been eggs. Or bread. If she still cooked.

"Isn't there a joke, we could have ham and eggs if we had *ham* . . ."

". . . and we had *eggs!*"

They laughed, repeated it, "We could have ham and eggs . . ."

Aaron took a bite of French toast and made a face.

"You love French toast, Aaron, so stop it."

"Do I?"

He was hunched over the dining-room table. There was a bath mat on the seat of his chair as well as a blue chux pad. Joy leaned over and straightened them.

"You going to work today?" he said.

"No, dear, it's Sunday."

"Oh yeah?"

He took a bite of French toast and made another sour face.

"Stop that," she said. "Anyway, you need a haircut."

"You going to work today?" he said.

Sometimes Joy thought he was doing it on purpose. "No, not today. Today is Sunday."

"Oh yeah? What is this, anyway?" he said, poking at the French toast.

"Your dinner."

"I'm not hungry."

Joy grabbed his plate and brought it to the kitchen and scraped the French toast into the garbage.

"Joy! Joy!"

She stuck her head back into the dining room.

"You going to work today?" he asked.

"If you ask me that one more time, I'm putting a bag over your head," she said mildly.

Aaron brought his face down to the teacup and took a sip, then looked fondly at his wife. He pointed to the cup of almost colorless liquid. "Join me, sweetheart?"

He began to sing in his once clear voice, now heavy and hoarse. *"Tea for two, me for you . . ."*

He sang pleasantly to himself while Joy fetched herself a cup of tea, and they sat looking out at the traffic's red brake lights, something they'd both always found festive as the evening drew in.

Molly had been a daddy's girl when she was very young. Her father was the only father she knew who had a beard, and the beard, a neatly combed beard that came almost to a point, was her pride and joy. He would carry her inside his coat, against his chest, like a kangaroo, and she would snuggle her face against his, against that extraordinary beard. Her father and his beard were so obviously superior to other fathers with their flabby pink cheeks. Her father was superior in height, as well. He was so tall that she and Daniel used him as a unit of measurement. How many Daddies high was that tree in the park? What about the elephants at the Museum of Natural History? It was Aaron who read to them when they were little. Push-me-pull-yous and the cat's meat man; bump, bump, bump down the stairs—books that had been his, books he wished his father had read to him. He bundled up the children and led them to the roof to look at the constellations. He took them out to the park to climb the rocks and along the river to the boat basin to play pirates and launch paper boats that tipped and sank while they sang "Blow the Man Down." It was Aaron who encouraged them, egged them on, when they begged for a dog, Aaron who went to the animal shelter with them to get a cat when Joy had expressly forbidden it. Aaron's father had failed him when he was a child, too busy steering the business out of the Depression. Aaron would never do that to his children, he told Joy. True to his word, she would say later: it was the business he failed.

Aaron and Joy were so different from each other that Molly and Daniel had been able to recognize the distance even as young children, Aaron sentimental and unreliable and brimming with love and obvious charm, a man who made you feel you did not have to work too hard because good things were coming to you, from somewhere; Joy distracted, forgetful, thoughtful, brimming with love, too, and oddly inspiring, causing Molly and Daniel to want to work their hardest because working hard seemed such fun. Molly wasn't sure why she compared them to each other like that, as if she had to make a choice, as if she could make a choice, because different as they were, there was no choice between them, no space between them. They were as one. They held hands when they walked down the street, they fed each other tidbits like lovebirds. It was embarrassing for the children, having such lovey-dovey parents. And reassuring. Like the trumpeters and singers in the Bible, they were as one.

———— 3 ————

Y ou'd better come home," Joy said to Molly on the phone. "Daddy's on the floor."

"He fell?" Molly tried to calm herself. "Is he okay? Did you call 911?"

"He slid out of his chair. I never should have gotten it in leather. I gave him a cracker."

"Mom!"

"The handyman's coming in a minute. He'll get Daddy up. Never a dull moment, right, Aaron?"

The phone was handed to Aaron. "Never a dull moment."

"Daddy, are you all right?"

"Your mother gave me a cracker."

"I'll be home soon," Molly said. She repeated it when her mother got back on the phone. "I'll be home soon, Mom. I arranged an extra week off in November."

"November?" A pause. "Oh." Then, "Wonderful, Molly! And how are your students this semester?"

Molly heard the strain in her mother's voice and hurried through a rundown of some of the more interesting students. "Anyway, nothing to write home about."

"Daddy's having a hard time, Molly. He gets confused sometimes."

"I know. But he does have dementia."

"Don't be disrespectful."

Joy didn't like the word "dementia." "Alzheimer's" was worse.

"Sorry," Molly said. "I just meant, you know, it's natural that he'd be confused and forget things."

"Well, he doesn't like it. He doesn't like it one bit. And he doesn't admit it. Which is tiring for me, I can tell you."

"Maybe—"

"We can't afford it."

"Well, what about—"

"Absolutely not."

"Not a *home*, exactly—"

"He has a home," Joy said. "His home is here."

Molly poured herself two fingers of bourbon, just as her father had taught her. No bourbon for him these days, just Ensure, many fingers of Ensure.

"I should be home," she said to Freddie. "I'm a horrible daughter. I might as well shoot myself."

Freddie thought, You are home, Molly.

"How many times can the doorman scrape him off the floor? At least she tips them at Christmas. I really have to go back. This is . . . it's . . ."

"What about your brother?"

"What *about* my brother?"

Now they would have a fight.

"I don't want to have a fight," Freddie said.

"Then don't mention my brother."

"Ever?"

"See? You *do* want to have a fight."

She went out to the garden, and Freddie followed. It was six o'clock and still hot, which was unusual where they lived, near the beach on the west side of Los Angeles. It had been an unusually hot summer, though. Molly brushed miniature pink petals off the chaise before sitting.

"Autumn leaves," she said, examining one blossom on the tip of her finger. She smiled. "What a place we live in, what an amazing place." She patted the cushion, motioned Freddie to sit beside her. "My brother is perfect," she said.

Freddie laughed. Molly's brother was off-limits. Absolutely, completely, utterly off-limits. She knew that. It was like criticizing Stalin in Moscow in 1939. Except her brother wasn't Stalin. More like a Dostoevsky innocent.

Molly's entire family, in fact, was off-limits. They were like a cult, one that did not accept disciples or converts. They had been through a lot as a family, it had drawn them together, but what family hadn't been through a lot? Well, every family has its myth, she supposed. The myth Freddie's family told itself was one of freedom. Her sisters and brothers were scattered across the globe, all of them—with the exception of Freddie—too independent and too far away to notice that their father wrecked the car three times in six months, or at least too far away (one hoped not too independent) to do anything about it.

The Bergmans, on the other hand, were a clan, tight knit and suspicious of strangers. They were tribal and closed, bound by blood. They were one, the world the other. Freddie was used to them now, used to their insular ferocity. She didn't often make the mistake of even implicit disapproval. There were worse things than loyalty and family love in this world. Sometimes she envied Molly her certainty, the way the atheist sometimes envies the believer.

"I know Daniel works very hard," she said. "I know he's incredibly busy. I love your brother, I think he's wonderful to your parents, and to us. I didn't mean anything, Molly. Really."

She did mean something, that Daniel was a son not a daughter, and they both knew it, but it wasn't his fault, and they both knew that, too.

"He can't be there every second," Molly said.

But neither could Molly, even if she was the daughter, Freddie thought, and the unspoken words hung between them.

"I could change my ticket, go to New York a week early. I could Skype my classes, right? I have to keep an eye on those two crazy old people. Check on their medications, clear up their bills, talk to the doctors, hire someone to come in, something. I have to do something."

"They won't let you hire anyone."

"I know."

"Maybe it's really time to start thinking about—"

"I'm one hundred percent sure you're not going to say what you're about to say, because no one is sending my father anywhere, okay? He would hate it. He'd be so confused. So please don't even mention it."

"Okay."

"Anyway, I already tried talking to Mom about it."

Freddie laughed again.

"She said he had a home."

"I wonder," Freddie said, "what would happen if they called them 'nursing hotels,' instead of 'nursing homes,' if people would be more receptive."

"You'd still get infections."

"Like a cruise ship."

Now and then Freddie wished someone would send her to a Home. Assisted Living—couldn't everyone use a little assistance in living? Three meals a day—nice comfort food, too. And a room of your own. You would be retired, of course, so you could read novels all day long without feeling guilty, assuming you could still see through the inoperable cataracts you might, at that age, have developed. Really, if people were sent to old-age homes at a younger age, they would get so much more out of them.

Freddie had already moved her own father into three different assisted-living facilities. The first time, he went to the Motion Picture Home in the Valley, an inviting-looking place with its gardens and neat paths and scattered terraces and benches, though no one could walk on its neat paths or sit on its benches or gaze at the fat roses from the terrace. It was simply too hot, it was always much too hot. Her father had been lucky to get in, though, hot or not—there was always a long waiting list. He was an actor, Duncan Hughes—a minor actor you might see in a party scene of a romantic comedy with Doris Day and Rock Hudson, lifting his martini glass above people's heads as he squeezed through the crowd and made a few humorous comments to the stars. He had been dapper and not quite dashing when he was young. Now his face showed the good life he had attempted to live. Decades of professional disappointment, as well as his attempts to comfort himself in that disappointment, had left their mark on his florid drinker's face.

Duncan had always attributed failure to bad luck. He was a believer in luck and had never reconciled himself to not having any. But at last, Freddie thought, he had hit the jackpot, not one he had expected, certainly not one he had dreamed of, but a jackpot nonetheless: the Motion Picture Home.

Duncan's memory had started to go even earlier. He had managed to sign with a new agent, however, a chatty man who operated out of a disreputable-looking office in a strip mall. It wasn't as if Duncan Hughes would get any parts, Freddie knew that. He wouldn't be able to remember his cues, much less his lines. But having an agent meant he could still hope for roles, which provided some continuity for him, as hoping for roles, Freddie thought uncharitably, had always been a dominant part of his life. And perhaps having an agent might keep her father sitting safely by the phone rather than driving all over town to open auditions. When he drove to auditions these days, he tended to total the car. The bottle of rye he kept on the passenger seat didn't help.

So on the day, a year ago, when Freddie got a call from her father asking if she could drive him to the airport, her first reaction had been relief—her father had finally agreed that he shouldn't drive! He was asking for help! He was reaching out! But then the rest of the request hit her.

"The airport? Why are you going to the airport, Dad?"

"To catch a plane, obviously."

"Where is the plane going?"

"It's going to Sweden, obviously."

"That's not obvious to me, Dad. Why is it going to Sweden?"

"That's where the commercial is being shot."

Freddie was devastated. Her father was having hallucinations, she would have to call his neurologist, the Aricept was clearly not helping. She called his agent first, just to ask if he knew of anything that could have triggered the hallucination.

"Well," the agent said, "I guess the fact that your father's been hired to do a commercial and is flying to Sweden—that could have done it." He chuckled at his joke. "It's legit, Miss Hughes. I just got the contract."

She tried to talk her father out of it, as she had tried to talk him out of driving. She tried to enlist the aid of his doctor, as she had tried to enlist the aid of his doctor in convincing him to give up driving. But she knew he was even less likely to give up a role than he was his car. He had been waiting a long time for a role. She remembered him waiting for roles through her entire childhood. She remembered the change of atmosphere in the house when he got a part, the relief, the temporary dispersion of clouds of disappointment and failure. Actors do not give up parts. She knew that.

She drove him to LAX, parked, and walked him inside to make sure he found the group. She imagined them all lined up, holding on to a bright yellow rope, the way the preschool children did on the sidewalk in New York. But the director and crew just stood in a loose bunch, most of them wearing safari jackets and baseball caps. Her father kissed her goodbye and made straight for an attractive young woman in the group who seemed to know him.

"Hello, handsome," she said, and her father, unable to help himself, gave his practiced half-smile and preened with pleasure.

"You will look after him, won't you?" Freddie asked the director, who did not seem to think it irregular to have hired someone showing clear signs of senility. But why would he? He was a man who thought it reasonable to cast a commercial in L.A. and fly everyone thousands of miles to shoot it in Sweden in English to then be dubbed into Swedish.

"Don't worry," the director said.

Her father called her that night from Chicago, where they were changing planes.

"Pretty soon you'll be in Sweden, Dad."

"*Sweden?*"

It was that trip that shocked Freddie into action. By the time he came home, three days later, a little vague about having gone at all, she had called the Motion Picture Home so many times and spoken to so many people that when she discovered a room had suddenly opened up there, she was sure it was because she had annoyed the director of the facility to such an extent that the director had taken it out on an employee who had taken it out on a patient who had consequently died and vacated a room.

It took only five months for the Motion Picture Home to realize it had made a terrible mistake.

"We are concerned about STDs," the director had said.

Duncan was now on assisted-living place number three.

"The social worker called again today," Freddie told Molly.

"What did old Duncan do today? Pinch the nutritionist?"

Freddie shrugged. "They decided to cut back his wine at dinner."

"They should just water it. Would he know?"

"That's what I told them. But the social worker thought that would be dishonest. Dishonest! So she had a talk with him, and of course he objected. He demanded to see a lawyer. He threatened to sue. I think this place may kick him out soon, too."

Molly held her drink out to Freddie. "Here. It's neat. The social worker has no jurisdiction in this house."

Freddie said, "I want to be cremated, Molly."

"I know, honey."

"No, I mean now."

"I know, honey."

Freddie said, "Let's go to the beach and watch the sun set instead."

It was a beautiful sunset, the brilliant red streaks of sky fading to gentle mauve. There was a full moon hanging over the parking lot, plump and orange. The wind blew and there was no one on the pier, just a few surfers below.

"We're so lucky to live here," Molly said as they walked back to the parking lot. She was radiant in the blinking light from a bar, her cheeks glowing red, then green, and Freddie had to agree.

— 4 —

They had been sorority sisters, and they were still friends—Daphne, Eileen, Natalie, and Joy. Daphne got on Natalie's nerves; Eileen got on Daphne's nerves; Natalie, who was bossy, particularly about her politics, which were of the radical right, got on everyone's nerves; but all three were extremely close to Joy, which had kept the group intact through all the decades and divorces. Every few months they would get together for a girls' lunch.

"I'm not happy about this old-age business," Joy said.

"I refuse to feel old," Daphne said. She slapped the table. "*Je refuse.*"

The silverware and coffee cups rattled, and Joy marveled at Daphne, not a bit different from the day they met, sleek, beautiful, noisy, every auburn hair in place. Natalie was, as she had been since college, wearing chic, expensive bohemian clothes, her hair cut in the same bohemian bob with bangs. Eileen had been less glamorous than the others, but she had grown into her looks as she got older, looking somber but dignified these days. They all still had their marbles, though only two still had their husbands. But pretty good for a bunch of old bags, Joy thought.

"We've been friends for sixty-five years."

"Our friendship could get Medicare," Eileen said.

Natalie began to explain how Obamacare was ruining America.

"How's the new great-grandchild?" Joy interjected, offspring being a successful diversion for any of the girls. Though she was asking Natalie, Daphne immediately began digging around in her bag, probably for her iThing with her own great-grandchild baby pictures on it.

"They want to name her 'Quiet,' " said Natalie.

"Convenient," Eileen said. "They can call her and discipline her at the same time."

"Mine is two years old next week," Daphne added, holding up a screen with a picture of a little girl with an ice-cream-smeared mouth.

" 'Quiet'?" Joy was saying. "Why don't they just name her 'No'?"

They started laughing and couldn't stop. They laughed until tears rolled down their faces.

"Oh, that felt good," Joy said.

All around them well-turned-out young women picked at their salads, preserving their waistlines, as women of Joy's generation used to call that mealtime behavior. Joy looked at them fondly, then slathered butter on a piece of bread, damn the torpedoes. She had no gallbladder, the surgeon had taken it out when he took out the colon cancer, "the blue-plate special," he'd called it, and never mind her waistline, she was not supposed to eat fat with no gallbladder. She sipped her espresso. That was verboten, too, atrial fibrillation. Delicious, though. It did not do to ignore the delicious.

"I love food," she said.

The tablecloths were pink and pressed. The napkins were large.

"I love napery," she said.

"Now, Joy," Daphne said, suddenly serious, "what are we going to do about Aaron?"

"I think he's dying," Joy said, and she began to cry softly.

Daphne put her hand on Joy's, which was an enormous gesture of support, Joy knew. Daphne did not like touching people.

"Nonsense," Natalie said.

"What do the doctors say?" Eileen asked.

Joy shrugged, and they waited for her to pull herself together and blow her nose.

"You have to take care of yourself, too, you know," Natalie said. "Even nurses have shifts."

"That's what my children say. They say I'm grandiose, taking care of Aaron myself."

"Children. What do they know?" said Daphne. "They think they know everything. But just wait."

Joy smiled. "They are so bossy, aren't they? I do miss Molly ordering me around, though." The smile disappeared. "Now that she's in California."

"What about Daniel?"

"Daniel is wonderful, but . . ."

They all nodded. Daniel was not a daughter.

"Anyway, I'm fine."

"Isn't there some sort of adult day care Aaron could go to?" Daphne was saying.

"No, god, no, he would hate that. He gets so disoriented. Then he gets frightened. Then he gets angry. He would hate it. What's he going to do? Sit in a drum circle? Make paper flowers?"

"What does he do at home?"

"Watch NY1. And eat. It's a wonder he doesn't weigh five hundred pounds. And a lot of time is taken up with, you know, showers and getting dressed and creams and applications of . . . things. I won't go into it. But trust me, a day goes by. And on the days I'm at work, who knows what could happen? I come home at lunch to check on him and I never know what I'll find, don't ask, and then, when I come back again at the end of the day . . ."

She went to the ladies' room. She put her bags down on a pretty little lavender table, shed a few more tears, washed her face, and sat gripping the arms of the lavender chintz chair, feeling faint. The doctor said these dizzy spells were nothing to worry about as long as she didn't fall. But what if she did fall? What was to stop her from falling? She could very easily have fallen *just now* . . .

"I know you all probably think he should go to a place," she said to the girls when she got back to the table, "but he would be miserable. He needs landmarks, needs familiar things, needs his schedule."

"But what about what you need?" they said.

"I'd be miserable, too. Visiting a nursing home? Every day? I'm exhausted just thinking about it. And they're not very clean, you know. Full of infection." There was something else, too, something no one seemed to realize: if Aaron went into a nursing home, he would be *gone*. "What about what you need"—Molly and Daniel asked her the same thing. But what she needed was so obvious. She needed Aaron.

"You're a saint," Daphne said.

It was not a compliment.

"One of those insane, self-destructive saints," Natalie added.

The kind who wander around in masochistic determination until they contract an incurable disease or are roasted on a fire or skinned alive, they all agreed.

"Joy, sweetie, at the very least you need to hire someone. *Hire* a saint," Natalie added.

When she got home, she noticed how gray Aaron looked, his hair, his beard, his face, and his hooded sweatshirt. He was not a man who was meant to be gray. Some men are, but Aaron ought to have been ruddy. He never had been, but he ought to have been. That's what Joy thought.

"You have to get some fresh air," she said.

He waved an enormous hand at her, as if he were swatting a fly.

"You'll get too stiff, sitting around all day."

He waved her words away again.

"Do you hear me? Where are your hearing aids?"

"WHAT?"

"Where are your hearing aids?" Joy repeated loudly.

"What are you talking about?" Aaron said. "Hearing aids!" He shook his head at her folly.

"I'm going to kill you, Aaron," she said.

"WHAT?"

"I'm going to kill you, I said!"

Aaron smiled. "So you say." He took her hand and kissed it.

" *'Joyful, Joyful, we adore thee,'* " he sang as she helped him up and over to the walker. He often called her Joyful.

"Well," she said.

" *'Hearts unfold like flowers before thee.'* "

Sometimes the songs were hymns, sometimes bits of British vaudeville from the last century, but mostly Baroque, mostly Purcell. The lyrics still came warbling out, even when he could not remember what the conversation was about, perhaps more so when he couldn't remember, couldn't keep up. Aaron had wanted to be a singer, a classical singer, but he'd gone directly into the family business instead. The Depression did that to people, made them think straight. Or warped them into shape, that was more the case with Aaron. It had taken Joy many years to understand that.

When they got outside, Aaron leaned heavily on his walker. It had wheels, which was a help. A shiny red walker with wheels. He called it his little red wagon.

"Lift up the front wheels," she said.

"Get away. I know what I'm doing."

"Tilt it."

"I'm tilting, I'm tilting. It's not moving. It's broken."

Joy took his arm. "Lean on me." She tilted the walker and got the wheels on the curb. "It's like a shopping cart."

They continued down the street toward Central Park. She could see the trees, still leafy and colorful. It had been a warm autumn. "Aren't they beautiful?" she said.

Aaron was breathing heavily. He was not singing. He was not calling her Joyful. He was not even answering her.

"This is ridiculous" was all he said, muttering it to himself.

She slowed her gait to match his, an excruciating shuffle. "Come on, come on," she said.

But he had stopped completely now and looked around him helplessly. "Where are we going, anyway?"

"To the park. You love the park."

"I hate the park. I'm going home."

"You love the park. I brought your camera."

"I don't know what you're talking about. Where are we going, anyway?"

They ended up stopping at the little park in the middle of Park Avenue at Ninety-sixth Street.

"You can sit here and rest," Joy said.

Aaron's chin immediately dropped to his chest.

"Are you asleep?" she said. "Or dead?"

"Which would you prefer?" he asked, his eyes still closed.

"I really wanted to go to Central Park."

Aaron opened his eyes and lifted his head. "Why?"

"Why? Because it's a beautiful day."

They sat for a few minutes silently.

"Pretty flowers," Aaron said, pointing a shaky hand at some late roses. "Beautiful, beautiful. Right here in the city."

Joy choked up a little. Because that was Aaron, her Aaron, the real Aaron. "Beautiful," she said.

"I should take a picture."

She handed him the little camera, and he fumbled with it for a minute, then said, "It's broken," and almost threw it back at her.

Joy put it in her tote bag. She had three tote bags, different sizes and different patterns. They hung on the handles of Aaron's red walker, two on the left, one on the right. She unhooked one of the bags on the left and stuffed it into the one on the right. "That's better."

"What have you got in there, Joyful?" Aaron said.

"I don't even know. But if I leave one bag home, it's always the one that has something I need."

He took her hand and held it. He stared off in the soft, blank way he sometimes had these days. His body sagged. The hand that held hers loosened and came to rest, like a large pale leaf, on his lap.

While he slept, Joy, too, closed her eyes. The afternoon sun was warm and comforting on her face. Sunlight was full of vitamin D. And cancer—that, too. Vitamin D, cancer . . . how to choose? She should have worn a hat. But how could a person walk around New York City in October in a sun hat? She refused to become an eccentric old lady padding around in bedroom slippers and a floppy hat. She pulled a thermos out of one of her bags, then another thermos. She shook Aaron awake. "Would you like a little Cream of Wheat?" she asked him. "I have an extra."

5

Daniel emerged from the subway and smelled the overripe fruit from the fruit stand. It would be just a quick visit to his parents, he had to go to a school assembly, he could not remember what sort, a concert, a play, a reading of the "books" the children had written. That was the most surprising thing about the school Cora and Ruby went to, the number of artistic events held there despite the absence of a budget for the arts. All those underemployed artistic mothers and fathers filling in the gaps. He bought some strawberries from the vendor for his parents and a banana for himself, which he ate as he walked to their building.

"For me?" his mother said at the door, taking the banana peel. "You shouldn't have."

He waited for the story of the time he had absentmindedly put a banana peel in the medicine cabinet. He'd been daydreaming about girls, probably. Sex. One did in those days. One still did.

"Oh, it was so funny, Danny," his mother was saying. "Do you remember that, Aaron? He was twelve or thirteen, just a little older than Ruby."

He wondered if Ruby daydreamed about sex. Terrible stray thought.

"I brought you strawberries," he said.

His father looked gaunt. He'd always been thin, a lanky cowboy sort of thin, and tall, too tall to reach sometimes. But he had never looked eaten away like this.

"You get a haircut?" Daniel asked him. "Tony still cutting your hair?"

When they moved to the East Side, his father had searched the neighborhood for a barber who could cut his beard the way he liked it. Daniel used to tag along when he was very small, and Tony would put a hot towel on his face.

"Tony?" his mother said. "Tony died years ago."

Joy began talking about all the people in the neighborhood who had died. If they hadn't died, they had gone out of business. She held the green plastic basket of strawberries and Daniel noticed her fingers were already stained pink with the juice.

"But we're still here," she concluded.

Daniel's father took his hand and held it. "You making a good living these days?" he asked.

"Pay no attention to him," said Joy. "I'd better wash the berries. Where'd you get them? On the street?" She licked a pink finger. "Now I'll get mad cow disease and Ebola." She went into the kitchen.

"I'm making a living," Daniel said. "Let's just leave it at that."

"I don't know why you work for that organization." He said the word "organization" with distaste. "Go where the action is."

"Where's that, Dad?"

"Just ignore him, Danny," his mother called from the kitchen.

"Wall Street."

Daniel rolled his eyes.

"Well, you can lead a horse to water," said Aaron.

Daniel left them sitting in the dining room eating the strawberries. As he closed the front door, he heard his father say, "Nice boy. Good work, Joyful."

"Wall Street?" she answered. "You want your son to be a crook?"

6

Aaron was lying on his side, turned away from her, when Joy got into bed. She put her arms around him and they talked about the past. He remembered unexpected things, digging clams in Cape Cod right after they were married, the poem he'd memorized for freshman English ("*how do you like your blueeyed boy / Mister Death*"). She talked about the children, about the grandchildren. A little bit about work, though he was no longer interested in her work, could not really follow what she was telling him. He was very romantic these days, more romantic than he had been in what she sometimes thought of as their real life, before he began to drift away. He called her darling, asked what the hell the colostomy pouch was, apologized for it, thanked her for putting up with it and him. Then they fell asleep. That was how it went most nights. Sometimes when she lay down on the bed with Aaron, her face pressed against the back of his head, she would cry. When he asked her what was wrong, she would say she missed her parents.

But one night, just as Joy climbed into bed, when Aaron pulled up his pajama shirt and poked at the pouch and said, "What the hell is this?" he yanked it out before she could stop him.

She cleaned him up. She changed the sheets. She settled him back in bed. He told her he loved her. She held him and cried, said again that it was because she missed her parents.

It began to happen frequently, regularly, sometimes twice in a night. *What the hell is this*, and a yank. Joy didn't tell anyone. That would have been disrespectful to Aaron. But beyond that, she knew if she told anyone, her children, her friends, they would tell her she needed to hire help or that Aaron ought to be in a nursing home.

"Please don't pull out the pouch tonight, Aaron."

"I'm hungry," he said. She'd gotten him into his pajamas but not into bed yet. He was in his chair watching television. The TV was on so loud she could feel the vibrations in her stomach. She brought him some ice cream, then canned pears. He smiled at her and asked for toast and tea. She imagined the plastic colostomy pouch puffing, swelling, being pulled off by his big restless hand.

"Look," she said, pointing to the pouch when she got him settled in bed. "Your colostomy pouch from your surgery."

"I had surgery?"

"It saved your life."

Aaron looked away from her. "Some life," he said with a sigh.

Joy rigged up the bed so that she could strip any wet or soiled sheets from his side without disturbing the king-sized bottom sheet. She put down layers of chux and towels and an extra sheet folded four times. They were not always necessary, he sometimes left the pouch undisturbed. But even then, he himself was disturbed, more and more, by noises, by movements, by Joy. The rustle of the sheets if she turned over, the click of the remote control if she watched TV, even with the sound off. If she got up to go to the bathroom, Aaron started, called out in fear.

Joy got very little sleep, even after she moved onto the lumpy living-room couch. If she was in the bedroom, she startled him and woke him up. If she was not in the bedroom, he woke up disoriented and called for her. She preferred the living-room couch. It gave her the illusion of distance and freedom, and the cushions seemed to fit her tired back perfectly. She slept like a cat, listening, curled in a ball, one eye half open. When her husband called, she woke immediately and leaped up. She did not slink gracefully from the room like a cat. She shuffled in her slippers and made small distressed murmurs, turning on lamps, holding the wall for balance. Sometimes, after soothing Aaron or getting him ginger ale or cleaning him up, she would be too tired to go back to the couch and she would fall asleep at the foot of the bed. Sometimes, as tired as she was, she couldn't get back to sleep until morning. Those predawn hours were excruciating at first. She paced and fretted and prayed for sleep. But after a few nights like that, she realized what a gift she was being given. She spread herself out on the couch and read whatever novel happened to be lying around. The time became precious to her. It was too late for anyone to still be out and too early for anyone to be out yet. The streets were hushed.

Joyful, Joyful, Aaron whispered. Their fingers were entwined. They lay on the cool sand. An orange moon hung dreamily on the horizon. We will visit every island on earth, Aaron said. We will go to Iceland and Corfu and Tahiti and Orkney and the Isle of Mull. We'll live in Tasmania and Ischia.

Long Island will do, Joy said.

There once was a man from Nantucket, Aaron said.

Poetry!

And the moon rose above them, growing smaller and paler as the night grew darker.

M y father is very ill," Molly said to the woman next to her on the plane.

"I'm so sorry."

"I'm going to New York to see him."

"I'm sure that will do him good."

Will it? Molly wondered. She thought of Daniel so many years ago, when he was so ill. He was just a kid, eighteen, younger than Ben, her son, was now. Younger than Ben and in the hospital for so long, almost a year. Then in a wheelchair for months. How had he stood it? The way he stood everything, she supposed—by ignoring it. Had it helped Daniel, had it "done him good" when Molly came home from college to sit with him in his hospital room? She had tried to entertain him, telling him amusing stories, family gossip. She'd read the newspaper to him, brought him milkshakes, too. And she'd given him novels, *Lucky Jim*, *A Handful of Dust*, which he was too sick to read. Did any of that "do him good"? There he'd been in his hospital bed, an unfiltered cigarette in his mouth, squinting against the smoke, smiling at her, laughing at her funny stories, but when it came time to leave, she'd see his eyes sink back into their blank gaping stare of pain. Oh, she'd had some good fights with the nurses about his painkillers, such as they were, not that anyone cared what a college girl said. Their mother had been even fiercer, but still the doctors refused to give him sufficient pain medication, insisting it was too addictive for a teenaged boy.

So had her visits done Daniel any good at all? Would this visit to her father do *him* any good? Would it restore his short-term memory? Would it give him back his strength, his balance, so he could walk? Would it replace the colostomy bag with his own intestine? Would it make him healthy, would it make him whole?

"You're such an absolutist," Freddie had once said to her, and she had said, "Yes. That is the goal, at least."

As soon as she got to New York she would call her parents' various doctors. She would organize all their medications in little plastic boxes labeled with the days of the week. She would order a lamp with a high-wattage bulb for reading, a telephone with big buttons and an extra-loud ring. She would put all their bank ac-counts online and arrange for deposits and payments to be made automatically. She would set up Spotify and program it to endlessly play Frank Sinatra.

She said these things to herself to make herself feel better, but she knew what would really happen. Neither her father nor her mother would be able to decide which doctor she should speak to or find their phone numbers. The medications she organized would be the ones they no longer took. There would be no place to plug in the new lamps with their bright lightbulbs, every outlet in the apartment, and there weren't many, sporting frayed extension cords already overloaded. They would change the appointments she did manage to arrange for them without telling her. Every television in the apartment, and there were too many, would not work. The radio would play only static, loudly. And then there was the computer.

"Why did you even talk to someone who called out of the blue and said he was from Microsoft?" she would ask her mother.

"Because he said he was from Microsoft."

"Mom, Microsoft doesn't call people like that to say your computer has a virus. They never call anyone. They don't even answer calls. It doesn't work like that."

"They said it was urgent."

It wasn't Joy's fault that an entirely new paradigm of communication and commerce had developed in her later years. Molly would say, "Okay, Mom. No harm done. As long as you didn't give them any information."

"Of course not! Just my name. I think just my name. Oh god, what if I gave them something else? Like my credit card number?"

"Did you?"

"I don't know. How can I remember everything like that? He asked me so many questions."

And her mother, her inspiring, unflappable, competent, hardworking, distinguished mother, would berate herself, berate the modern world, then sigh helplessly. "I don't know why Microsoft called in the first place," she would say. "I really don't."

Molly sat in the taxi from the airport anticipating Central Park, heavy and loamy and full of autumn. As Manhattan came into view, she experienced what she always felt on approaching the city from JFK: a mixture of excitement and calm, a sense of totality; of perfect, living, vibrant, chaotic peace. She opened the cab's bleary window and breathed in the lights and the skyscrapers, the sky lit from below, the river.

The taxi driver popped the trunk and pulled her bag out for her. Before she could grab it, the doorman was already rolling it beneath the canopy to the door. When Molly was growing up here, the doormen were such a normal, essential part of her life. She had never really gotten used to living without doormen. They always knew where your parents were, when they'd be home, if the dog had been walked, if your brother had friends with him—an early alert system for family life. If you lost your keys, they let you into the apartment. They handed you packages. They told you the mailman had come when you were waiting for college acceptances and refusals. When she was little she had loved their uniforms with their names stitched on the chest, their smart hats like policemen's hats, but unlike a policeman, they picked you up and swung you through the air and lent you a quarter if you needed it for candy. She'd known some of them, the older ones, for what seemed like her whole life.

"Hi! Hi! It's so good to be here!" she said, then realized she did not actually know this particular doorman and had greeted him too warmly. He did look familiar, perhaps because of a strong resemblance to Mussolini. Squat head, square jaw, wide frown. He was probably too young to know who Mussolini was. The name stitched on his uniform was Gregor.

"The Bergmans," she said. "I'm their daughter. I have a key. They're expecting me."

A novel by James Patterson was spread-eagled on the console. He glanced at it longingly as they went to the elevator, saying, "Your mother will be glad to see you." He spoke in a heavy, clouded voice, just as she would have expected a Mussolini look-alike to speak, though the accent was wrong, Eastern European. "She's had a rough night."

"Is she okay? Did something happen?"

"Oh," said Gregor, and he cleared his throat. "*She's* fine, but . . ."

"My father? Oh god. What happened?"

The elevator doors opened.

"They're both home, safe and sound," Gregor said as the doors closed.

Home? Of course they were home. Where else would they be at midnight?

Molly burst through the door, unlocked as always. "Mom! Mom! What's going on?"

Her mother was lying on the couch in the living room, though Molly had trouble locating her at first, she was so swaddled in down. A down comforter, a down robe beneath it, down booties, and, which was new to Molly, a down hood. "I'm here," the little face said. "I'm fine, darling."

"But Daddy?"

"I'm trying to warm up. What a night. Your father is okay now, back in bed where he belongs." She took a sip of water from a paper cup on the side table. Why did she use paper cups? Molly wondered. To make the apartment seem more like a hospital?

"I was reading, I guess I fell asleep—"

"Mom?"

"A really deep sleep, which I have not had in weeks, believe me. I checked on your father at ten, before I went to bed. I made sure he went to the bathroom to pee, I checked the colostomy pouch . . ."

Oh, please spare me those particular details, Molly thought guiltily, knowing her mother could not spare herself those details.

"And he was comfortable and quiet. So I came back here to my nest."

It did not look like a nest, that undulating pile of pillows and comforters, more like an avalanche from which long-lost hikers might at any moment emerge, shaking themselves off, wondering how they ended up in this Manhattan living room. "And?" Molly said, rather sharply, moving her hands in circles as if to speed things up.

Perhaps, Joy thought, Molly's authoritarian nature came along with the work she did, a professional hazard, like Marie Curie being exposed to radiation. Molly was exposed to so many pottery shards. They were not radioactive, but there were so many and they were minuscule and each one might turn out to be the important one, but who could tell, they were so small and filthy, and so you had to gather them up as if they were diamonds, then separate them, then put them back together again. Well, you would have to be officious, wouldn't you, with all those shards depending on you? Joy had been so proud when Molly decided to study archaeology, when she got her Ph.D., when she went off to Turkey to dig up ancient pots. It was like an Agatha Christie novel. It was like Agatha Christie's life with her archaeologist husband, minus a husband, of course, but that was another story. You had to clean the dug-up bits and pieces with a soft toothbrush like the ones for people with diseased gums. This thought always made Joy shudder, as if the pottery shards were in fact old decayed teeth. Then the discoveries, such as they were, would have to be labeled on bits of paper like the slips in a Chinese fortune cookie. Then they would end up buried again, in drawers in a university or museum, never to see daylight for another thousand years or so. No wonder Molly was always trying to organize Joy. She even tried to organize her own body, stretching this muscle, strengthening that one. If Molly could number the hairs on her head, Joy was sure she would, she was so busy trying to order the world. She had been the same as a child, not particularly obsessive or compulsive, although she did refold her clothes when Joy brought them up from the laundry room, come to think of it. But it was more a show of strength, this insistence on order, her own order, a demand rather than a need.

That would keep anybody busy, never mind her job. Look at her, poor dear, so antsy-pantsy. She was looking good, though. Fit. Always fit. An obsession. There were worse obsessions. She resembled her father with that long face. Sculptural, Joy liked to think, though others might call it craggy. The face was frowning ferociously now. Of course! Joy hadn't told her about Aaron yet. No wonder! "Where was I? Oh, I came here into the living room and I read a little and then I must have fallen asleep—"

"Mom!" Molly snapped. "Could you just tell me what actually happened, for god's sake?"

Her mother glared at her and snapped back: "Your father got out of bed and pulled his urine-soaked pajama pants and adult diaper down around his ankles and went out, like that, with his urine-soaked pajamas and adult diaper around his ankles, into the elevator to the lobby, okay? The doorman brought him back."

"Jesus."

"*Gregor*—Jesus retired last year. All right? Okay? Direct enough for you, Molly? Delivered quickly enough? Sorry I was not as concise as you would have liked. I'm sorry I didn't describe your father's humiliation with the clarity and alacrity you demand . . ."

Molly sank onto the downy couch beside her mother. "Oh, Mom," she said tenderly. "I'm sorry, Mom. I'm so sorry."

They sat like that for a while, quiet, together, and she snuggled against her mother, then went into her parents' bedroom. Her father was asleep, the quilt pulled up to his chin. He had aged since she last saw him, not that long ago despite her mother's admonitions, two months. But Aaron, breathing noisily, his face otherwise so still, looked old, like an old, old man. Molly kissed his forehead.

"I'm sorry you walked in on such a drama," Joy said. They were squeezed in at the table in the kitchen drinking the house specialty, decaffeinated tea, weak, lukewarm.

"I'm sorry you have to deal with this, Mommy."

"Gregor is a nice young man. He and his wife just had a baby."

"Do you think maybe you should lock the door? At night? Then, if Daddy gets up—"

"What if there's a fire?" her mother said, appalled. "You're not thinking, Molly."

Molly stirred her tea. The sound of the spoon against the teacup was musical, like bells.

"I hate being such an old ruin," Joy said softly.

"You're not an old ruin. You're still working, for heaven's sake. You take care of Dad all by yourself. I don't know how you manage, honestly. And you look beautiful, too. Old ruin. That's a joke."

"Well"—Joy was obviously mollified—"I *am* old."

No one at work knew her real age. Eighty-six. That would give them a jolt, all those potbellied men planning their retirements at sixty-five. Of course, she couldn't afford to retire even now. She'd cut back to part-time since Aaron got so sick, which was hard enough on the finances.

"I only work three days a week," she added.

"That's plenty."

"Plenty of *tsuris*."

The room that had once been Molly's was now her mother's office and her father's study. Those were the terms used by them both, and if an office is a place where you store cardboard boxes of unopened mail and a study is where you sit between spires of those boxes on a convertible sofa and listen to your transistor radio, then those terms were accurate.

Molly transferred the piles of boxes from the sofa to the floor, leaving a little path to the door, and began removing the sofa's newly visible pillows before she realized that other towers of boxes on the floor would prevent the mattress from unfolding.

"Oh well," Joy said. "Storage is a problem in New York City. Sleep in Danny's room."

Daniel's room had originally been a maid's room, a remnant from the days when the building had been built, the days when families had maids. The room was so narrow that the only bed that would fit there was a special narrow maid's-room bed sold, once upon a time, in some of the better New York department stores. This one was very old, perhaps forty years old, lumpy and somehow inviting. Daniel had always loved his room, fixing it up like a cabin on a boat. In fact, he had made it so cozy and inviting that Molly had tried to get him to switch with her, but he had contemptuously refused. Aaron called it the Nookery, a Dickens reference, he said, and that had clinched it for both children: Daniel had the best room in the house. It even had its own bathroom, the size of a phone booth, with a toilet and a skinny shower.

The sink was in the bedroom, which Daniel one day announced was very European, enraging Molly, who was stuck in her conventional American bedroom with its big closet and large windows facing the tree-lined street. The small window at the head of Daniel's maid's-room cot faced another building, but he had managed to make a friend across the air shaft and they rigged up a pulley system and paper cup telephone, so even that turned out to be an advantage.

Molly pulled the old cotton quilt around her. She felt far away, missing Freddie, and she felt comfortably at home. Outside, an ambulance went screeching along somewhere in the distance.

She heard her mother padding around in the kitchen, the pop of the toaster, the refrigerator door opening, closing. She would have to check the refrigerator tomorrow, search for the squalid, liquefying slices of tomato, the curled, desiccated turkey slices she knew would be tucked up somewhere in there. She had to make sure her parents were eating properly. There were boxes of Vienna Fingers and saltines on the counter. Minute Rice. Rice Krispies. Cream of Wheat. If it was an empty calorie, her parents were sure to stock it. But she had also seen a banana and a few oranges in a bowl. A good sign. She had tried once to arrange a regular delivery of decent produce through an organic food website. It had not been a success. Her mother did not like the dirt on the vegetables. Her father did not like the irregular shapes. Neither of them liked rutabagas.

Molly had come a week earlier than either Freddie or Ben, neither of whom could get to New York until Thanksgiving Day, and Joy was glad. It gave her a little time to be alone with her daughter. From the kitchen table, she watched with pleasure as Molly grabbed parcels from the refrigerator and threw them into a large garbage bag.

"Mom, this is disgusting."

Joy nodded. Molly's movements, so abrupt and assured, charmed her. It was as if Molly were a little girl, a busy, officious little girl, as she had sometimes been, bossing her brother around, arranging the spices in the kitchen alphabetically as soon as she learned the alphabet.

"It's wonderful to have you here," Joy said.

Molly looked up from the garbage bag. She smiled.

"I miss you terribly," Joy said.

The smile faded. "That makes me feel kind of guilty, Mom."

"Would you prefer that I didn't miss you?"

Molly pondered that. "I don't know. Maybe. No."

"Good. Because I do, whether you like it or not."

She watched Molly spray the kitchen table with Fantastik and scrub it vigorously with a sponge, her elbows almost banging into Joy's face.

"Should I move?"

"You're okay."

Joy did not offer to help. Molly did not like help. Joy watched her with growing satisfaction. The chemicals in the spray made her eyes sting, but she said nothing. The sticky circles left by teacups and jam jars disappeared. Molly gave her a quick kiss on the head as she put back the saltshaker, the sugar bowl with one of its handles broken off, the portable radio, then quickly took them off again and scrubbed them, too. She scrubbed the blackened windowsill.

"That will never come off," Joy said.

"I miss you, too, you know," Molly said.

"I should hope so."

Joy listened to the water run as Molly took a shower in Danny's minuscule bathroom. There was life in the apartment, echoes of her old life, echoes of life before she was old.

"Aaron," she said that night as she tucked him in, wrapping her arms around him and pressing her face against the back of his head, "I love you."

He said, "I love you, too, my darling."

The words echoed in the apartment full of echoes.

Joy left for work at 9:30. She never knew what she would come home to, but Aaron tended to sleep during the day and never went near the stove, so she told herself. She was a conservation consultant for a small museum on the Lower East Side that specialized in Jewish artifacts. It was, she had once observed, years ago, not unlike Hitler's Museum of an Extinct Race, but with less stuff. Aaron was shocked when she said this. They were in Prague at the time, entering a museum beside the old synagogue, a museum that was piled with candlesticks and spoons and silver spice boxes stolen from Jews by the Nazis and stockpiled in anticipation of Hitler's museum.

"Joyful, darling, a little perspective," Aaron said.

A museum like hers was a record of the past, not a trophy of genocide, certainly that was true. But Time was so cruel and so thorough. It made her sad sometimes as she examined her own museum's jumble of dented tin *pushkes*, Sabbath candlesticks brought from the Old Country, telegrams, newspapers, photographs, the wheel of a pushcart, a deck chair from the Catskills. Where did they belong now? Nowhere. It was an extinct world that passed through her hands and into the Lower East Side Museum. Joy would examine each item donated to the museum or acquired, each fragment of this lost world, to determine if it deserved to be found or to be lost again, to be tossed back quite literally onto the dust heap of history. This choosing which item lived and which died, so to speak—that was the part of her job she did not relish, separating the wheat from the chaff.

"Who am I to judge?" she said to Aaron. "If the pope said that about his flock, is it any wonder I feel that way about my flock of artifacts?"

"I don't know how to tell you this, my love, but you are not the pope."

Joy wanted to save everything, every scrap, as if it were a soul. A museum was not a warehouse, however, and a conservator was not a hoarder. Collections had priorities, strengths. Every Houdini flyer did not need to be preserved. One Houdini flyer was quite enough. Yet she had been trained to save, not to choose.

A mother of small children with a bachelor's degree in Art History, she had volunteered at the museum two days a week as soon as Daniel started nursery school. It wasn't until that first bankruptcy that she'd gone to work there full-time as a secretary, assisting the conservator. Both he and the director of the museum encouraged her to go back to school. She couldn't give up her job to go full-time, but she managed, working during the morning, going to school in the afternoon, so she could be home to make dinner and put the children to bed. She worked long and hard for that Ph.D. The museum hired her as a conservator even before she finished. She loved the battered pots and pans, the sewing machines, the Yiddish-to-English primers, liked to handle them. She knew others would like to handle them, too, and so she protected them from the loving caresses that would, as in a myth or a fairy tale, eventually destroy them.

The director had a bit of a crush on her, though he had never bothered her after that one time, and even then she had been able to fend him off with a pretense of utter ignorance and innocence, one of her favorite strategies, no hurt feelings or embarrassment. It had been a long time since she'd had to act as though she had no idea what a man meant when he spoke in a husky voice and happened to rest his hand on her knee. That was one piece of the past she'd been only too happy to consign to the garbage.

The conservator who had encouraged her had died years ago. The director had retired. The field of conservation relied more and more on computers and software and technology, or so she read, she could not possibly employ all the new techniques, it was hard enough for her writing emails. The museum was changing with the times, too, growing bigger and more professional, and Joy had begun to identify with her artifacts, out of date, obsolete, left behind.

Joy had already gotten Aaron dressed. All Molly had to do was bring her father his breakfast and his lunch, and make sure he didn't wander or fall.

"For once I can relax at the office," Joy said. "Goodbye, Aaron. Goodbye, Molly. Don't drive each other crazy. I'm off to the salt mines."

Aaron poked at the lump in his sweatshirt and asked what it was doing there. Molly explained about the colostomy bag at great length, as if a longer explanation would stay in his head longer, but at a certain point he just waved his hand at her, a dismissal, and she left him in his chair and washed his dishes. By the time she was done, he was calling for her mother.

"She went to work, Daddy," she said from the doorway.

"Is that so?"

"Yes, that is so."

He called for Joy ten minutes later, and ten minutes after that, until Molly decided to stay in the bedroom with him.

"No wonder Mom is going nuts," she said to him.

"*Who can from Joy refrain,*" he sang, "*this gay, this pleasing, shining, wond'rous day?*"

By two o'clock, the apartment was driving Molly insane, the banging radiators and stifling steam heat, the television's endless loop of NY1 weather and politics and interviews of off-Broadway dancers. She had to get out.

"You have to get out," she said to her father. She bundled him in his jacket and herded him and his walker to the door. "Come on. It's so hot in here. With the TV grinding on and on. I can't stand it."

"Well, I can."

"You need fresh air."

"You sound like your mother. Where is your mother? Joy! Joy!"

"She went to work."

"Oh, she did, did she?"

He often took on this joshing tone when he was confused. Molly hustled him into the elevator.

"Well, where's your mother, anyway?" His voice had gone from joshing to desperation. "Joy? Joy! Where are you? Where's your mother?"

They made it to the park, and Aaron stared at the evergreen bushes.

Molly sat on a bench beside him. The air was cold and wet. "So," she said. Before the dementia, he had been a kind of genius at small talk, always able to chat and charm. That gift had been lost, gradually, but even so he had continued to enjoy a good attack on the mayor. She mentioned the mayor now, and he said, "All a bunch of crooks," but did not elaborate. Molly moved on to the grandchildren. He liked to hear anything at all about them, laughing and calling them spitfires or *wisenheimers*.

"So Cora and Ruby go to public schools," she said.

"Imagine that."

"I hope they're really good ones."

Her father nodded. "Yes, indeed," he said.

"I thought Ruby would go to private school for seventh grade for sure. Not that anyone asked my opinion. Of course no one can afford the tuition anymore. Except Russian oligarchs."

"Well, now."

"*Are* there any good public middle schools?" she soldiered on. "There weren't when Daniel and I were that age, that's for sure."

"Is that so?"

Molly tried a couple of other topics, but none of them, not the state of the CIA or health care or water quality, sparked more than a nod, an all-purpose phrase: You don't say; imagine that.

Oh, Daddy, Molly thought, and tears came to her eyes. She was a useless, selfish daughter, dragging her father out into the cold against his will so that she could get some fresh air, so that she could breathe, so that she could escape when she knew he could never escape what was happening to him, not if she made him stumble behind his red walker as far as the North Pole. And to top it all off, in these precious moments at what was surely the beginning of the end of his conscious life, she couldn't even think of anything to say to him. To her own father.

She tried reminiscing. Older people loved to reminisce. "Remember when you had to drive up to Vermont to take me home from camp?"

"You don't say?"

"Yup. Twice, actually. Because when you got there the first time, I had already changed my mind and wanted to stay. But by the time you got home again, I had changed it again and wanted to leave. I was so bossy. Why did anyone listen to me? I was eleven, for god's sake."

But her reminiscences were apparently not his reminiscences. He smiled and patted her gloved hand with his gloved hand, his expression blank.

"Now, look, Daddy," she said, "you drove all day. I *know* you remember. You have to. You were so annoyed, but then you just laughed. That got me really upset—that you laughed at me, that my situation was comical and I was just one of a million little girls who did this, just an ordinary, predictable child. You have to remember all that. I got mad when you laughed, and you somehow understood and stopped laughing and pretended to take me very seriously, and then I was happy."

"Imagine that, imagine that."

Then another old man with an identical red walker appeared, and Aaron seemed to come alive. He stood up, with great effort, and offered the man his hand. "How do you do?" he said.

The slow determination of his movements, the difficulty and awkwardness of them, lent them a seriousness, almost dignity. Why don't we revere the elderly? Molly wondered briefly. She knew why. They were difficult and inconvenient. But how brave her father was just by standing up, by insisting on the code of conduct he'd been brought up with, by being, simply, polite. He still tried to open doors for Molly, his hand shaking. At first she told him not to, afraid he'd topple over. But then she saw it mattered. It was what a man did, a man brought up when he was brought up.

Aaron put out his hand to shake the newcomer's and with some formality introduced first Molly, then himself. There was a cookie crumb in his beard. Molly saw it and thought, for a flash, how foolish he looked, then recanted. The cookie crumb was not foolish at all, it was a battle scar from a battle to exist in a world that insisted on changing if he so much as blinked.

The other man introduced himself as Karl. "And this," he said, gesturing toward his plump, red-cheeked caretaker, "is Marta. She is kind, though strict."

"I go coffee," she said in a heavy accent, Polish, Molly guessed.

"Would you like coffee, too?" Karl asked. "Marta, can you get this nice young lady and her delightful father a cup of coffee?"

Molly pulled her wallet out, but Karl put up his hand and said, "My treat."

He was a good-looking old man, silky gray hair nicely cut, beautifully dressed. Molly shot a glance at her father. The cookie crumb had been dislodged. His beard could use a trim, but it wasn't too bad. Her mother took very good care of him. Better than she took of herself, but there are only so many hours in the day, as Joy said when Molly pointed this out to her.

Marta returned with four cups of coffee, and they sat there drinking the scalding coffee in the cold November air.

"Chilly for two old geezers like us," Karl said to Aaron.

"Not like the war," Aaron said, shaking his head.

"I don't know why people call them flying rats," Karl responded. "Listen to them. They coo like doves."

Neither Aaron nor Karl seemed to mind the gaps, the non sequiturs, in their conversation.

47

"We had cold showers in the jungle, but boy oh boy, we sure didn't mind."

"Just listen to them cooing. Like lovebirds. They're pretty, too. Don't you think?"

"*Oh that I had wings like a dove!*" Aaron said. "*For then would I fly away and be at rest.*"

"Dad? That's beautiful. Is that a poem?"

But her father had no answer for her. He smiled and turned his face up to the golden autumn sun. Molly looked on, a little envious, as the two men sat in a companionable silence, side by side, while the pigeons cooed like doves.

9

When the groceries arrived on Thanksgiving morning, Joy was astonished. "What are all these boxes? There's no room for them!"

"Don't worry," her daughter said.

"Don't worry," her daughter-in-law said.

Joy allowed them to usher her into the living room. Her original plan was to order Thanksgiving dinner from the coffee shop, but Molly had given her that you-are-crazier-than-I-thought look.

"Don't look at me like that. The kitchen gets too hot when you cook in it."

"I'll take care of everything," Molly said soothingly, as if that were reassuring. But Joy did not want her daughter to take care of everything, she wanted to take care of everything herself. As she always had, but no longer could.

"The coffee shop has wonderful turkey. Moist. And it's sliced."

"That is so depressing, Mom."

Joy knew she should find Thanksgiving turkey from the 3 Guys coffee shop depressing, too, but she found the thought comforting instead. Everything would be done, there would be no banging of pots and pans and oven doors; there would be no grease, no smoke; there would be calm instead of chaos. And she would be in charge.

She said, "I can't take the disorder of cooking a Thanksgiving dinner, the crazy mess, the hot steam in the kitchen, the millions of dishes. It's too much for me, Molly. But I don't want to give up my place as the matriarch, I suppose. What foolishness. But it's true."

Molly looked at her with interest. Then she laughed and said, "So the 3 Guys will be the new family matriarch?"

"I said it was foolish."

It was Danny's wife, Coco, who came up with a compromise. Coco liked to smooth the waters in the family. She was a fidgety intellectual woman who had a fondness for any problem she might be able to solve—her children, for example, presented wonderful puzzles. It was the chemistry teacher in her, Aaron used to say. Coco suggested they order everything ready-made from one of any number of high-end grocery stores. "Zabar's, Fairway, Fresh Direct. We live in New York City, people. We'll get a whole turkey, it's not carved, but you don't have to roast it, and everything else comes with it. You just heat everything up. No cooking."

Joy could not really see the difference between cooking and heating everything up, but she agreed. When there were no problems available for Coco to handle, Joy felt uneasy, almost guilty. Her daughter-in-law's intervention in the Thanksgiving-dinner difficulty provided a rush of satisfaction.

But Joy had not expected so many boxes.

"Where is Aunt Freddie?" Danny's daughter Ruby asked. She had just turned twelve. Her sister, Cora, was eight. Ruby and Cora—Joy never could understand how two nice little Jewish girls had been given such names, the names of women who waitressed in diners in 1932, but then, they thought her own name was odd, so there you were. Such sweet, pretty girls, flowering vines, wrapped around each other as usual, the two of them giggling and tangled on the couch.

"She's coming soon," Joy said. "She took a red-eye."

"A red-eye," Cora said. "Ew."

"It means a flight at night and you have to stay awake all night and your eyes get red," Ruby said.

"Aunt Freddie has blue eyes," Cora said. "So there."

Joy had marveled at first at how blasé the girls were about their Aunt Molly marrying a woman. She still marveled. *It's very strange*, she wanted to say sometimes. *Don't you see?* "Aunt Freddie will be here soon, in plenty of time for dinner," she said instead.

Ruby had recently gone through a Katy Perry phase, mercifully short, when she wanted to dye her hair blue. She settled for a blue wig on Halloween. Then, just a week ago, she'd done an about-face. She still dressed in incomprehensible combinations of sparkly garments. She was wearing such an outfit now, an undersized flared skirt in a strawberry print, each strawberry a collection of layered red sequins, leggings decorated with clown faces, a gold-and-pink-striped lamé T-shirt. But she was now reading *Tom Sawyer* with the same intensity she'd previously reserved for Katy Perry songs and gossip, and she was now intent on getting a pet frog.

"No more Katy Perry karaoke?" Joy asked. It had been cute, Ruby lip-synching the pop songs, until she began shaking her hips in suggestive ways.

"I don't want to be stereotyped," she said.

Daniel flopped down beside his mother. "As what? A teen pop star?"

"Don't tease me," said Ruby. "Mommy said her father teased her about the Beatles and she never got over it."

"Mommy's a stereotype," Daniel said.

Joy listened to the noises from the kitchen. Plenty of banging and crashing, but she found she didn't mind as much as she had anticipated. Still, they didn't know where anything was, those two,

Coco and Molly. Joy got up and went into the kitchen, pointed out the roasting pan, the carving knife. The women smiled at her tolerantly until she went back into the living room. Fine, fine, let them look high and low for platters and gravy boats. If they needed any more of her help, they knew where to find her. She would sit and put her feet up and watch her grandchildren. That was matriarchal, too.

Ruby pushed her younger sister away and kneeled on the floor at the coffee table. She pulled an ornamental wooden box toward her and began to rummage through old photographs that were kept inside. Two years before, Ruby's teacher had asked the class to construct their family trees. Ruby had formed an immediate attachment, bordering on obsession, with the heavy ancestral mustaches, the billowing knickers, the bows and fancy perched hats. She still gravitated to the photographs when she came to see her grandparents. She knew the names of every second cousin on both sides of the family. The old man with a long white beard spread across his chest who was wearing a fur hat was Aaron the First, as she put it—her grandfather's grandfather. He had eyes like an angry crow.

"Why do you like him?" Cora asked. "He's scary. And he's dead."

"So?"

"So he's scary and he's dead."

But Ruby only shrugged and gazed fondly at the old man. He had sent his children to New York for a better life, six of them, holding only one back to take care of him and his wife in their old age. That daughter had died of cholera at sixteen. Tragic, Grandma Joy told her. Ruby thought, *It served him right*, but she said nothing.

"Is the turkey cooked or not?" Joy said, back in the kitchen. "I don't understand."

"Mom, you did plenty. Just sit down and relax. Coco and I can do this part."

Joy had helped set up the extra table and the folding chairs, she'd helped Molly get the good dishes down, the good silverware, all the linens tucked away in boxes lined with tissue paper. That, plus everything she'd done to get Aaron ready—she *was* tired. In the living room, she watched as Aaron trudged in behind his walker. The girls looked up from the box of photographs.

"Do you want to look at your ancestors?" Ruby asked him.

"I'm too old to have ancestors."

"That's silly, Grandpa."

"I'm too silly to have ancestors," he said. He threw two kisses at the children. "Catch!" he said, and they both jumped and raised a hand, as if they were catching a butterfly. "Good," he said. "Sometimes they get away."

Joy helped him sit on his chair. He threw her a kiss, too. "Tough to be an old Jew," he said.

"I'm Jewish," Cora said.

Her sister rolled her eyes.

Cora showed Joy a photo of a man wearing a woman's bathing suit.

"That's my father," Joy said.

"Why did he wear a girl's bathing suit?"

"All the men did."

"There's a girl in my class who used to be a boy. But I've never seen her in a bathing suit."

"Dear god."

"Sometimes people get born in the wrong bodies," Ruby explained to her grandmother.

Joy checked to see if Aaron had been following this, but he appeared to be, mercifully, asleep.

After a while, Cora began her ritual search for spare change, running her small fingers beneath the seat cushions of the sofa. Mostly she encountered grit, but she did come across a few bobby pins. Beneath the cushion of a chair, she discovered a clear plastic bean with a tiny wire. She was so disgusted when she realized that it was her grandfather's hearing aid that she put it back. She moved onto the floor and lifted the sofa's skirt. There, among the dust balls, she saw a ballpoint pen she could not reach.

She moved on to the ashtrays.

"What are ashtrays for?" she said.

Ruby looked at her incredulously. "For ashes."

"For dead people in India?"

"You girls are very odd," Joy said.

"For ashes from cigarettes. And cigars. And pipes," Ruby said. "Don't be so stupid, Cora."

"But nobody smokes cigarettes or cigars or pipes."

"Well, they used to."

"Don't call your sister stupid," Joy said. "How would she know that? How do *you* know that?"

"Hasn't she ever seen a movie?" Ruby said, turning back to a black-and-white photo of her father in the bath as an infant.

But Cora was no longer interested in the conversation. The heavy blown-glass ashtray in the front hall that was full of keys and paper clips was too high up and too heavy for her to lift with any confidence, so she stood on tiptoe and scrabbled through the loose keys and stamps and sample tubes of sunscreen until her fingers felt the cool of silver coins, quarters, quite a few this time. She sat down on the floor and counted them, piling them in towers of four. Nine quarters and then, in a small dish on the dresser in the bedroom, four rather sticky pennies. Her grandmother gave her an eyeglass case with a snap to use as a wallet.

Back in the living room, clutching her eyeglass-case purse, she approached her grandfather in his red chair that looked like a Chinese throne, or what she imagined a Chinese throne looked like after she once heard her grandmother say, "Just sit in it and stop complaining. It's an antique. From China."

Her grandfather looked uncomfortable. He shifted his weight back and forth.

"Grandpa, want to see my money?"

He gave a short laugh. "You rob a bank?"

"I discovered it."

She unsnapped the eyeglass case.

"Whatcha got there? New glasses?" he said.

She thought he was playing with her. She took out two of the sticky pennies and held them over her eyes, the case safely clutched in her armpit.

"Don't do that," her mother said sharply. She had appeared suddenly, the way she often did. "Stop."

"Why?" Cora put the pennies back, her lower lip protruding, sullen. "I was just fooling around."

"Because the Greeks put pennies on dead people's eyes," Ruby said. "To pay the ferryman."

"Coco," Joy said to her daughter-in-law, "your children know far too much about death rituals."

Cora sat on Ruby's lap. "But, Ruby, I'm not Greek," she said. "And I'm not dead."

"*Kaynahora,*" Ruby said, looking up from a picture of a skinny elderly couple inside an old-fashioned grocery store. "That means you shouldn't get the evil eye."

"In Greek?"

Now their mother laughed, said, "You two. Honestly," and returned to the kitchen.

"So, Grandpa, you want to see my money?"

He gave another little snort of a laugh, just like the last one, then said, "You rob a bank?" He looked at the eyeglass case. "You wear eyeglasses now?" Then he began to sing: "*My eyes are dim, I cannot see, I have no-ot brought my specs with me-ee-ee . . .*"

"Grandpa, who's this?" Ruby held up a black-and-white photograph of a long-eared dog standing in front of a screened-in porch. She handed it to Aaron.

"That's Prince," he said. "That's my dog Prince."

He brought the photo closer to his face. Ruby thought he was looking at it more closely, but no, he did not bring it to his eyes.

He whispered, "Prince. My dog Prince," brought the photograph to his lips, and kissed it.

When Freddie arrived, Aaron recognized her, but he did not seem to remember her name.

"Look who the wind blew in!" he said.

Molly's son, Ben, got there a few hours later.

"Look who the cat dragged in!" Aaron said.

Ben did look a little like a cat at that moment, a scraggly alley cat. He had gotten a ride from New Orleans with a friend and they'd driven all night. His hair, not very clean, stuck up at unexpected angles in unexpected places. His clothes were wrinkled, even his parka. He had grown a beard, which disconcerted Molly for a moment. She worried about Ben, down there in a violent city with a job that kept him out so late. She worried that he drank too much, that he wasn't doing anything with his life. Sometimes she welcomed the concern about her parents as a distraction from her concern about Ben.

"You look handsome," she said. Ben Harkavy, bartender and handsome alley cat, the kind that rubs against your leg, then hops a fence and disappears.

Ruby and Cora, who loved Ben in a way that reminded Molly of her feelings for her father when she was a child, a reverential physical ownership, threw themselves at him for a double piggyback. Molly gently pushed them aside so she could give Ben a hug. Her arms around his neck, her face on his coat still cold from the outside air, she felt herself relax. Ben was a good boy. Ben was healthy and dear and safe in her arms. And with Ben here as well as Freddie, at last she would be able to make some order in her parents' lives.

"The cavalry," she murmured. "Thank god."

"You miss me?"

"God, yes."

"Don't make him feel guilty," Joy said. "Your mother doesn't like it that I miss her."

Ben hugged his grandmother and said, "You can miss me, too. Instead of missing her. I don't mind."

"I miss you the most," Cora said.

"You're just his cousin," said Ruby.

"So are you."

Ben squatted down and pulled them to him, one in each arm, and the apartment was boisterous and gay. Coco and Molly had used the dessert plates for the salad, but Joy found she didn't mind. The children were playing a game that involved pulling the table-cloth as hard as they could, but she didn't mind that either.

"To Mom and Dad," Daniel said, raising a glass of wine.

Aaron gave a bloodcurdling howl.

"Grandpa," said Ben, jumping up, kneeling beside Aaron. "What happened?"

"What are you talking about?" Aaron said.

Molly saw Ben go white. He had not seen too much of his grandfather in the last year, and when he had, Aaron had always managed to simulate conversation.

"Grandpa forgets sometimes," Ruby whispered to Ben.

He smiled at her. "Thank you." But he was obviously shaken.

"What's going on?" Aaron said, looking around with wild eyes. He swatted Ben away with his enormous white hand. "Off your knees, soldier." He caught Molly's eye. "I'm fine," he said. Then that awful sound, again.

By the time Molly brought out the apple pie, the sound had taken on an alarming volume and pitch.

"What do we do?" Molly said.

"Joy, what should we do?" Coco said.

"Mom, has he ever done this before?" said Daniel.

"Aaron," Freddie was saying, "where does it hurt?"

"I don't know what you're talking about," Aaron said.

Joy had not spoken. The room looked blank to her, as if it had emptied. The sounds were muffled. Except for Aaron's. He was hazy beside her, enormous, ashen, opalescent. But the sounds he was making were not.

"Aaron, eat some pie," she said. How stupid: Eat some pie. But it was all she could think of. She shoveled some pie onto a fork and held it to his mouth. "Delicious pie."

Aaron opened his mouth and allowed her to tip the pie in. He chewed. He smiled. He swallowed. The noise stopped.

Joy looked up at her family and smiled, though she could hardly breathe.

"Pie," she said.

Then the sound began again.

As Molly steered Aaron and his walker through the lobby, the doorman said *Pow! Pow!*, pretending to box. It was his favorite doorman, Ernie, but Aaron did not say *Pow! Pow!* back. Ernie looked solemnly at Molly as he opened the door, then he hailed a cab. Aaron's long, lanky body, always so thin and flexible he seemed to be made of pipe cleaners, was now stiff and unyielding. He sat on the seat of the cab, his legs out, feet still on the pavement. The doorman went around to the other door and tried to pull him over by his shoulders, sliding Aaron across the seat. His legs stuck straight out the door now, feet in the air above the street.

The driver got out, and he and Joy tried to bend Aaron's legs while Molly watched them as if she were witnessing a natural disaster, struck dumb, stuck in place.

"Well, hold my bags, at least," Joy said.

Molly took the three heavy bags.

"No problem, no problem," the taxi driver was saying. "Slowly, slowly."

We are in a cab, Molly texted Freddie. *The coffee is decaf, in case any-one asks.*

Getting Aaron out of the taxi was even worse. The driver, a

wisp of a man who said he was from Bangladesh and had a grand-father and knew how to respect the old, was holding him up beneath his armpits. Joy and Molly each took one arm, but Aaron began to sink to the ground, slowly, inexorably, the stiffness gone, as if he were melting.

"I can't, I can't," Aaron said.

"Nice man, do not give up," the taxi driver said. "For the sake of the nice ladies, do not give up."

Aaron's knees buckled, he was squatting, held up only by the two women and the determined driver. He sank lower and still lower, until Joy, shaking beneath the weight, was sure she would have to let him sink to the ground.

Just at that moment, two enormous arms wrapped themselves around Aaron, lifting him easily.

The two arms belonged to a security guard who was even taller than Aaron and far bigger, a muscular giant of a man. He held Aaron aloft, dangling him, Aaron's feet just touching the ground.

"We forgot your shoes," Joy said in horror. Aaron was wearing bedroom slippers. He was out on a cold rainy day in his bedroom slippers. "Your shoes, your shoes," Joy said.

"Mom, it's okay, he won't need them, it's the hospital . . ."

"Your shoes, Aaron. I'm so sorry." It was all Joy could see, his large feet, clodhoppers he always called them, brushing the pavement in the wool cable-knit sock slippers with deerskin soles. He hated them, but they kept him warm and they weren't slippery. "Oh, sweetheart, you hate these slippers. But why, Aaron? I ordered them from Hammacher Schlemmer . . ."

"He'll be in bed, Mom. It's okay."

Another security guard came running out with a wheelchair and Aaron was folded awkwardly into it. He was so weak he was not even moaning now. But his feet in their warm slip-resistant slippers were off the sidewalk, placed on the footrests by the two security guards, one guard per foot. Seeing the men handling the big feet, seeing each foot on its footrest, made the slippers seem less out of place, and Joy recovered herself.

"There you are, Aaron," she said, holding his hand. "There you are." She ran her other hand along the arm of first one guard, then the second, as if she could gather strength from them, Molly thought. Or for good luck, the way people stroke a talisman.

"You came to our rescue," Joy said. "And on Thanksgiving!" She looked around at the gathering, the first security guard an African-American, the second a giant as pale as Putin, clearly Russian, both towering over the Bangladeshi taxi driver and over her, a Jewish lady, and her daughter, a lesbian lady.

"New York is so cosmopolitan," she said as they wheeled Aaron in after more effusive thank-you's. "Isn't it, Aaron? We've always liked that. Aaron, do you want to be near the window while we wait? We can people-watch."

10

Daniel went to the hospital at lunchtime. He ate a sandwich, a very old-fashioned sandwich, he noticed—bright white bread, a few slices of pink boiled ham, a slice of orange cheese, a piece of pale iceberg lettuce, mustard the vivid yellow of newborn baby poop. The sandwich was a little stale, but comforting, and he wanted to be comforted. His father, the man who sang sea shanties in stormy weather, the tall, skinny father who'd swung his son onto his shoulders as if he'd been a scarf, this man of his childhood was lying in a hospital bed looking like another man entirely. Except for the beard. But even that was uncharacteristically shaggy.

Daniel finished the sandwich in four enormous bites, then answered emails while his father slept. Monday, a workday after the Thanksgiving weekend, so much to catch up on at the office, but his boss said he should stay at the hospital all afternoon if he needed to, working from his phone. If his mother came in, he'd have to put the phone away. She had an aversion to his phone, he wasn't sure why. He hoped she wouldn't come to the hospital, and not just because of his cell phone. He had noticed for some time, months, how tired she was, and this episode with Aaron had really knocked her off her pins. He looked at his father, at the gray beard and disheveled gray hair, the big hawk nose. He turned off his phone.

"Dad," he whispered.

His father twitched, but didn't wake up. His breathing was loud. Sinister red lights blinked above him accompanied by beeps like strangled birdcalls. It was too familiar, the beeping and blinking and labored breathing. Daniel stood up quickly, ready to make for the door.

Aaron opened his eyes.

"You'll be fine, Daniel," he said, reaching out a stringy arm and taking Daniel's hand.

"Me?" Daniel smiled and sat down. "How about you?"

"Where the hell am I?"

"Hospital."

"Don't worry, now. You'll be out of here in no time." Aaron heard the word "hospital," saw Daniel, and put the two together. They had, after all, been a pair, an intimate pair, Daniel and hospital.

"Thank you, Dad. Thank you for worrying about me. But I'm okay. That was thirty-five years ago. Remember that? Bad times."

Aaron nodded. "Terrible."

You were not much help, Daniel thought, in spite of himself. He'd convinced himself he'd put it all behind him, the worst year of his life, the year he was eighteen and developed osteonecrosis out of the blue, a year of searing pain, conflicting diagnoses, the year he couldn't walk, the year he spent in the hospital. His mother had practically moved into his hospital room to look after him. His father had not visited much. He was preoccupied, planning another business, squandering whatever was left of his own father's money. And he didn't like hospitals.

No one likes hospitals, Daniel thought now.

Maybe, Daniel's mother had said, maybe it's just too painful for him to visit. You mean he's too weak? Daniel answered. Yes, said his mother. Yes, I guess that is what I mean. But someone weak can love you, and he does.

"That was a long time ago," Daniel said. "This time, it's you we have to look after. Are you comfortable, Dad?"

"Who knows."

"Well, you, presumably."

"Don't believe everything they tell you," Aaron said.

For a weak man, he was physically strong. His hand still held Daniel's, and Daniel felt the grip tighten.

"Dad?"

Aaron moaned.

"Pain?"

Aaron moaned again. He couldn't speak. He looked pleadingly at his son.

When the nurse arrived, she tipped a pill into Aaron's mouth from a small, pleated paper cup. "Now drink up," she said, handing him a plastic cup of water.

Aaron looked at her with wide-open eyes—eyes full of fright. Did she notice? Daniel wondered.

"It will help the pain," Daniel said.

The moans got louder, a crescendo of misery. Daniel thought he had never heard anyone in such misery.

His father's face seemed to shrink with the pain, his eyes growing wider, fearful, his ears standing out from his head like little elbows.

"Dad, I wish I could do something for you."

The moaning stopped. "You got a stick of gum?"

Daniel put his head in his hands. He waited a few seconds, breathing deeply. "Dad," he said when he looked up, "how is the pain now?"

"Nobody tells me anything," his father muttered, then drifted off into a robust, drugged sleep, snoring deeply.

Aaron was supposed to come home from the hospital soon, and Molly tried to talk to her mother about how she would manage once Molly went back to Los Angeles.

Freddie was gone already, back to her sleepy undergraduates. Her semester started a week earlier than Molly's, and Molly envied her that roomful of hungover boys and girls, students forced to sit and listen. You could test students, grade them, fail them if necessary; you could tell what the correct answer was. Your mother was another story.

Molly tried, she really did. She ran through all the things her father could no longer do, all the things Joy would have to help him with, even writing them down on a large legal pad in broad black letters. Aaron could no longer stand up by himself. He couldn't get himself into bed or out of bed or out of a chair or into a chair. He could not walk by himself, though he often tried, which meant he could not be left by himself for even a minute. Joy would have to dress him, and Joy would have to undress him.

"This is not news to me, Molly."

He needed to be bathed, frequently. And dried. And powdered. He required ointments and unguents. He needed all the attention to pouches and adult diapers that Molly was so queasy about, as well as the rashes and sores they produced, and even so, the bed linens often had to be changed in the middle of the night.

"I can cope. I have *always* coped. Haven't I? Admit it, Molly. Through everything."

"Yes, you cope, but can't you cope with some help? Just keeping him fed is exhausting."

"I order in," Joy said.

Molly had noticed that. In the days leading up to Thanksgiving, her father was given the remains of the same turkey meat loaf dinner from the coffee shop for days, interspersed with the remains of the roast turkey dinner and the turkey burger deluxe, for variety. Joy had tried to feed Molly endless teaspoon-size portions of turkey leftovers, too, but Molly had rebelled and insisted on cooking. Both her parents pronounced her chicken too spicy and her green beans undercooked, then turned rather loftily back to their scraps.

"Next thing I know you'll be sending both of us off to assisted living," Joy said to her now. "To a facility."

"A locked ward."

"In the meantime, I need you to fix the computer. I hate the computer."

She said the words "the computer" with categorical disdain, the way someone might say "Tea Party."

Molly felt the buzz of her phone and went into the bathroom so she could check the text without incurring her mother's rage.

"Help," said the text from Daniel. "Dad thinks I'm in the hospital."

"You are," she responded.

"He thinks I'm the patient."

Daniel was waiting when she got to the cramped café ten minutes later. She swept in, looking harassed, windblown. She always looked harassed and windblown, he thought, even when she was reading a magazine on the sofa or sitting in a restaurant at dinner. Her clothes were always pressed and tucked in and perfectly, overly, coordinated; yet she always appeared to be weathering a great storm. Maybe it was the way she moved—big, jumpy gestures.

"Mom is going to have a nervous breakdown and die," she said.

"Hello to you, too!" He stood up and kissed her. She rested her head on his shoulder for a moment, relaxed and soft. Then he felt her pull herself up. Back on duty.

"Those two are killing each other. What are you eating? I want a panino."

He laughed. A panino, singular. She did like to be correct, Molly did. "I already had a sandwich at the hospital that was prepared in

1958," he said. He ordered an espresso. "A good espresso place in our old neighborhood. Imagine that."

"Imagine that. You sound like Daddy."

Daddy. He liked it when she said that. It made everything seem softer, kinder than it was. "He's in agony one minute, and then the next minute he forgets he was in agony. It's like a backward curse. Or a Greek myth: Dad-alus."

They talked about Coco and his kids for a few minutes. Ruby had turned twelve a couple of months before. Many of her friends were studying for bar and bat mitzvahs. She was not interested. Even the lure of a party and gifts did not entice her. Religions caused wars. Religion was mass hysteria. Like soccer fans, but worse. Cora, on the other hand, was already planning her party, five years to plan it, that ought to be enough, Daniel said, laughing. Then he remembered he should probably ask Molly about Freddie. "How's Freddie?" Molly started to tell him how Freddie was, and he nodded, not listening. Molly said, "Are you even listening? You never listen, Daniel." Molly always told him he didn't listen, and it was true. How else did people get through the day? Daniel's notion of a perfect afternoon was to sit in a garden in the warm sun with bees buzzing lazily around him, his eyes half closed, a battered Panama hat comfortably situated on his drooping head, like the scene in *The Godfather* with an ancient Marlon Brando. Daniel had no interest in being ancient just yet. He just didn't like to rush. He gazed idly at the glass display case and wondered if the cookies were any good. He held his hand up to summon the waiter.

Molly thought, He moves like an old Chinese man on a hill doing tai chi, dignified in the dawn. His expression was serene, self-possessed. But Molly knew he was merely distracted, constantly distracted.

"Wake up," she said. "What are we going to do, Daniel? About Them?"

He shook his head. What, indeed? "I do come up to the apartment every Saturday," he said. "And I bring the girls, too, sometimes. We go to a museum first and then come for dinner. Mom never wants to come with us to any of the museums, though. She doesn't like to leave Dad, although all he does is sleep in front of the TV. I've tried to get him to go in a taxi and then a wheelchair, but he never wants to. Neither of them is very cooperative. They would have such a good time, watching Ruby sketch—she loves Picasso."

"She *would* love Picasso," Molly said, laughing. "But walking around museums at this point . . ."

"Cora is so into the minerals at the Museum of Natural History. Not just the ones that look like jewels. I think she has a scientific bent . . ."

"Come on, Daniel. She's eight. She likes rocks. Which I think is fantastic, I like rocks, too. But what are we going to do when they let Dad out of the hospital? Mommy can't take care of him anymore."

"I don't want them to be old," Daniel said.

"The alternative and all that . . ."

"Maybe."

"We can't put pillows over their faces."

"No," Daniel said. "We would miss them too much."

11

Joy went to work the Tuesday after Thanksgiving. She was expected, and if she was honest with herself, she could not stand another day sitting in the hospital with Aaron.

The museum was in the process of moving to a new building that week. The little neighborhood museum devoted to preserving a small, vibrant, gritty slice of New York life, the life of pushcarts and sweatshops and vaudeville and Tin Pan Alley, was moving into a new building in a different part of town. It was going to be incorporated into a larger organization, to become a section of the City University system, where there would be more room, more money, more prestige. It was as if the drab middle-aged museum had snagged a rich dentist.

"Dr. Bergman! There you are." The new director was a nervous, suspicious woman with a heart-shaped face instead of a heart, that's what Joy had told Aaron, and he'd laughed. She usually introduced herself as Miss Georgia, as if she were a beauty pageant winner. "Out with the old, in with the new," Miss Georgia was known to say. It was her mandate. It had to do with grants.

"Packed up and ready to go?" she said when she saw Joy. "The new year approaches. The movers wait for no man."

Then, like a schoolmarm or a politician or the Wicked Witch of the West, she shook her finger in Joy's face.

Joy, a little taken aback, recovered and jauntily waved her finger in Miss Georgia's face in response.

By Wednesday, they were in the new building.

"It's big and bulky and it's cement, it's sort of like being inside an inverted swimming pool," she told Aaron. She smoothed his hospital gown. "There are no windows that I can see. The stairs were made by giants for giants. And inside, I couldn't decide whether I was about to be overcome by claustrophobia or agoraphobia. Help! I wanted to say. I'm just an old lady looking for my cabinet of old tchotchkes."

Her new department was called City Collections.

"Like a sanitation-truck company," she said to Aaron.

She had arrived at the new building out of breath and a little confused. Her bags were heavy and she tilted noticeably to the left. Lopsided or not, she thought, here I come.

"But this is a closet," she said when Miss Georgia showed Joy her new office.

"A storage room," the director corrected her. "But it will do nicely. Look at all the . . . storage."

The narrow, windowless room was lined by expensive-looking built-in file cabinets. There was also a table, very white and modern, and a rather worn gray chair on casters.

"But I do need a desk," Joy said. "I mean, after all, a person needs a desk."

"But that is your desk," the director said, pointing to the table.

"But it has no drawers. There isn't even a drawer for a pencil."

"Perhaps you have a nice mug," the director said, patting the table encouragingly. "For your pencil."

"Do you think they're trying to get rid of me?" Joy said to

Aaron. "I don't think they can fire me for being old, so they'll just torment me, right? Until I leave of my own free will."

She spooned some ice cream into his mouth.

"They'll see how easy it is to get rid of me," she said. "They're in for a surprise, aren't they, Aaron?"

Aaron was prescribed various painkillers that teenagers in shrinking Midwestern towns abused. But when asked what the pain was from, the doctors were as canny and cautious as politicians. Molly wanted to shake them. *Tell us what is wrong so we can fix it*, she wanted to say. *He is suffering. And I have to get back to L.A. to teach.* She bombarded the doctors with direct questions, but the doctors always managed not to answer directly. Aaron had bladder cancer—they would concede that much, but everyone already knew that much. Heart failure, colon cancer, bladder cancer, Alzheimer's. Yes, yes, but what was causing this pain?

"Daddy wants a pastrami sandwich," Joy said, coming out of Aaron's hospital room. "Honey, did you hear me?"

Molly had just asked the resident how long her father had to live. The resident said he could die tomorrow. Or not. He could live for a year. Or not. Or more. Or not.

"New York pastrami!" the resident said. "Good sign. A man with an appetite."

In fact, Aaron had eaten nothing but a spoonful of ice cream in days, and when Molly arrived with the sandwich, he said there was a disgusting smell in the room, waved his big hand at her, and made her take it away.

She took the pastrami sandwich, which she had gone all the way to Zabar's to get, to the cafeteria and split it with her mother and brother.

"It shouldn't go to waste," Joy said.

"That doctor said Daddy could come home in a day or two," Molly said.

Joy wagged her head noncommittally.

"So we have to think about that."

"You do need some help, Mom," Daniel said. "Maybe someone to live in. Just for a while."

"Molly's here."

Molly said slowly, clearly, " 'Help' as in 'You can't get good help these days,' not help as in 'My daughter is a great help.' "

"And Molly has to leave on Friday."

"I'll cope," Joy said. "I always have."

"And when you're at work? Do you want Daddy crawling down Park Avenue with no pants on? He needs someone to watch him."

Joy sensed that Molly was right, but she wondered if it was necessary for Molly to bark at her like that. It was certainly ex-peditious, that bark, for even when Molly was not right, people tended to listen to her. But not this time, Joy thought. "I'm not sending him to a home," she said. "Period."

"Maybe we can get a nurse's aide to come in," Daniel said.

"I don't want those people in my house. A different person every day . . . strangers snooping around."

"But it would be so 'cosmopolitan,' " Molly said, her voice full of sarcasm.

"What are you, sixteen years old, Molly? Give me a break."

Molly did not give her a break, how could she? "You have to hire someone, whatever it costs. What have you been saving for all these years? A rainy day? This is the rainy day."

Daniel said, "If it's the money—"

"Of course it's the money."

"—then we can help you out, right, Molly? I mean as long as Ruby gets into a good public high school and Cora gets into a charter school for middle school and . . ."

"Take from my children?" Joy made a disgusted, dismissive sound. "Out of the question."

"Well, then you could always sell Upstate," Daniel said.

A horrified silence.

Then, "Never."

Joy had inherited the little house Upstate when her mother died. She had fought to keep it safe from . . . well, from Aaron. There was no other way to put it, though she had tried at the time. We're putting it in a trust, she had declared. A trust in my name. To keep it safe from creditors, she'd said repeatedly. But they all knew what she meant. Safe from Aaron. The house sat on a hill above a stream in Columbia County, New York. Upstate, Joy's mother used to say. We're going Upstate this weekend. Upstate was where the noise and worry of the city disappeared and the stream gurgled, where the birds sang. Upstate was the fruit of her father's labors, that's what he used to say when he stood on the porch and looked out at the maple tree and the three birch trees and the weeping willow by the stream. It was also the fruit of his frugality, and finally of his generosity. He had worked so hard, supporting every stray uncle or aunt or cousin who wandered through his door, and there had been a mob of them. Then the Depression ended and he was a manager, and then the war ended and he was a vice president. Spend a dollar, save a dollar, he said. And one day he announced that he had a surprise, and they drove out of town and into the country to the white-shingled house. He had saved and he had invested. Upstate was his reward, a reward he left to his wife and she left to Joy.

"I am not selling Upstate. It's all I have. Do you want me to have nothing? Nothing?"

"Yeah, Daniel. Do you want her to have nothing?" Molly said.

"Of course I don't want her to have nothing. I just want her to hire some help."

"So do I. But we can't sell the house. It's our family house."

Daniel noticed that Molly said "we" can't sell the house. But it was their mother's house, not theirs. Molly spent ten days a year in the house, if that. What difference did it make to her? Daniel spent every summer there with his wife and children. He loved the house. But love and sentimentality were two different things, or they ought to be.

"It's part of who we are," Molly was saying. It was true she no longer spent any time there, but she thought about the house all the time. It was an anchor of some kind, an East Coast anchor. It was there, stable and firm, even if she was not.

"Why are you fetishizing this house? Mom and Dad need help, they need money to pay for the help, the house is an asset that can be liquidated. Do you want them to live in squalor so you can idealize a house you never use?"

"Children! Stop it right now."

Molly and Daniel were quiet. They looked at her sheepishly.

"You can argue about the house after I'm dead."

"Mom . . ." they both said.

"You can squabble about it then. I need peace now."

Daniel wondered if the house was even worth anything. But it had to be worth the salary of an underpaid health-care worker.

"We just want you to hire—"

"How can I hire? I have no money! Why are you talking about real estate when your father is so sick?"

Daniel left, wanted to get home before the girls went to bed, and Molly walked with her mother back to Aaron's room. She knew she was being selfish about the house. She did not like to think of herself as selfish.

"You know," she said, "whatever you have to do about the house, I'm fine with it."

Joy said, "Enough, Molly."

"Not that you have to consult me or anything," Molly added. "Or ask my permission."

"I'm not selling the house with or without your permission."

"Well, good, good. But if Daniel is right and you need money . . ."

"I am leaving the house to both of you. It's all I have, and I want to leave it to my children."

"Oh, Mommy," Molly said, her voice tearful. She took her mother's hand and squeezed it. "You know you don't have to leave Daniel and me anything."

"So you *do* want me to die with nothing."

They got back to Aaron's room just as Aaron was being hoisted from the floor beside the bed, soaked and soiled. He had lowered the bed rail. "Get off me," he was shouting at the nurse. White, shaking, he was maneuvered back into bed by Joy and the nurse. Joy wiped him down as gently as she could, but he was a mess.

"Stop bothering me," he kept saying. "Leave me alone, all of you."

Joy helped the nurse attach a clean pouch. When the nurse had gone, she smoothed the sheets and poured some water, which Aaron refused to drink.

"We'll be safer with this." The nurse reappeared with an armful of nylon webbing. She began calmly to strap Aaron to his bed.

"What are you doing to him?" Joy cried.

"Get away from me!" Aaron said.

"Get away from him!" Molly said.

Joy lunged for the netting, trying to pull it off Aaron, but the nurse blocked her and continued with her task, saying, in the same calm way, "It's for your safety, Aaron."

Aaron struggled against the restraints. "Get me out of this!" His eyes rolled like a frightened horse's. "Help! Help!"

"Nurse, please, why are you doing this? I'll stay with him every minute, I'll watch him, I'll hire someone to watch him."

"Maybe if you had arranged that earlier," the nurse said. "But it's too late for tonight. This is for safety, Aaron," she said again as she wrestled him into the restraints. "Your *safety*."

Aaron thrashed and scratched at the orange netting. "You!" he said, poking out a finger and aiming it at Joy. "You can't do anything right! You can't do anything right!"

Joy pulled her hand back from the strap she had been trying to unbuckle. The soiled towels she had used to clean him fell from her other hand to the floor.

"You can't do anything right!" Aaron yelled again. He kept yelling: "You can't do anything right," his face distorted with rage. "You never do anything right! Never!"

"Aaron . . ."

"You did this! *You* did this to me! It's your fault!! You do everything wrong! Everything!" He twisted in the netting like a huge, dying fish. His voice was hard. Spit flew from his cracked lavender lips. "You can't do anything right," he roared. "You can't take care of anything."

"Daddy, stop it. For god's sake . . ."

He sneered at Joy now as he struggled in his webbing. "You can't take care of anything, you know that? You can't do anything *right*. Nothing. You can't do anything . . ."

Molly steered her mother out of the room. Her father's enraged screams followed them down the hall. "Okay," Molly said, holding her mother's arm, feeling the bone of the skinny arm beneath Joy's sweater. "Okay," she said again, but her mother said nothing, and Molly found herself looking away, ashamed, almost as if she'd walked in on her parents having sex. Or something. "Okay."

Her mother turned on her, yanking her arm free. "I've had it," Joy said fiercely, as if Molly were going to argue with her.

"Yeah," Molly said. "Yeah. Jesus."

"Am I not flesh?"

"I know. He's not himself."

"If you prick me, do I not bleed?" her mother continued. She was crazy-eyed now and walking quickly, waving her arms.

"Mom . . ."

"Don't Mom me. After everything I've done. Everything I've lived with all these years. Everything I've had to do. I am a human being!"

Shylock, the Elephant Man. Her mother was pulling out all the stops. And why shouldn't she? Molly felt as if she had just seen a horror film, a monster movie, and her poor father was the monster.

She coaxed her mother to a couch in the waiting room.

"I've had it," Joy kept saying. "I've had it, I've had it."

Then, almost in slow motion, she slumped forward.

She said, "Had I, haa . . . I . . ." She stopped.

"Mom?"

"Haaa daaa. I haa. I, I." She stopped again and looked at Molly in alarm.

12

What was that awful smell? The smell was almost a parody of a fresh smell, a little like chewing gum or floor cleaner, but sickly and decomposed, as if someone had tried to cover up the stink of decaying flesh. Was it decaying flesh? Was it gangrene? Joy thought of wiggling her feet to make sure they were there, but they seemed far away and she was so tired. She heard Molly badgering someone. She heard Daniel's voice, too: "But I thought you said she'd had a stroke."

Oh yes, now she remembered. She was in the hospital visiting Aaron. Someone must have had a stroke.

"She did, a mild one. But we also think she has a highly contagious antibiotic-resistant infection called Clostridium difficile. C. diff for short," said a male voice Joy did not recognize.

But who had had a stroke? Who were they talking about?

"C. diff is common in older patients being treated with antibiotics in the hospital or in a nursing home," the male voice continued. "Has your mother been in a nursing home recently?"

"No," Molly said. "But she practically runs one."

"That's why she's in an isolation room. The C. diff."

"Excuse me, Doctor," Daniel said. "It's just that there's another patient here. In this isolation room."

Daniel was always so polite, using someone's title, his voice soft, though Joy could hear the frustration and anger. She worried about him hanging around a hospital after what he'd been through. He should go home to his family. She would look after Aaron.

"Well," the doctor was saying, "we believe the other patient probably has C. diff, too."

"You *believe*?" Molly said. "They both *probably* have C. diff? What if one has it and the other doesn't? The one who has it will give it to the one who doesn't."

"Then they'll both have it," the doctor said, his voice a little impatient with Molly's absence of scientific method. "That's why they're in isolation."

C. diff. Joy knew she had heard about C. diff somewhere. On the radio, perhaps. Did C. diff cause a terrible odor? The smell, that was what was worrying her.

Molly and Daniel stood together in the blue paper gowns and caps and booties, the white masks and the almost transparent gloves they had to wear in their mother's room. It was hot in her curtained-off portion and rivulets of sweat ran down Molly's back. The woman in the next bed, who may or may not have had C. diff, was small, even smaller than Joy. Her face was caved in around her missing dentures. Her skin was dry and yellow and mottled and tight as a cadaver's. She looked very much like a cadaver. She nearly was a cadaver. A man, Molly presumed it was her son, sat beside her, rocking forward and back, saying, "Mommy, Mommy," and for the first time in her life Molly wondered if it was bizarre that she still sometimes called her mother Mommy, because this man was as old as she was and he was saying Mommy and he was surely bizarre. "Nurse! Doctor! Help! Help!" he would occasionally cry out, running into the hall. He had a disturbing voice, flat and desperate and loud. "My mommy's not answering me," he would say, wringing his hands, when a nurse appeared. "My mommy's not talking!"

The nurses did not like this odd middle-aged man who be-haved like a child. And they did not like coming into the room, because of the smell.

"What *is* it?" they asked each time they entered.

"What *is* it?" Molly and Daniel asked each other.

Molly was glad of her paper mask. She got up to check the trash can one more time, but it was still empty.

"What *is* it?"

A strange raspy sound came from the woman in the other bed.

"It's a death rattle!" her son cried. "Mommy, don't die."

He ran out of the room and returned with a nurse, who threw on a gown, snapped on gloves, and examined the emaciated woman.

"It's a cough," the nurse said gently. "Don't worry. It's just a cough." She patted him on the shoulder.

Then she said, "What is that nasty, nasty smell?" She pulled away from him. "No wonder this poor woman is coughing." She sniffed at him, like an unfriendly dog. "Is that your *gum*?"

"Gangrene," Joy said.

"Mom's awake!" Daniel said. "Mom said gangrene! Did you hear her, Molly? Nurse? Hooray! She said gangrene!"

The other woman's son was sniffing at his own arm. "Bengay?" he said.

"Bengay?" Joy said, actually sitting up. "Good god."

"I put it on every morning," the son said, eyeing the nurse warily. "After my shower," he added with sudden defiance.

"You mean like moisturizer?" said the nurse.

"Good god," said Joy.

"Bengay. That's a new one," the nurse said as she left the room.

"Mom, I'm so happy to see you back to yourself," Daniel said.

"Welcome back to the world," said Molly.

"Why are you dressed like that?" Joy asked.

"Isolation," said Molly.

"You can be alone even in a crowd," Joy murmured, and fell back to sleep.

Soon another nurse came in.

"Sir," she said to the man in Bengay. "I'm going to have to ask you to leave. I'm sorry, but the smell of your, um, ointment is disturbing patients and staff and visitors up and down the floor."

"Yes, but do you have the C. diff test results yet?" Molly asked the nurse. "I think both patients deserve to know why they're in isolation *with each other.*"

"Sir?" The nurse ignored Molly. "Sir, please go home, wash it off, and then you can come back. You don't need to use so much, you know. Just a little bit. Why don't you try it at night, before bed? But for now . . ."

"Excuse me, Nurse, but if his mother catches something from my mother," Molly said, "you will have more to worry about than Bengay."

"I use it every day," the man said. "I can't leave Mommy. I can't. Mommy is very sick." He began to cry a little. He covered his face with his hands. "I can't."

Molly patted his back. The smell was less upsetting now that she knew what it was, but it was just as strong. It burned her nostrils. It stung her eyes. She said, as mildly as she could, "You don't want your mother to catch something from my mother, do you?"

He shook his head.

"And if my mother catches something from his mother," Molly said to the nurse, "you should know that my brother is a lawyer."

But it was as if Molly were not there. The nurse, a small, even dainty woman, emanated authority, and she wanted this man, the source of disturbance on her floor, to go away. "Sir?" she said, her hands on her hips. "I really don't want to have to call security."

"I don't think you understand," Molly said. "This man will not be bullied and neither will we. We are in this together." She stood in solidarity beside the unhappy, redolent man. "Aren't we?"

He stopped crying and took his hands away from his face. He

seemed afraid to look at the wee, mighty nurse, but he made eye contact with Molly, brief, furtive eye contact. Then he looked down at his mother. She didn't move. The only sound in the room was her rasping breath. He gazed at her for what seemed a long time, then he squared his shoulders.

"Mommy," he said, "we are calling your doctor."

And he led the way to the nurses' station.

When Molly got back to the room, the Bengay man was headed home and arrangements had been made to separate the two potentially infectious patients.

"Strength in numbers and the desire to get that poor guy off the floor."

Daniel was holding their mother's hand. She was awake again. "Good job!" he said to Molly.

Molly laughed. "That's the voice people use for their kids. And dogs."

"I don't know what you're talking about," Joy said weakly, reminding herself of Aaron, which made her worry suddenly and viscerally how he was. "Daddy! How is Daddy?"

"Dad's doing fine," Daniel said. "He's out of the hospital, how about that? He's home."

"But who's looking after him? What is he eating? How is he—"

"It's all taken care of, Mom," Molly said. "You'll see."

13

The apartment was full of voices, all timbres, tones, and accents. It was like an orchestra. The cushions of the sofa cradled her aching body. She listened to the voices: a deep, male, harsh African musicality; the free-for-all vowels of Portuguese English; the loops of female Polish. And Aaron, his intermittent wailing reaching back to Middle Eastern chanting in its cadences, as if all his ancestors were crying out at once.

Joy opened her eyes. A man the color of ebony smiled at her as he walked past the door toward the kitchen. He stopped to confer with a boxy woman in wide capri pants. And there was Elvira, too, the Bergmans' housekeeper, tall and thin as a daddy long-legs, behind the boxy lady, nodding. It was such a lively group, the three of them speaking together, one more incomprehensible than the next, incomprehensible to Joy, presumably to one another as well.

Joy closed her eyes again and listened to the languages she could not comprehend. It was as though she could comprehend nothing at all, drifting comfortably on the soft outskirts of comprehension. Eventually Danny introduced the compact, quiet black man. His name was Walter. Danny said that Walter came at night. Joy smiled at Walter. How kind of him to come at night to care for Aaron. To care for her. Lovely, she said when Danny introduced her to Wanda, the woman shaped like a UPS package. Wanda emitted a gurgling laugh. Thank you, Joy said. Wanda emitted the gurgling laugh again. She spoke only Polish. Joy said, How kind of you.

"Wanda and Walter are trained in changing the colostomy bag," Danny said. "And they taught Elvira."

"Lovely."

"You absolutely cannot do it anymore. The doctor said you can't even touch it. That might be how you got C. diff."

"C. diff is very, very dangerous." She remembered now, she had heard about C. diff on *The Joan Hamburg Show* on the radio. "Treacherous."

"So you really have to take it easy, Mom. Will you be able to do that? Just rest and let your strength come back?"

"Danny, you're so good to me. You and your sister are so good to me."

"Molly will be back in a few weeks."

"She's a good daughter. I am so lucky."

Daniel smiled. She reminded him of his daughters when they had a low-grade fever. How sweet they became.

"You're okay with not touching the pouch? Molly and I were a little worried. We know you like to take care of everything, especially about Dad, which is admirable, completely understandable. But this is really important. No pouch."

"Lovely," Joy said, closing her eyes. "Lovely."

She could remember, in a soft, foggy way, the motions of taking care of Aaron, gathering his pills, counting them, explaining what each one was, then explaining again, helping him out of his wet pajamas, squatting down to get each of his enormous feet into his pant legs . . . And then the pouch, removing it, emptying it, washing Aaron, drying the hole, affixing the new pouch . . .

Each night Walter helped her to the bathroom. He brought her things to eat and helped her move the spoon from the bowl to her mouth. What a kind, kind man. When he appeared in the room carrying a tray or a basin of water, she was always pleasantly surprised. There was that kind man again.

When it was not night, there were the other kind people. Elvira, wiry and fast as a greyhound, whisking into the room and whisking out again. She had worked for Aaron and Joy for many years, coming every other week for a few hours. But now, Danny explained, she was coming in three mornings a week. She had insisted, he said. She didn't trust the others. Joy smiled when he said this. She smiled when he said anything. She really did not care what he said or what anyone else said as long as she did not have to move, as long as she could lie on the couch and rest. Never had fatigue been this heavy, never had it been this welcome. Lovely, she said when someone spoke to her. Thank you, she said. How kind of you.

"So kind," she said. "Everyone is so kind."

14

Could Molly have ever convinced Freddie to move to New York? Of course she could have. Even though Freddie had a tenured position teaching English at UCLA while Molly had been an adjunct at a community college in New York. Even though Molly had a better position here and was paid more, too. Even though her new Catalina Island investigations, unlike the work she'd been doing in Syria, were not likely to get her kidnapped or beheaded. But she did not want to convince Freddie to move to New York.

She thought guiltily of her mother and father trapped in their apartment. Freddie's father, Duncan, was old, too, as Freddie sometimes had to remind her, but that had not entered into Molly's decision. He did not weigh on Molly's mind as he should have, meaning she often forgot he existed.

But he did exist, he was old, and now he had fallen.

Freddie spoke to the paramedics, who said they'd thought at first that Duncan's hip was broken, but he was standing on it, so it couldn't possibly be broken. "The pain would be unbearable," they said. "Take him to the doctor, though, just to make sure there are no sprains."

The assisted-living facility where Duncan lived was called Green Garden, so Freddie and Molly naturally called it Grey Gardens. When they arrived, Molly waited in the car while Freddie went upstairs and got her father into a wheelchair.

"We going to the track?" Duncan said.

"No. We're going to the doctor. Because you fell."

"I'd rather go to the track."

It turned out you could stand up with a broken hip, after all. Duncan Hughes could, anyway. After the doctor saw his X-rays, Duncan was taken to the hospital in an ambulance. Freddie and Molly followed in the car. Freddie was too shocked to say much. A broken hip for a man in his late eighties. That was pretty much it for her father. Pneumonia would come next, and he would die. That's what always happened.

"He's not like other people," Molly said, as if she'd read Freddie's thoughts. "He'll walk out of there, Freddie. You'll see."

Freddie called her brothers and sisters. One brother lived in Melbourne, one in Hong Kong. Both sisters lived in Rio. They ran a boutique together.

"They all said the exact same thing," Freddie told Molly. " 'Keep me informed.' "

"They came for his eighty-fifth birthday. I guess they think that's enough."

"So then they'll end up coming for his funeral, and it won't make any difference because he'll be dead. People should have pre-funerals."

But Molly turned out to be right: Duncan was not like other people, there was no funeral, and he returned to his room at Green Garden.

"He seems happy to be back. Although he thought the name was Green Goddess. And he still wants to go to the track."

"We should take him. Maybe his luck will hold out. We'll win some money."

15

Daniel took Ruby and Cora to the Museum of the City of New York. He thought they would like the Victorian dollhouse, but they preferred an exhibit on graffiti. Then they walked down Fifth Avenue, past the hospital, toward his parents' apartment, and the girls insisted on getting ice cream from a vendor although it was windy and cold.

"Let's sit in Grandpa's park," Ruby said. "Maybe we'll see the rat."

They sat on the cold bench and watched pigeons fluff themselves against the wind. There was no one else there. Daniel wondered if his father would ever see the park again, if he would ever leave the apartment again. For all he knew, his father was slipping into a new stage of dementia, leaving the park, the apartment, the entire world. Leaving Daniel forever.

The world without Aaron Bergman was unimaginable to Daniel. Even this pocket park, where he sat on a bench in a swirl of dead leaves with his daughters, was confusing without Aaron. Why was the park here if not for Aaron? Why were any of them in the park if not for its association with Daniel's father?

"It's weird without Grandpa here, isn't it?" he said.

"Do you think raccoons come here?" Ruby asked.

"Or the coyote?"

His father was the embodiment of the word "entitled," Daniel understood that. It was a kind of strength, he understood that, too—Aaron's sense that whatever the world had to offer, it was certainly on offer to him, and deservedly so. Daniel envied him that confidence. Perhaps it arose from being born into a well-to-do family. But it had stayed with Aaron even when he lost his fortune. A small fortune, but Aaron had lost it, lost a profitable, solvent, well-run family business.

My daddy was a gambler, Aaron used to sing, and Daniel would joyously sing along. They listened to Woody Guthrie records while Aaron's business swelled up into a big balloon of impossible debt and then, one day, just like that, popped and shriveled and disappeared. Daniel had been quite young, so young he didn't really remember being well-off. What he remembered were the years afterward, one surefire scheme after another, his mother getting a job, taking any freelance work she could rustle up even as she went back to school. He remembered the need, not for the family to live—there was always, miraculously just enough for that—but the need inside his father, the need for money, and for money to make money, and for that money to make more money, and for the lost money to reappear as borrowed money and the whole thing to start over again.

"*I've been doing some hard travelin', I thought you know'd*," Daniel sang in a nasal country-Western voice.

"Daddy," Ruby said. She tugged at his arm. Things about him had started to embarrass her.

"*Hard travelin', hard ramblin' . . .*"

"*Hard gamblin'*," Cora joined in.

"You both make me sick," Ruby said. But she joined in eventually, too. There was no one to hear them. Just an old man with the same red walker Aaron had, and by the time he reached the bench, the song was over.

16

Freddie could not decide whether or not to go to New York for Christmas. She loved going East for the holidays, it was still a novelty for her, it always would be—the snow, the cold, the lights on Fifth Avenue.

"Everything you hate about it," she said to Molly, "like the crowds, for instance—I love that. I love being a tourist there."

"You go to New York and see my father, I'll stay here and see your father. They won't know the difference."

As soon as she said it, Molly wished she hadn't. "I'm sorry. It's so easy to dine out on them. Cheap joke. Why don't we both stay here this year?"

But Freddie knew that Molly's family Jewish Christmas was somehow their most important holiday. They celebrated Hanukkah in a haphazard way, lighting candles on the nights they remembered. But Christmas was a time they all got together, all of them, even Molly's ex-husband and his current wife.

"And Ben will be there," Freddie said. She had said the magic word, the defining word, the name of the son. She watched Molly's face grow almost beatific.

"Ben," Freddie said again, just to see the effect, to see the benignity intensify.

Then Molly caught her at it. "Oh shut up," she said.

Freddie started to laugh. "The idea of you staying here for the holidays—it's pretty funny, Molly. Go see your cockamamie family and I'll stay here and look after my cockamamie father. We will long for each other across the wide continent."

———— 17 ————

In her parents' bedroom, it was dim and cluttered with medical apparatus. Her father sat in his leather recliner, a blanket spread neatly over his knees. He grabbed Molly's hand and motioned for her to lean down, then put his lips close to her ear.

"There's a black man in the house," he whispered, obviously alarmed.

"That's Walter, Mom's nurse's-from-when-she-broke-her-ankle-ten-years-ago's son-in-law's cousin's mother's friend from church. Or some such thing. He's from Ghana." He was a very gentle man with a beautiful smile and a staccato, musical accent. He knew how to change a colostomy bag. He was strong. He was kind.

"What's he doing here? There's a black man in the apartment, I tell you," he whispered again, sputtering now. He pulled on her arm.

"Walter. From Ghana," she said, louder.

"No one from Ghana is named Walter," he whispered. "He's a fraud. Get him out."

She straightened up and looked down at her father. His beard was trimmed. His hair was combed. Even the hairs in his ears had been trimmed. His nails were clean. His shirt was unstained and buttoned properly. And that blanket on his lap—he could have been a gentleman taking in the salt air on an ocean liner.

"Daddy, he's here to help you."

"I don't need help. What are you talking about? Help? I don't need help. You're the one who needs help."

"Well, Mom needs help. You don't want her back in the hospital, do you?"

"Hospital? Nobody tells me anything. Where's your mother?"

"She's resting. Do you want her to drop dead from exhaustion? Then who would take care of you?"

He looked pointedly at her.

"*Me?*" she said. "I wouldn't last two minutes."

"Honey?"

"Yes, Daddy?"

He motioned her to lean down again. "There's a black man in the house," he whispered.

"I knew he was a Republican," she said later to Freddie on the phone. "But he never struck me as any more racist than anyone else his age. The uncomfortable kind of racism, not the suspicious kind."

"He's not himself, though."

"I hope not." That didn't come out right. "Anyway, he's incredibly difficult one minute, then he just switches over to sweetness. When I left the room, he and Walter were sitting side by side eating vanilla ice cream, watching NY1."

"That's the real Aaron, the vanilla ice cream one."

Freddie was a gracious person. It was one of the things Molly loved about her.

"Thank you for being a gracious person, Freddie," she said. "Even in the face of ghastly in-laws."

Freddie laughed. How lovely that laugh was. How close Freddie seemed.

"They could have stopped with the telephone . . ." Molly said.
"Who?"

". . . No television, no cars or planes, no computers. Just telephones, the invention that allows me to hear you from so far away, the magical telephone. It would have been enough."

"That and penicillin," Freddie said.

When they hung up, Freddie called her sisters. They were the first and second children, born only eleven months apart. They liked to call themselves Irish twins, though they were not even Irish. Freddie was the youngest, separated from Pamela and Laurel by almost a decade, but they acted like little sisters to Freddie's mind, giggling and teasing each other, trading clothes, trying each other's lipsticks, doing each other's hair. Freddie had never paid much attention to them, two squealy older girls off on their dates, counting their sweaters. It was no surprise when, both divorced, they opened a boutique together, though why they chose Rio de Janeiro she could not fathom. They must stand out in that city like two sore thumbs, two plump pink sore thumbs, she thought. They resembled Freddie's mother, though they did not remind Freddie of her mother. They were pinker than her mother, who had skin that was soft and blushing, and they were chubby. Freddie's mother had spoken like an adult woman who hoped someone might listen to her now and then. Her older daughters spoke like girls at a slumber party, breathy and secretive, then shrieking with laughter. And now, presumably, in Portuguese. Freddie could not envision them among what she imagined to be the slender, sophisticated bronzed beauties of Rio. They had done well with their boutique, but when Freddie tried to picture them in their store, she saw only the two of them selling clothes back and forth to each other.

She had been closer to her brothers in age and in temperament. But they had grown up and gone their own ways, like her sisters. If any one of them had moved any farther away from Los Angeles, they'd have ended up being home again, the world being round and all.

"I'm keeping you informed," Freddie said when Pamela answered. Laurel immediately picked up another extension. How quaint, Freddie thought. Like our grandparents.

"He's a marvel," Pamela said.

"What are you two doing for Christmas?" Laurel asked.

"Well, Molly had to go to New York to see her mother, so . . ."

"No, I meant you and Dad."

"Oh."

"He won't know what day it is anyway," said Pamela.

"I could take him to the track."

Neither of them thought that was a good idea, but they were sure Freddie would come up with something.

"I picture you two sitting in front of the fire at Green Garden," Laurel said.

"Oh, perfect!" said Pamela. "Drinking eggnog. Just the thought of you and Dad in front of the crackling fire makes me nostalgic."

Freddie did not tell them Green Garden had no fireplace.

She called her brothers next, but she got the time wrong and woke one up, and the other did not answer.

"Molly, I miss you," she texted.

"Never again" said the text that came back.

There were certain things about the Christmas Hanukkah season that Coco did not like. First of all, she felt guilty for having a Christmas tree, not because she was Jewish, but because it was such a waste. A living thing cut down for nothing.

"I understand not eating meat," Daniel had said the first time it came up, when Ruby was two. "I understand being a vegetarian. But you're *not* a vegetarian. And even if you were a vegetarian, you would eat vegetables. Vegetables would die so you could live. Isn't a Christmas tree like a vegetable? It grows out of the ground. It's like a big stalk of broccoli."

"We don't eat Christmas trees. It doesn't die so I can live. It dies so we can decorate it."

"We could eat it. We could chop it up and cook it after Christmas."

"Very funny."

Coco hated waste. It was that simple. The death of the pine tree was not the issue. She was not a fool, she was a science teacher, and she understood the importance and beauty of decomposition, how it brought new things to life. But the planting and cultivating and harvesting of what was essentially a big bauble, a bauble on which to hang other baubles—that was unconscionable.

"It provides employment," Daniel said.

"Those Canadians who drive down every year and sell them on the street?"

"It provides enjoyment!" he said, pleased with the rhyme.

She sniffed her disapproval.

"Ruby really, really wants one."

Then, of course, Coco said "Okay!" instantly. For Ruby, anything.

And now she made a big, happy fuss over the tree each year. She did love the smell, the look of them lined up on the sidewalk, the ritual of carrying the tree home. Once it was standing in the living room, though, and opened its fragrant branches, spreading the outdoor smell through the house, Coco had to fight off a flicker of sorrow. Like any useless bunch of carnations or daisies, the Christmas tree would shrivel and die. She cheered herself with the thought that the city now had a policy of gathering the trees up and using them for compost.

Choosing presents helped to cheer her up, too. Each potential recipient of a gift presented a puzzle to be solved. This year, she had solved two problems at once—a gift for Ruby, who was so unpredictable and in-between these days, and a more immediate use of the Christmas tree than compost.

She'd been a little unsure about the kit of science projects she'd gotten the girls. It used marshmallows, which of course they would like. It was, however, educational, and educational gifts sometimes fell flat. But when they opened their gifts on Christmas Eve, the science kit was both Ruby's and Cora's favorite. Cora immediately took herself off to watch marshmallow after marshmallow swell prodigiously in the microwave. And because the kit included a slingshot, Ruby, in her new Tom Sawyer phase, was delighted. The rubber tubing, the patch of leather, the plastic Y-shaped stick did the trick. She had been lobbying for a frog for Christmas, but without any real conviction.

"Best of all," Coco said, handing her another package, "you can make a new, stronger slingshot from the Christmas tree!" It was a whittling knife.

"This is the best Christmas we ever had," Coco told Daniel that night. The tree had been put to use, Cora went to bed wearing every wearable gift and clutching a new stuffed dog and a bag of marshmallows, and Ruby went to bed clutching her knife.

"I hope Ruby doesn't cut a finger off in her sleep," Daniel said.

"It's a jackknife. It's all folded up. Would you say that if she were a boy?"

"No. Then I'd be sure there would be cut-off fingers. Don't let my mother see the knife."

"Didn't you have a jackknife when you were a kid?"

"They said I could have a BB gun when I was twenty-one."

"Typical."

"I had a *compass*."

It was too difficult to load Aaron into a taxi this year to go down to Daniel and Coco's, so the family gathered for Christmas Day at the apartment uptown instead.

"Grandpa, look. I made a slingshot. And I'm whittling a new wooden handle for it, too. A slingshot uses kinetic energy."

"That's a dangerous weapon," Aaron said, handling the stick.

"My father would have murdered me if he knew I had a Christmas tree."

"It only shoots marshmallows."

"We always had a tree," Molly said. "Grandpa Bergman didn't mind."

"Like hell."

Ben had been sitting on the floor playing with the Spirograph he'd gotten the girls. Now he examined Ruby's knife. He put it in his pocket.

"Thank you, Ruby. I've always wanted a pocketknife."

She chased him around the apartment and Cora chased her. Joy watched them fondly. But the noise was pounding in her ears, the laughing and happy screaming. Wrapping paper flew around them, ribbons trailed from the girls' shoes, stuck to the soles by tape. Cheerful children, she said to herself. A blessing. She repeated it silently several times to chase away the other things she was thinking, which were, Shut the hell up, Stop it, Why must you be so noisy, You are not on the street, You are driving me crazy.

Ben's father, Doug, came with his wife, Lisa, a sweet youngish person with long, lank hair and a nervous laugh. Who would not laugh nervously, Joy thought, thrown into the bosom of your husband's ex-wife's family? She greeted the woman with as much warmth as she could muster. It wasn't Lisa's fault that Molly had left Doug, it wasn't Lisa's fault that modern mores compelled all these exes to gather together and exchange gifts, it wasn't Lisa's fault that Joy missed Doug and held Lisa responsible, even though it was *not* her fault, it was Molly's, but of course Molly had the right to be happy, of course she did.

Molly threw her arms around Doug when she saw him. I love you, Doug Harkavy, she thought. I will always love you, you are Ben's father and there was a time when we planned our future and our future died yet here we are, and I will always treasure those days and I'm so glad I'm no longer married to you and I bet you're glad you're no longer married to me.

"Whaddya get me?" she said to him. She realized she was a little drunk. Ben had made a cocktail with apple cider and bourbon.

"Where's Freddie?" Lisa said politely.

"Home with her own dysfunctional family. Well, just her father, really. She couldn't leave him. He's been ill. Men-tal-lly ill." Oh dear. She was truly drunk.

"Okay, Mom, sit yourself down right here and drink this big glass of water, that's a good girl."

Molly beamed at Ben. She beamed at Doug and Lisa. Good old Lisa. She beamed at her mother and her brother, at Coco and the two little girls. When her gaze got to her father, she stopped beaming. He was tugging at the colostomy bag.

"Daddy, don't."

He looked up at her. He shrugged.

"You should eat something," Ben said, but Molly was no longer drunk, not even tipsy. She was sad, suddenly and thoroughly sad. She shook her head at Ben, afraid if she spoke she would cry.

"Marshmallows," said Cora. "Eat marshmallows."

"I don't have marshmallows," Joy said. "But I have Mallomars. Would anyone like a Mallomar?"

"Shoot a Mallomar, Ruby," Cora said excitedly.

Ruby said, "I ain't botherin' with suchlike nonsense."

"Ruby is channeling Tom Sawyer," Coco said proudly.

"Sounds more like Slim Pickins," Molly said.

"We used to say '"Ain't" ain't in the dictionary,'" Daniel said to Molly. "Remember? But it turns out it is."

Joy started telling Ben her story of when she had polio as a child.

"They were all so hysterical," she said. "My mother fainted, my grandmother had to tend to her, and for all I know, it wasn't polio at all. Maybe my leg fell asleep."

"But you were in the hospital, Grandma. They put you in the hospital. It must have been something."

"Oh, who knows, they were all so hysterical."

They ate Mallomars while Cora explained Boyle's Law as she understood it, which Coco said was brilliant, until Cora began speculating on volume and pressure in the bowel, at which point Coco interrupted and said the bowel was not a closed system, and Molly involuntarily glanced at her father and thought of his system, definitely not a closed one. He had fallen asleep in his chair, his chin on his chest.

"Do you want to try the experiment, Grandma? You put marshmallows in a syringe."

"Well, I don't have any syringes on hand, sweetheart. Maybe another time. You'll teach me."

Aaron's head jerked up and he said, "You can't teach an old dog new tricks."

"I bet you can," Cora said. "Can we try? Can we get an old dog? From the ASPCA?"

"But what if it really won't learn any new tricks and the saying is true?" said Daniel.

"And we're stuck with an old dog with a low IQ?" said Coco.

"Well, at least it won't live very long," Ruby said. "If it's so old." Cora started to cry.

"Ruby, really," Coco said. "Was that necessary?"

"I'm very sensitive," Cora said between sobs.

"Death is natural," Ruby said. "No dog can live forever, especially an old one."

Daniel rocked Cora on his lap. "Our dog can't ever die, Cora sweetheart, because we don't have a dog."

But that made her cry harder.

On the walk home from the subway, Ruby kicked the snowdrift and waited for her parents and Cora to catch up. Cora was crying and dawdling because she was cold. If Cora would hurry up, she would be warmer, their mother explained, embarking on what Ruby thought was a clear and reasonable, though rather long, disquisition on the relationship between heat and energy. Ruby had tried hugging Cora from behind and duck-waddling along against her to provide some insulation, but there was no satisfying Cora when she was in this mood.

"Hurry up! I'm freezing!" Ruby called.

The snow that had piled up at the edge of the sidewalk was not really a drift. It had been pushed there by snowplows the night before, and it was already specked with black smuts of city dirt. Ruby scooped up a handful of dirty snow and packed it into a ball and took a few steps up the side of the mound of snow. She put the gray snowball in the leather pocket of the slingshot and let it fly, but it fell apart and disappeared into the dusk.

She shuffled her feet on the icy sidewalk. The wind blew and the sky was dark. Cora sniffled and shambled beside their mother. After two more blocks, she again refused to move, demanding a taxi. While her mother and father argued with her, Ruby pushed off and slid on the ice all the way to the next corner. There, the great berm of snow created by the plows took a right angle. She was boxed in by three-foot walls of snow. A narrow path of foot-prints ran up the snowbank. Over the course of the day it had cut into the bank like a mountain pass. It was frozen now, the bumpy pattern of boot soles shining in the street light. Ruby struggled to the top and surveyed her territory. "I'm the king of the world," she hollered into the wind. Nobody heard her.

She bent down and pried loose a small rock that had been plowed up with the snow, then fitted it with frozen fingers into the slingshot.

The hole it made in the plate-glass window of the corner mar-ket was small, like a bullet hole in a windshield in a television show. The cracks around the hole were the cracks around the hole in the ice on the skating pond in a movie and the little girl slips in, mittens flailing above the cold black water, and drowns.

Ruby stood, three feet above the sidewalk in the freezing wind, and stared in surprise at the hole in the window. The hole severed the stem of the letter *T* in the word MARKET. MIKE'S CORNER MAR-KET. Ruby felt her mother yanking on her arm, but did not see her. She saw only the mouth of the man who owned the store, Manuel (not Mike, there was no Mike), a nice man who sold her candy and Doritos. His mouth was moving, his missing tooth appeared and reappeared, a blink of dark space. Like the hole in his window. His face was contorted in mystified rage. He slapped the top of his shiny bald head with an open palm.

"What were you thinking?" That was her mother's voice. "Hand it over this minute." That was her father. They were all inside the store now, all of them in the narrow space between the counter and the racks of chips and boxes of power bars, in a line— Ruby, her father, who was pulling her slingshot from her frozen grip, her mother, her sister, who was white and awed but still wailing, Manuel, and a man Ruby did not know. Manuel's voice was speaking Spanish. Manuel's hand was pointing at the man who stood in front of the cash register. He was a tall man in a navy blue parka. His hair was soft and dark and fell over his forehead like a boy's, but he was not a boy, he was a young man. He was wearing a small beanie, the Jewish beanie, she forgot the name. His eyes were bright and blue. He was holding a Kleenex to his cheek. It was bright red. Red with blood. He was the handsomest man Ruby had ever seen.

The Spanish words and the words of her mother were all mixed together with Cora's wails. The noise was amplified by the constricted space, and the warmth was overwhelming after the windy street, and Ruby was sweating and crying, and her mother was holding her shoulders and shaking her, not very hard, and Manuel was slapping his head with both hands, and Cora was gulping her sobs down.

I'm sorry, I'm sorry, Ruby thought, but no words came out.

And then the handsome man put one hand on Ruby's mother's shoulder and one hand on Ruby's shoulder, the hand with the bloody Kleenex. The blood was so bright. It was the color of the paper stuck in the bottom of the plastic container of raspberries. It was almost pink. The tissue had sucked the color up. It flapped like a flag. A horrible, bloodstained flag. Ruby stared at it, and she didn't even hear herself scream, but she screamed, screamed bloody murder, as her father said later. And everyone else was suddenly quiet, even Cora.

Ruby screamed for quite a while, but eventually she heard what the handsome man was saying. He was kneeling down on the dirty bodega floor, and he hugged her and said, into her cold ear with his warm breath, "You didn't mean any harm. I know that. Accidents are everywhere, just waiting for us, aren't they? This accident is over now. No one was hurt. No one was hurt."

She did not remember her father reassuring Manuel that they would pay for a new window or Cora telling her she would be paying for it from her allowance for the rest of her life.

The handsome man held her hand and walked home with them. He was a rabbi. Call me Rabbi Kenny, he said. That's why he was wearing a beanie, she supposed (yarmulke, that was the name, she remembered). That's why he forgave her. He was a man of the cloth. Manuel had given him a first-aid kit he sold in the shop, no charge, and it had two gauze pads, which the rabbi had unwrapped and placed over the cut. He asked Ruby to apply the Band-Aids to hold them in place. There was no blood coming through them. No more blood, said the rabbi. See?

"You might need stitches," Daniel said.

The rabbi said, "No, I don't think so. Ruby did an excellent job patching me up."

Ruby's mother gave Ruby a cold glance.

"Why did you do that?" Daniel asked for the tenth time.

Rabbi Kenny said, "It was a mistake, a lapse in judgment, and Ruby seems like the kind of person who learns from mistakes."

"Well, that's true," Coco said. "She does. But we're so sorry, Rabbi."

Ruby was thinking how kind it was of the rabbi to refer to her as a person, rather than a little girl. Or a monster.

"I'm sorry, too," she said, the first words she had spoken since what she already thought of as the Incident. "I'm really, really, really sorry." She looked into her victim's lovely blue eyes. She wanted to say, Forgive me, Father, for I have sinned. She had seen it on so many TV shows. It was obviously inappropriate for a rabbi, which seemed a shame, for she *had* sinned and she *did* want his forgiveness.

"People should wear helmets," Cora said.

Rabbi Kenny lived a few blocks away with his wife and two small children. His synagogue was around the corner. They had passed it millions of times, but never gone in.

"We're not exactly observant Jews," Coco said.

"Daddy says monotheism is the greatest disaster to befall the human race," Cora said.

"Well, Daddy said Gore Vidal said that, sweetie," Coco interjected quickly. "I don't know that Daddy thinks that himself."

"He said." She stopped and folded her arms and glared at her father.

"A clever but simplistic sentiment," Daniel said, "and like everything Gore Vidal said, it's a little bit true, that's all I was saying."

"Daniel!" Coco was clearly embarrassed.

"Daddy!" Ruby said.

Cora gave a triumphant "ha" and moved on.

"I still remember my haftorah," Daniel said to the rabbi. "I'm not a complete pagan."

Rabbi Kenny laughed. "Well, if you're ever locked out of the house or something, pop into shul."

Molly burrowed into the pillows, eyes closed, a cool scented breeze blowing in through the open window. She listened to the crows in the neighbor's sycamore. The deplorable tree shed darkness and elephantine leaves, but high in its branches there lived a family of crows, an exemplary family, crow sons and daughters from the year before helping out with their new siblings, all sober as a portrait of Queen Victoria and her own mob of children.

There were pomegranates and grapes growing over her neighbors' fences. One house had a garden of neon-colored succulents, another a cheery garden of pink and yellow roses. Molly never argued with anyone who described Los Angeles as a jumbled and incoherent city, a nightmare of traffic bordered by jumbled, incoherent rows of houses in every architectural style known to man. Its flora was jumbled, too, incoherent and abundant palm trees and pine trees, roses and cacti. The place was a foreign country as far as Molly was concerned. And after almost sixty years in New York, years of Manhattan in all its might and frantic momentum, every day felt like a day of blessed vacation in a faraway vacation land. Work did not interfere with this holiday feeling. She could hardly believe her luck. Some sky above her, some sun. Some crows.

She thought of her mother shivering and feeble in the biting January wind. A disconcerting tableau: her lovely mother, her lively mother, bundled and drained, shuffling like a refugee in her own life.

Molly had always thought of her mother as someone sharp and bright, someone light and airy, full of color and warmth and intensity. A kind of maternal sun goddess, always there whether she showed herself or not, always there behind the inevitable clouds of Molly's life, of the family's life. Like Aaron, Joy had been both attentive and absentminded as a parent, but to Molly the periodic negligence was freedom, it was privacy, independence. If Joy worked late or was out of town at a conference and the cupboard was bare like a nursery-rhyme cupboard, Daniel and Molly rejoiced, for that meant hamburgers or pizza or Chinese food or a trip with Aaron to the market to buy the makings of eggplant Parmesan, his specialty. The pressure from such kind and consistently inconsistent parents was negligible. Joy and Aaron held, for reasons the children did not understand but did not question, an unshakable faith in Molly and Daniel. If either child stepped out of line, the line moved accordingly. Even now, Molly could feel Joy trying to forgive her, to understand her act of geographical treachery. But Molly could hardly understand it herself. She had fallen in love. She had been offered a job. She woke up happy every morning. Those were facts. Why did she feel she had to explain them, excuse them; why weren't those facts the explanations in and of themselves?

Molly called her mother every day. She never mentioned the sunshine and the soft breeze. It would be in bad taste to call Joy's attention to the glorious physical reality of Los Angeles. Joy called Molly every day, too, sometimes more than once: she was still so weak from the C. diff, the wind was ferocious, the mayor said something appalling. Sometimes she called to tell a funny story or report on the medical progress of someone Molly had never met, to urge Molly to watch something on television, to discuss her health or Aaron's behavior or a doctor's report or a possible side effect of a pill neither of them was taking. "I told Dr. Moritz he gives me a reason to live," she would say after a dentist appointment. "I have to live many, many years to amortize the cost of these new implants." Molly would laugh. Her mother often made her laugh. Just as often Molly listened annoyed and impatient, yet even then she found herself soothed by the inconsequential drip, drip, drip of the conversation. Her mother's voice made her feel safe, safe from the loss of her mother.

"You're too far away," Joy said.

"So are you," Molly said, but she said it gently, and she meant it.

She also meant to visit every six weeks. It did not work out to be quite that often.

"Don't come, don't come, this is the worst winter we've ever had, it's not even safe to go outside," Joy told her, and Molly pretended she thought her mother meant what she said. She put off her visit for two weeks, three weeks, then a month. The snow fell in New York, then fell again. "The sidewalks are sheets of ice," Joy would say. "Treacherous sheets of ice." The weathermen warned the elderly to stay inside. It was too cold, too windy, too icy. "I went downstairs just to stick my nose out the door, just to get some fresh air, just a walk to the corner, but the doorman wouldn't let me leave the building. Not one step. Far too dangerous."

"The doorman takes better care of my parents than I do," Molly said to Freddie one morning, a beautiful morning, the air brilliant and blue.

Freddie handed her a cup of coffee. "Thank god for those doormen."

"My mother says she has cabin fever. You know, I couldn't do anything about that even if I were there. I can't change the weather. And she won't come out here, even to visit, even for a week. Well, how could she? She can't leave Daddy, and he certainly can't come. So what good would I be there anyway if they can't leave the house? I mean, I spend more time with my mother on the phone now than I ever did in person when I lived in the city."

Molly was talking to herself, Freddie understood that, and she sat in the winter sunshine not quite listening. Her own father had a new girlfriend. It was causing ripples of resentment in the facility, and not only from his former girlfriends. The social worker seemed somehow offended, too. "They're all over each other," she'd said in the last call.

"Am I supposed to leave my job? Leave you? Leave my whole life?" Molly was saying. "Well, maybe she thinks since I did it once, I could do it again, just roll the film backward . . ."

"I don't like the direction in which this monologue is going," Freddie said. "I really don't."

". . . Of course, that's not what she wants, which is good, because it's not going to happen, because how could I even get my old job back, and what job would you be able to get in New York . . ."

Freddie stopped listening again. It was indecent to intrude on such desperate thoughts. She tried not to worry that Molly might someday approach her with a serious plan to leave L.A. A few times when she had taken Molly at her word and thought the guilt outweighed everything else and suggested they move to New York, Molly had been horrified and said, "Can't I feel guilty in peace?"

—— 19 ——

For Joy and Aaron, the months were long and cramped, though not without excitement. The apartment teemed with people in rubber gloves, and the atmosphere was pungent and gurgling with strange cuisines, sausages and beans, African pumpkin and foo-foo, fish heads floating in soup pots, chicken feet protruding from stews. Joy's eyes burned from the spices in the air. She was afraid to look in the refrigerator.

She was still tired, more tired than she had ever imagined a person could be and still rise up and stand on two feet. Her hearing was going, too, she was sure of it. "I'm deaf, Paw," she said to Aaron, and he smiled because he knew he was expected to, not because he thought she was funny, she could tell. There were days when she was glad of losing her hearing, the babel of languages and the sounds of pain thereby muted and dulled. The cold and snow continued morning after morning, afternoons of snow dissolving into snowy nights. Joy and Aaron, trapped inside, migrated from one end of the apartment to the other and back. Aaron could no longer use a walker, and the one time they had tried to push his wheelchair in the snow, before the temperature really dropped, the wheelchair bucked and slid and crashed into a bank of snow.

The wind blew and iced branches fell. The sidewalks dwindled to slippery tracks. The days, short and dark, seemed endless. Joy wondered if Aaron suffered from choking claustrophobia, too. She couldn't ask him. He no longer said more than a few stock phrases. For Joy, the way one indistinguishable hour ran into another was frightening. She came to cherish the arrivals and departures of Walter, Elvira, and Wanda. They were like the chimes of a clock, like church bells, dividing the day into its proper parts.

On one afternoon when the sun peeped out and the temperature rose to just below freezing, and Joy could stand the seclusion no more, she bundled Aaron up in a heavy sweater and the parka she'd gotten him on sale at McLaughlin's, which looked so good on him.

"We have to get out of our cloister, Aaron. We are going to breathe some fresh air."

She adjusted his cap, a tweed driving cap that did not cover his ears.

"Your big ears are going to freeze," she said.

"Watch your language." It was more than he had said in days, and Joy pulled off the hat and kissed his head.

"There."

Sometimes she wanted to put her hands around his neck and squeeze the last lingering pretense of life out of him. More often, she wanted to bury not him but herself—bury herself in her down duvet and never show her face again. She missed him terribly.

She put on her warmest coat. Wanda pushed the wheelchair to the front door and Gregor made a fuss over them, shaking Aaron's hand, then high-fiving him. Though the days of Aaron walking to the park with his little red wagon were gone, every cloud had its silver lining, that's what they said, and Joy, unsteady and weak, took possession of the red walker herself for their outing.

"Won't Coco be pleased, recycling and all," she said to Aaron as she followed him out the door. She leaned down and whispered in his big ear, "I feel like the red caboose of the Old Jew train." She turned to Gregor. "I'm the caboose," she said.

"Good for you, Doctor," Gregor said.

She often wondered if he thought she was a real doctor. He held the door and smiled and nodded encouragement.

The shock of the cold almost stopped her. The snow, banked up on the sidewalk, looked ponderous and old. But the sunlight and the sky, that blaze of blue sky, were miraculous after so many weeks of looking out the window at sky the color of an old nickel.

They turned into the park where Aaron had spent so many afternoons.

"Isn't this nice?" Joy said. "Oh dear god, we're free!"

Aaron, inside his heap of warm clothing, said nothing.

"Okay, Aaron." She sighed, disappointed in spite of herself. "Have it your way."

She sat on a bench blinking in the sunlight like a night creature.

"Koffee?" Wanda said.

Whenever Wanda said coffee, it seemed to Joy that the word began with a *k*.

"No," she said. "Thank you, but I dare not." Dare not. Where had that come from? A book she'd read? Her grandmother? Did all grandmothers use the same phrases no matter what era they lived in? "My digestion," she added primly, as if Wanda did not know their digestive behavior, hers and Aaron's, intimately.

"You go," she said to Wanda. "Go get your koffee. I'll watch Aaron."

And that is what she did, gazing at him with the love of decades past and the angry exhaustion of a sleepless night and the terror of the days and nights to come.

I dare not think that way, she said to herself. I dare not.

The air smelled cold, but the sun gave the illusion of warmth. Snow that had piled on the bushes dripped, just a bit. It was almost like spring, which is just what the man approaching, pushing a familiar-looking red walker, said.

"It's almost like spring!"

He was accompanied by a pink-cheeked woman who immediately began to speak in Polish to Wanda. This must be Aaron's friend, Joy thought. She watched as the man settled himself on the neighboring bench. He adjusted his gloves and his hat and his scarf, then turned to her, obviously about to speak. Instead, he stared.

"Joy?" he said. *"Joy?"*

"Karl? Oh my god. Karl!"

They clambered to their feet and embraced.

"Sixty years? I think that's how long it's been, Karl. I can't believe it. I can't believe you recognized me."

"Sixty-six years," he said. "I would know you anywhere."

They sat down again, on the same bench this time. So this was Aaron's park friend Karl. This was *Karl, her* Karl.

"Karl," she said. "You really are Karl."

He was better-looking, in a way, than he had been as a young man. Old age suited his angular face. His face had been awkward for a young man's face. Now it was distinguished. He wore a beautiful overcoat, and his scarf was elegantly tied. He exuded prosperity and confidence. Even the red walker looked natty. It matched his luxurious silk scarf.

"I wondered if I'd ever see you again," he said.

She had wondered, too. "The world is strange," she said.

"Wondrous strange."

"You have met my husband," Joy said, putting a hand on Aaron's sleeve. "Aaron, your friend Karl is a very old and dear friend of mine."

Aaron nodded affably.

"I've heard about you from Aaron. But I had no idea you were you."

Karl lived right down the block. He was a lawyer, or had been until he retired.

"I'm still working," Joy said.

"It's something you love," Karl said with such assurance that Joy felt buoyed.

"Yes, I do." Must remember that.

They talked until the clouds washed over the sun and the cold could no longer be ignored.

"Very much money," Wanda said to Joy, when they were out of earshot, rolling her eyes toward Karl and his caretaker.

"He was poor as a church mouse when I knew him."

But Wanda's English did not include church mouse or the past tense. She said "Yes" emphatically, and they made their way home.

20

Danny arrived at the apartment for dinner an hour late, but Joy had expected as much. He worked hard, such long hours. But since Aaron had become so sick, Danny made sure to have dinner with her at least once a week, no matter how busy he was. He did it to be nice, she knew. Which both touched and saddened her. We all prefer to have someone visit for our company rather than be kept company, but she must not be greedy, she reminded herself. He was here, and as always when she saw him in the doorway, she was happy, deliriously happy. Sometimes she thought she would swoon with love for him. He put his arm beneath hers to walk her to the dining room, and she felt safe for the first time in days, since he had last been to see her, to be exact. He comforted her, just by being in the same room.

On the other hand, there he sat, expecting to be fed. Thank god for Wanda, because Joy had forgotten to arrange anything for dinner. She tried to remember what exactly she had done all day that kept her from taking care of dinner for Danny, sweet exhausted Danny coming from work in the cold.

Aaron was in bed. He'd had his dinner already, leftover turkey meat loaf from Joy's ordered-in dinner the night before. He used to laugh when Joy fed him from the various dinners they had ordered in, saying she was a genius at assembling and rearranging garbage. Wanda had made stuffed cabbage and a cucumber salad for Danny, which she made him every time he was there, despite the fact that neither Aaron nor Joy could possibly digest that particular meal. Danny never seemed to notice he was the only one eating it. Joy was having the meat loaf left over from the leftover meat loaf she'd given Aaron. She watched Danny wolf down the stuffed cabbage in huge, animal mouthfuls. She really ought to have taught him better table manners. It had somehow not held him back in life: he did have a wonderful wife and wonderful children and a successful career. But his table manners . . . disgusting.

"Mom?" he said, and gently wiped the corner of her mouth with his napkin. "Catsup."

"Dribbling?" she said. "Time to put me out to pasture."

She was excited tonight, Daniel noticed. She folded and refolded her napkin. She absentmindedly picked up a lipstick from the cabinet behind her and applied it at the table using the back of her spoon to make sure it was not on her teeth.

"Going somewhere?" he asked.

"What? No!" She put the lipstick back. "No. Where would I go?"

"Well, it's great you were able to get out to the park yesterday, anyway. Was Dad's friend there?"

"Oh yes. Mmm-hmm. He was there."

"Nice, isn't he?" he said.

"Oh yes."

Joy wondered why she didn't tell Danny who Karl was. She certainly had nothing to hide. "Daddy just lit up when he saw him."

Karl had been so gentlemanly, waiting at the gate to the park to let her and her entourage out first. She thought wistfully of Aaron, what a gentleman he had always been. He still was sometimes, an instinct that had outlived his memory. Joy noticed it when she stood up from the table, the way he tried to stand up, his hand reaching out to help her pull her chair back.

"Good," Danny was saying. "Maybe it will warm up for real sometime soon. This weather is ridiculous. And people don't understand it's a symptom of climate change, just like global warming. They think it counters global warming . . ."

She listened contentedly as he talked about energy, how we squandered it, how there would be no energy left.

"I have no energy. Can you people help me?"

"Mom."

Danny had devoted his professional life to combatting climate change. If he occasionally lost his sense of humor when it came to the environment, you couldn't blame him. She just forgot now and then, forgot not to tease him.

"Danny, I'm sorry. That was glib."

"Sorry, Mom. It's just that I deal with these idiots all day long . . ."

He patted her hand, and she had the urge to put her cheek against his, to press against his cheek, to kiss it, to grab both his cheeks with both of her hands and kiss him some more.

She could see he was getting restless.

"Wanda gave Daddy too much fruit today," she said.

"Did she?"

Joy simply did not want to mention Karl, that was all. It would start up a whole conversation, wouldn't it? All about the past. The past was too alive to her as it was without stirring up memories.

Danny kept looking at his phone, pulling it out of his pocket, staring down at it as he held it below the level of the table, as if that made it somehow more discreet, like holding a napkin in front of your mouth when you picked an annoying bit of food from between your teeth.

"It's very rude, what you're doing," she said. "Is this the way it's going?"

"Is this the way what is going?" Danny asked, still looking at his phone.

"Civilization. Everyone always looking at those electronic things."

He looked up. "Sorry." He looked back at the phone.

"People are going to forget how to talk to each other. That's all."

"I *said* I'm sorry."

Joy could feel the tears welling up. She took a deep breath. Danny was dog-tired, he was overburdened at work, he had so much on his mind. The changing climate, the melting polar ice, droughts and floods, the girls getting into decent schools . . .

"How are the girls?" she asked.

Danny gave her a suspicious look.

"They're very busy, Mom. They have a lot of homework."

And birthday parties, Joy thought. It was mathematically impossible, the number of birthday parties those little girls went to. Homework and birthday parties, a balance of a sort. "I know, sweetheart. They work so hard. So do you."

"Yeah," he said, mollified. "We do."

Joy hadn't seen or heard from her grandchildren in over a month, but that was not why she asked about them. Danny was prickly about his family, as if any inquiry were a veiled criticism. She had asked about the girls because she had suddenly pictured them, like two kittens, their big eyes and silky hair, the way they snuggled into each other like kittens, then batted each other away. They were beautiful, sweet, eccentric girls. It was only natural that she missed them. Only natural that she asked about them. She understood they had their lives and that their lives were imperative and irresistible in that way that a child's life is.

"I'd love if they called. You know, just to say hello."

He laughed unkindly. "You sound like Grandma Bergman. *Your finger broken? You can't dial a phone?* I mean, you can call them, too, Mom."

Joy could not explain this to her son, would have been too ashamed even to mention it, but when she did call his house, every-

one there was always so busy. It made her feel awkward and intrusive, out of step.

"Grandma Bergman," she said. "Them's fightin' words."

But there were circles under his eyes, his shirt was wrinkled
and his tie rumpled, he'd been up since five, and still he made time
for this visit. She got up to spoon out his ice cream herself.

She stood at the door watching as Danny, large and wilted and
fiddling with his phone in his pocket, waited for the elevator,
and she was glad for once that the elevator was so slow. She could
not take her eyes off him.

"Your briefcase is so heavy, Danny. You should get one with
wheels."

He laughed, walked back, gave her another hug. Over his
shoulder she could just make out the elevator door opening. She
said nothing, holding her big, tired son in her arms. The door closed
and the elevator began its slow ascent to some other floor. A high
floor, she hoped, her face against his chest. Maybe the penthouse.

That night, Joy pressed her back against the cushions of the
sofa. It was late, after 3 a.m., but it was not dark. It was never dark
in New York, and tonight the cloudy sky reflected the city lights
in a pale green glow. It was quiet, though. Those few hours when
all the creatures of the city, the screeching, roaring buses, the
howling ambulances, all seemed to take their rest, when the garbage
trucks had not yet trundled out of their caves. She could hear Walter
changing Aaron's colostomy bag. God bless you, Walter, she thought.
May the lord bless you and keep you and shine his countenance
upon you.

But who will pay you? Not the lord. And there was no version
of arithmetic in which Joy and Aaron's social security was sufficient
for the parade of helpers each day. It seemed almost Victorian, having caretakers. As if she and Aaron were large estates. She would
have to go back to work soon, that's all, maybe go back to full time
to help make ends meet at Bergman House. How she would find

the strength she did not know. Even with the caretakers there was so much she had to do for Aaron. She wasn't complaining, she told herself stoutly, just being honest, though how she longed to complain sometimes, to let loose and curse the gods. She had tried it out on the children. The response had not been entirely satisfactory.

"I'm lonely," she had said. "Even though Daddy is right here and even though I never feel as though I get to be alone."

"You should get a dog!" Danny had said. "That would be perfect!"

Oh, Danny, another helpless creature to tend to? Yes, dear, perfect. And Molly! When Joy said her head was muddled and she sometimes was so tired she could not breathe, but so worried about the cost of the caretakers that she could not sleep, Molly suggested she go to the 92nd Street Y's poetry readings. Poetry. They meant well, they did. But *they fuck you up, your son and daughter,* Joy thought, pleased with her clever Philip Larkin allusion, 92nd Street Y or no 92nd Street Y. *They may not mean to, but they do.*

21

The light in the synagogue was far too bright for a holy place. The atmosphere was meant to be one of velvet darkness illuminated by sunlight streaming from windows high above, like the church they had visited on their trip to Paris. There were ten rows of chairs divided by a center aisle, six chairs on each side. Sixty in all, but only half of them filled: Rabbi Kenny would be disappointed. Ruby chose the fourth row, the two seats closest to the aisle on the left. She wanted to be able to see.

"Won't the rabbi be surprised to find us here," her mother said. "I'm surprised, too."

"Aren't you glad? Don't you want me to be Jewish?"

"You are Jewish, you know, already."

"That's kind of racist, Mommy."

"Some people think *Huckleberry Finn* is racist. Do you?"

But Ruby was not to be lured back to Mark Twain.

"Tonight is Shabbat," she had said when she got home from school that afternoon. "The service starts at seven, so we should eat early."

"What service, sweetie? Is there a memorial for someone at

school?" Every now and then, a terrible tragedy struck one of the families at school and the other families got together to raise money or protest a law or clean a flooded basement apartment.

"The Shabbat service, Mommy."

Daniel was worried. "Ruby, I know you feel bad about the slingshot, but the rabbi understood it was an accident. He's an awfully nice guy. He wouldn't want you to punish yourself, honey. And Mommy and I would never make you go to services. I had enough of that when I was little, believe me."

"You're not making me. I want to."

"I understand that you feel guilty, but . . ."

"Daddy, I'm going to shul. It's not guilt. It's inclination."

"No one has the *inclination* to go to services," he said to Coco when they were alone in the kitchen. "Especially not a twelve-year-old."

"I had a Joan of Arc obsession. And I was a Taoist."

He groaned. "I can't do it, Coco. I can't sit there and listen to that stuff. I did my time. I had my bar mitzvah."

"It's your ADD. It's a wonder you can sit through a movie." Daniel was constantly jiggling his legs and rattling the change in his pocket. He paced, too, up and down or in tight circles if the room was small.

"Don't blow the candles out, Daddy," Ruby said to him as she left the house with Coco. "You have to let them burn down. I read it."

"Here he comes," Ruby whispered. The bandage was gone and there was no scar that she could see. Rabbi Kenny came up the aisle greeting the congregation on his way to the bimah. "Mrs. Simkowitz, hello, how did Lev's Series Seven exam go? Mr. Krauss, you look so much better. And . . ."

He stopped when he got to Ruby and her mother. He smiled broadly.

"Are you armed, Ruby?"

Ruby held her hands out, empty.

"It is an honor to have you both here. Welcome."

Ruby listened to the prayers. A secret language, a secret alphabet, secret incantations. She could have been in a room of whirling dervishes or monks in saffron robes, it was that exotic, that exciting. Her mother mumbled along with some of the prayers.

"Wasn't it beautiful?" Ruby said afterward. "Did you like the singing? The songs sounded so sad."

"The cantor has a beautiful voice. She seems a little glitzy for a cantor."

"She could be on Broadway. *Les Mis!*"

"Exactly. And I do prefer male cantors, generally."

"Mommy, that's sexist."

"Nevertheless."

They walked around the block to their building. They passed the corner market with its sparkling new pane of glass. Ruby held her breath the way she did when she passed a cemetery.

"Manuel's insurance paid for it," Coco said. "That was a relief."

"Can I have my allowance back?"

"No."

"Mommy," Ruby said as they reached their building, "we need to get another set of dishes."

"I love our dishes. Daddy and I got them on our honeymoon in Italy. They have a few chips, but really, Ruby, why would we want a whole new set, you can be a little extravagant, that's from your father's side of the family . . ."

"You really don't understand anything," Ruby murmured as her mother went on and on. She patted Coco's arm with fond pity. "May god forgive you."

Ruby sat on the floor of her grandparents' living room, her legs stretched under the coffee table. She had spread out the photographs of her ancestors in approximation of her family tree.

"Now she wants to keep kosher," she heard her father say. "With two sets of dishes. I'm all for the bat mitzvah, I'm proud of her, a sudden change of heart, but kosher?"

"I don't think Tom Sawyer kept kosher," Grandma Joy said. "How does she even know about keeping two sets of dishes?"

"The Internet. Google. Wikipedia."

"Aren't there parental controls on those things?"

There was a picture of Grandpa Aaron as a young soldier in the decorative box. Ruby showed it to Cora, who sat on the couch behind her, kicking her gently.

"Dad didn't say anything when I was in there with him," her father was saying.

"Nothing. For days. Almost a week."

There was the muffled sound of weeping. Ruby turned the photos over, facedown, as if they were playing cards, moved them around the table, then guessed which was which, turning them faceup one by one. Cora slid off the couch and cuddled beside her. Ruby felt her breath on her cheek.

"Quit it," she said mildly, and the shove she gave Cora was mild too.

Their mother appeared in the doorway.

"Girls, we're going. I think you should say goodbye to Grandpa."

Ruby and Cora held hands. With the big bed pushed against the wall to make room for a hospital bed, their grandparents' room looked off balance, cluttered, a showroom for things no one wanted to see. The blinds were old venetian blinds, pulled down, a few of the metal slats bent, allowing in shafts of winter light. The bathroom door was open, and a big white booster seat rose up from the toilet. Pajamas hung from a hook on the back of the door, threadbare and limp.

"Do you know a prayer or something?" Cora whispered.

Ruby shook her head. "Not a whole one. Not yet."

Their grandfather's nose was bigger and thinner than ever. It rose up monumentally from his sunken cheeks. His eyes were closed. His lips were almost white and gave a small puff with each breath.

"Grandpa," Ruby said, because she was the older. "Grandpa, it's us, Ruby and Cora."

He did not stir. There were brown bottles of pills and twisted tubes of ointment on a flowered porcelain tray on the dresser. There was a fat roll of gauze and one of white tape, some baby powder, a box of rubber gloves. Cora took out a rubber glove and blew it up like a balloon.

"Udders," she said, handing it to Ruby to tie. They both giggled, then stopped and shifted their feet.

"We have to leave, Grandpa," said Ruby softly.

Cora poked him. "Grandpa!" she yelled.

"Cora!" Ruby whispered. "Shhh."

"Well, what if he's . . ."

"Don't be silly. He's asleep. Look at his mouth. Listen."

They could hear him breathing.

"Grandpa, we're here, we're here," Cora said. She rattled the aluminum bed rail. "Me and Ruby."

"Ruby and I," Grandpa said. He opened his eyes.

"Everyone, everyone! Come quick! Grandpa talked!" Cora pounded down the hall.

Joy rushed to his side. "What is it, sweetheart? What is it, my darling?"

"Chipped beef," Aaron said.

"You're kidding me, Aaron. Aaron, darling . . ."

"In a jar." And he slipped back into silence.

It was three in the morning. Joy went into the bedroom. Aaron had not moved. He was asleep on his back, the covers pulled up to his chin. The only sound he made was a rhythmic quiet groaning.

Walter, who had been in the next room on the pullout bed that would not pull out, appeared at the door.

"Okay?" he said.

She nodded. "Go back to sleep."

There was a kitchen chair beside the hospital bed, and Joy sat down on it. She reached beneath the blanket and found Aaron's hand. His hand was cold. "There, there," she said. A useless, irrelevant comment. "There, there," she said again. Not every comment had to be useful or relevant. Some words were useless, irrelevant, words that meant I'm sorry, I'm so sorry, I wish I could help you, I love you and I have for so many years that I even love you when I don't; words that meant I didn't mean it when I said I was going to put a bag over your head if you asked me one more time where your ice cream was when it was right in front of you. "There, there," she said.

Aaron, eyes still closed, opened his mouth, and through his strained breathing, he said, "There, there," too.

—— 22 ——

When Joy called Molly and said, "It's your father," Molly thought, My father is dead. It was a strangely distant thought, as if it couldn't be true.

"Daddy's dead," Molly said.

"Molly! How can you say that about your own father?"

Daddy was not dead. Daddy was about to start palliative care.

"He's in so much pain," Joy said. "And we can't get him to the doctor's anymore. He's too weak. So now the doctor comes here. Nurses come, too. It's a very good service. Your father is thrilled."

Daniel went to grocery stores all over the city to no avail. He finally tracked down some chipped beef, online. It was frozen, not in a jar, but he ordered a package anyway. Aaron had first eaten creamed chipped beef on toast in the army. They called it Shit on a Shingle. It was one of his favorite dishes. But when the frozen chipped beef arrived from Wisconsin, next day mail, no one prepared it, and no one ever would. His father was dying. He had been dying for a long time, but now he was actively, earnestly dying. Daniel could see it. Aaron's skin was the skin of the dying. His eyes had clouded like the eyes of a fishmonger's fish. He was cold to the touch. He never moved except to raise a hand a few inches from the white blanket, then let it fall back.

"I know what palliative care means," Molly said to Freddie.

"I hope it means he'll be more comfortable."

"It's a euphemism for hospice care."

"Hospice care is its own euphemism."

"It means they can't do anything else for him."

"But you've been saying that for a month."

"But they never said it. Now it means they won't even try to help him."

Freddie put her arms around her and said nothing, another thing Molly loved about her: she said nothing when there was nothing to say.

But within a week, Aaron had gone from palliative care to hospice care. It was snowing in New York when she and Freddie arrived on a red-eye and the dawn didn't really happen; the horizon was too leaden. The ride into town was excruciatingly slow. The sight of the skyline, so grand after the long drab strip of funeral homes in Queens, shocked Molly as it always did, though the buildings were faint, veiled, soft in the storm. Freddie paid the driver and Molly hauled their suitcases across the sidewalk, the wheels leaving tracks in the snow like sleds. She thought back to the snow of childhood, the white hillside Upstate, the wooden sled with red metal runners they waxed with soap, her father seating himself on the sled, then arranging her and all her winter bulk in front of him, the rush of air on her face, the snow whispering beneath the runners, her father's arms around her, his snowy beard against her cheek as he lifted her off the sled, his enormous glove closing around her mitten as he led her and the sled back up the hill. Oh, she was crying now, yes she was, sobbing as the snow landed on her cheeks and her nose, the tears hot, each one identical in the way snowflakes could never be. She was sobbing as she hauled the suitcases through the front door past the doorman, who offered to help and whom she shook off with a quick head motion. The elevator shuddered with her sobs, the melted snow pooled at her feet, her suitcase fell on its side and lay forlornly on the wet floor. Molly kicked it. Freddie kicked it, too, in solidarity, then righted it.

Daniel was sitting in the chair beside the hospital bed. "The hospice nurse said he'll last a day, maybe two."

"Don't say that in front of him, Danny," their mother said. She had appeared in the bathroom doorway.

Daniel was looking at Molly the way he did when he wanted her to tell him what he should do.

"Aaron," Joy said, "look who's here. It's Molly."

Molly stood up straight. She kissed her mother. She kissed her brother. She took her wet coat off and hung it on the doorknob.

"Oh, Molly, really," her mother said, grabbing the coat and taking it out of the room. "You of all people."

"Hi, Daddy," Molly said.

His eyes flickered. Maybe. She took his hand and kissed it.

"It's me, Molly," she said softly. She bent over and kissed his forehead. It was rough and fragile, like cheap paper.

"Speak up, honey," Joy said, back in the room. "He doesn't have his hearing aids in." She began rummaging through drawers. "I'm sure they're here somewhere. You hate them, Aaron, I know, but they do help."

Hearing aids? Don't forget your orthotics while you're at it, both essential components of hospice care. "I don't think he can hear me anyway, Mom. He's kind of out of it, isn't he? All that morphine . . ."

"What do you mean? Of course he can hear you. Of course you can, Aaron."

"It's me!" Molly said loudly.

The eyes flickered again.

"See?" said Joy. "Don't go borrowing trouble, Molly."

That night, Molly straightened the medicine bottles. The hospice nurses had lined them up neatly already. Molly reorganized the reorganization. Molly Mixinovitch, Aaron used to call her when she got like this.

"It's a pick-me-up, isn't it, Aaron? That Molly energy. And her friend Freddie, what a lovely person."

Should she have said wife? "Well, wife, then." She put on her reading glasses and found the ointment for Aaron's lips. "Wife," she said softly. "I am your wife, Aaron. Mrs. Aaron Bergman." She began to say, Till death do us part, but stopped. "Nothing can part us." Even death could not do that after so many years.

They had been Aaron and Joy for a lifetime. Joy contemplated the word "lifetime." How sad that a word meaning a full span of experience, meaning a whole life, should carry within it the end of a life.

Marrying Aaron had been a triumph, the goal of her existence, of any girl's existence in those days. A handsome, well-heeled man, that was part of it. A handsome, well-heeled man who didn't care about money, that had been another part of it—he was an artist, a singer, contemptuous of the grubby world of commerce. On their first date he had lifted her up and carried her through the park singing. It was like a movie. She was swept away. She did not know the difference between carefree and careless in those days. She learned. There were trials and tribulations along the road. "We've had some sickness and health, haven't we, Aaron? Some richer and poorer." She dabbed the ointment on his lips. "Never a dull moment." It didn't seem possible that Aaron's lips were so dry and cracked, lips she had kissed when they were practically a boy's lips, nice well-formed lips, when she and Aaron were both young. Aaron's young lips had been replaced, magically, by these chapped and papery ones. How proud she had been, proud of being in love, of finding love, as if love were a prize on a treasure hunt. Aaron smiled at her as they stood at the altar fumbling with their rings, a crooked smile he never turned on anyone else, until the grandchildren were born. It was a dangerous smile, full of promise and play. "That's you, playful and full of promises." He did not keep his promises, perhaps, but he never stopped making them, and that had been a different kind of honesty and keeping of the faith.

Molly threw the package of chipped beef away. Joy retrieved the package when Molly wasn't looking. She put it back in the freezer.

Freddie and Molly took the girls to the Museum of Natural History to get them out of the apartment for a little while.

"They look so real," Cora said. The enormous Alaskan bear loomed over her, a wounded seal at its feet.

"They are real," said Ruby.

"They're dead."

"They're still real."

Freddie stepped away from the existential discussion to answer her phone. She backed against the case of the skunks. "Laurel, is anything wrong?"

"Not that we know of," both sisters said at once. "But we thought we'd come see Dad in June. It's a slow month for us. It might be the last time we see him. We have to be realistic."

"He'll be thrilled."

"We have a very good package at the Disneyland Hotel for three nights, and then the Beverly Hills Hilton. Doesn't it sound like fun? A night in Palm Springs, a quick trip to Vegas—we've got it all planned out. You let him know we're coming. We'll send you our itinerary. And, Freddie, we're gluten-free. Just so you know."

"Maybe *you* should call Dad and give him the good news. I'm sure he'd love to hear from you."

"What if he didn't know who we were?" Laurel said. "It would be so awkward. But you'll know how to tell him. After all, Freddie, you see him all the time. We don't."

Freddie smiled a little at that. When she found Molly and the girls, they were examining the naked Neanderthals. Molly was distracted, worried about her father. Ruby and Cora were hungry.

"I still say the animals are not real."

"Are they fantasies?" Ruby said contemptuously.

"Well, they are in a way," Freddie said. "Nineteenth-century fantasies of everything wild. In their glass cases."

Molly snorted.

Cora said, "Snort again!"

"If I went inside one of those cases and kicked one of those kudus," Ruby said, "I'd hurt my foot. A fantasy wouldn't bang my foot. A real kudu would. A dead, real kudu."

"You refute Berkeley thus, Dr. Johnson," said Freddie.

"Death is the only thing that's real," Molly said softly. Only Freddie heard her. She took Molly's hand and they walked silently home across the park. Cora and Ruby skipped and cried out in English accents, "I'm Berkeley and nothing is real; I'm Dr. Johnson and I refute you thus," kicking stones.

23

This is a general picture, the pamphlet said. Then it said that the skin turns a gray or green or bluish hue. Her father's skin was gray and green and bluish. He is off-color, Molly thought, like a joke. *As you hold his hand you may notice that it feels cold.* Her father's hand was as cold as ice, as death.

He was dead.

Joy came into the room.

"Oh, Mommy." Molly pressed her face against her mother's shoulder and cried in ugly dry heaving sobs.

"Molly, Molly." Joy patted her back, kissed her cheek. "There, there, Molly. You must be so tired." She turned to Aaron, lying still on his hospital bed. "That terrible jet lag," she said to him.

"But Daddy . . . Daddy's . . ."

"Come," Joy said gently. "Aaron, we're going to get some tea. Back in a minute!"

In the hall, she closed the door to the bedroom and said, "Now, what is it, sweetheart? I don't want to have any sad discussion in front of Daddy."

"But . . ."

"The booklet said you must always act as if he can hear you. Hearing is one of the last senses to go. We have to be careful not to scare him. He can hear what we're saying even if he doesn't seem to."

"But, Mom—"

"The booklet said so," Joy said fiercely. "It's disrespectful to talk about dying in front of him. Do you understand?"

"Mom, his fingers are blue."

"He's chilly."

"Do we get a mirror or something?"

"This is not television, Molly. Go wait in the living room. I want to chat with your father. Just the two of us."

Molly found Daniel and Freddie in the kitchen. "I think Daddy died," she said through her sobs. "But Mommy doesn't want him to know."

She slid down the wall and sat on the floor. She wished she could breathe. She watched Daniel make his slow careful way toward their parents' bedroom. Maybe her father would be alive again by the time he got there. Maybe her mother would have talked him back to life.

"She thinks he's still alive and she's talking to him," Molly whispered.

Freddie slid down and sat beside her. "Is he? Maybe he is."

"But he's green. And waxen."

When he came back a few minutes later, Daniel said, "She's holding his hand. They're having a quiet conversation, she said."

"So he's alive?" Molly asked.

"I don't know." Daniel started to cry.

Freddie and Coco, the in-laws, went in to take a look as more neutral observers.

"He's awfully stiff-looking," Coco said. She emitted a tiny, nervous laugh, then shook her head.

"Is he still green?" Molly asked.

"Bluish green," Freddie said.

"Is he moving?"

"Of course he's not moving. If he were moving they would know he wasn't dead," her brother snapped.

By the time the hospice nurse came for her afternoon visit, rigor mortis had set in. *Rigor mortis*, she said in her rolling Jamaican accent. *Rigor mortis*.

But still Joy could not be sure. Death? How could anyone be sure of something as unlikely as death? Death made no sense. Where was Aaron if not there? Who was that if not Aaron? Why were the children filing in to say goodbyes as if he were about to take a journey on an ocean liner? She sat on the edge of the bed where she and Aaron had slept and looked at the silent, still man in the hospital bed. Who would take care of him now that he was dead? Who would get him his tea and see him sneak three spoons of sugar into it and pretend not to notice? Who would make him wear his hearing aids? Who would buy him warm sweaters? He would be so helpless and so alone now that he was dead and she could no longer look after him.

She supposed she was crying. Her sinuses were swollen and painful. Her face was wet with tears. She heard uneven sounds, hoots of sorrow, and suspected they came from her. She heard sirens and turned toward the window. It had stopped snowing. She stood up and gazed at Aaron on his hospital bed, his arms now crossed over his chest. Perhaps the nurse had done that, because Aaron, she had to admit, certainly had not.

24

There was chaos and urgency in the Bergman apartment. Daniel said, *We have to call a funeral home, don't we?* Molly said, *Well, they aren't going to call us.* Daniel said, *I'll call the one on the West Side.* Joy, with furious conviction, said, *The one on Madison is so convenient.* Molly said, *It's not your health club, it's not the subway stop, you don't have to carry him there yourself,* and she must have been screaming, because Freddie took her hand and squeezed it with what was surely excessive force and, in her annoying Yoga voice, told her to breathe.

"I'm a widow," Joy said. "Show some respect."

"Okay, I'll call the one on the East Side, then." Daniel reached for the phone.

"No! Not yet! Not yet!"

"Rigor mortis," said the nurse.

"Mr. Aaron, Mr. Aaron," Wanda cried.

"Grandpa," the little girls were wailing. "Grandpa!"

Molly marched into Daniel's old room and called the East Side funeral home on her cell phone. She told the man who answered that they would want a Jewish ceremony, as soon as possible, did they have an opening, as if she were calling to have her hair colored. Like the hair salon, the soonest appointment the funeral home had was in two days. But two days was Saturday and you could not have a Jewish funeral on Saturday.

"Of course," said the man. "Well, we do have a spot on Sunday afternoon."

Aaron was zipped up in a black bag and placed on a wheeled stretcher, then steered out by two silent men, the discrepancy in their heights comical, their clothing almost theatrically grim: shabby black suits, white gloves like footmen. One wore a fur cap; the other, the little one, a yellowed straw fedora with a grimy brim and stained brown hat band. Ernie, the doorman on duty, had come up to say goodbye; the grumpy super, too. He was a fine man, said the super. A gentleman, said the doorman. They stood with bowed heads while the family wailed in anarchic waves of hysteria and grief that emanated from every side of the room, then bounced back from the walls, rolling, echoing, as the little girls clutched their mother's waist and Coco said shrilly, desperately, "Who wants cake, I brought cake."

That was how Molly remembered it. Joy didn't remember it at all.

Wanda and the hospice nurse stripped the hospital bed. They pushed it against the wall. Joy refused to go into the room. The room did not exist without Aaron.

She went into the hall bathroom, which Aaron had used as his own. Wipes and pads and pouches in boxes. Creams and lotions and powders. Tubes and rubber gloves. Where would she put them? Aaron was in a refrigerator on Madison Avenue, but what about all of Aaron's supplies? They would not be buried with him, he was not King Tut and they were not treasures. They were garbage. Expensive garbage. How sad that she had all these costly medical supplies and no one to use them. Most of the boxes had not even been opened.

"Daniel, quick! Look on your phone. Where can I donate? I have colostomy pouches. Perfectly good! Someone needs them! Hurry! I have to donate!"

That was what Joy remembered.

She rushed to the phone and said, "Operator! Dial the hospital. I have urgent equipment to donate." Daniel took the phone from her hand gently. "The operators aren't there anymore, Mom. No more operators, remember?"

"She's in shock," Molly said.

"Should I slap her?" Cora asked.

"That will not be necessary," her father said.

Ben came in the unlocked front door and saw immediately that he was too late.

"He's gone," Molly said. "Oh, Ben, he's gone."

He put his arms around her and they both cried.

Joy called her friends to let them know. Natalie first. She always called Natalie when something happened, good or bad. Sixty-five years of good and bad, and now this, which was very bad. She called Natalie to tell her, just as she had called Natalie when she was married to a man who was alive instead of to this man who was dead. She told Natalie Aaron died. She listened as Natalie said such nice things about Aaron. She stopped listening and took comfort in the voice, the same voice, hoarse with cigarettes, that had been bossing her around since college, that had bossed her around during all those days and weeks and months of Daniel's illness, through the depths of Aaron's financial ruin, through chemo appointments, the voice that inevitably called to cancel lunch dates and dinner dates and any date that involved the pleasant, the unnecessary, the routine encounters of a social life, but never failed her when things got tough.

"Oh, them," Natalie said when Joy mentioned the funeral home where Aaron now lay. "They're crooks. They're all crooks. I plan to be cremated and set in a tin box on my own mantelpiece next to my mother and father and dog and two cats in their tin boxes.

Now, let me think. I read something. A nonprofit funeral home on the West Side. Community-based and nonprofit . . ."

Joy imagined a community center, a rec room with Ping-Pong tables and battered metal folding chairs. "That sounds horrible. Like they hand out cheese sandwiches. Oh, I don't care anyway. He's gone. What does it matter?"

As soon as she said it, Joy knew it did matter, that it was all that mattered, there was nothing else. The funeral was Aaron's funeral, the last thing she could do for him. She had to do it properly. Not just properly, but perfectly, in just exactly the way she suddenly and clearly visualized it: "There will be a violinist. The violinist will play klezmer as people file in."

"It's not a wedding," Molly said.

"Never mind your sarcasm, Molly."

"I know what you mean, Mom," Danny said. "Sad, beautiful, Yiddish melodies."

"Why not get a string quartet? They could wear white tie," Molly muttered. "While you're at it."

For a fleeting moment Joy saw the string quartet, three men in evening dress and a woman in a black gown—the violist, probably—before the tone of Molly's voice registered, and Joy began to cry.

Molly made up with her mother within minutes. Of course she did, and she didn't need Freddie to open her eyes in that exaggerated way to get her to apologize, either, for heaven's sake.

Joy was now in a terrible state, trying to decide whether or not to change funeral homes. Another friend had been to the rec-room funeral home and said it was lovely, the downstairs chapel in particular, all wood, like a Reform synagogue from the sixties.

She decided to move Aaron. They had been so happy on the West Side. When the Madison Avenue funeral home told her what they would charge even if the West Side funeral home came and got Aaron that afternoon, Joy said, "That's highway robbery. I would not bury a fly at your funeral home," and arrangements were made to strike camp and head to the West Side.

The funeral director on the West Side extolled the virtues of a nonprofit funeral home just as if he were selling them a fur coat. Ladies, ladies, he said, when Molly took Joy there to take a look, we will take care of everything. Our reputation is how we survive. A plain pine coffin? Of course, of course, every size, immediately available. A rabbi? Naturally a rabbi, and not just any rabbi, a wonderful man, tops, a top rabbi.

"It was very sudden," Joy said, "and yet not sudden at all. Do you understand?"

The funeral director sighed and looked at that moment not like a funeral director or a furrier but like a human being. "I do," he said. "I'm afraid I do." He put his hand across the desk, across the price lists to be perused and the papers to be signed, and he patted Joy's hand.

Her eyes full of tears, Joy gave a small smile. "You *will* have a coatrack," she said, "in case it rains?"

25

Some people had implied, even said outright, that it would be a relief for Joy when Aaron died. Tactless, Molly had thought then. But now that her father was gone, she wondered. The stress of looking after Aaron had been so fierce. Without it, Joy seemed calmer, softer. Even on the phone from California, Molly could sense it, as if her mother's voice, her whole temperament, were gently muted.

Daniel, who went to see Joy every day after work, confirmed this.

"How is she?" Molly asked him. She often called when she knew he would be at the apartment.

Daniel, phone to his ear, poked his mother, who sat beside him at the dining-room table. "Mom," he said, "Molly wants to know how you are."

"As well as can be expected," said Joy.

He nodded. It had been three weeks. "As well as can be expected," he said into the phone.

"Oh good!"

He wasn't sure what was to be expected in three weeks, but he did not say that to Molly. It was hard for her, being so far away. It was hard for him, too, being so close.

Joy had been quiet in those three weeks. She didn't complain. It was almost as if Aaron's death were a liberation, once the funeral and all the hubbub associated with it were over, if a sad smile and general acquiescence to everything Daniel said or proposed meant liberation. He hoped it did. Yes, he was sure it did.

When he told his mother he had to get home, he saw her panic for a second. Then she said, "Off you go."

"Sorry I can't stay for dinner."

Joy looked confused, as if dinner were a rarely performed ritual.

"Maybe tomorrow," Daniel said.

"Tomorrow?"

Joy shuffled in her slippers to the front door.

"Mom, are you okay? Really?" He held both her hands and kissed the top of her head from what appeared to him a great distance. She seemed to have decreased. Not just in height, but in volume.

"Absolutely."

"Oh. Okay. Good. You're a trooper."

"Absolutely," she said.

26

Molly called her mother every day, which was admirable, Freddie thought, and often inconvenient, happening when they both got home from work and should, theoretically, have been talking to each other. Freddie called her father, of course, but not as frequently. Often, when she did call, he wasn't in his room. He was a social person and he had found several of the ladies of Green Garden willing to be social with him. Her father was so social, Freddie told Joy, that the social worker at Green Garden seemed to devote a good portion of her working life to him. So when Freddie got a call from the social worker telling her that Duncan was feuding with a woman in a room down the hall, Freddie was not surprised.

"He's become verbally abusive," the social worker said.

"Oh, that." Freddie breathed a sigh of relief. "Yes, he told me there's a lady who shouts at him when he walks by her door."

"His language is out of bounds."

"Did he call her a crusty botch of nature? That was always one of his favorites."

"I don't think you understand how serious this is. It's disturbing the entire facility."

"But that's from *Troilus and Cressida*."

"It was very upsetting for Mrs. Barsky."

"Mrs. Barsky?" Mrs. Barsky had been his regular dinner partner some weeks back. Now he was sharing his table with another lady. Freddie suggested to the social worker that this shift in dining companions might have something to do with the arguments, but the social worker kept coming back to her father's elaborate curses.

"He called Mrs. Barsky the slander of her heavy mother's womb and, let me see, I wrote it down somewhere, here it is: a swollen parcel of dropsies."

"*Henry the Fourth*, Part I. You know that's why I became a Shakespeare scholar? To keep up with him."

"They're revving up to kick him out. I can feel it," she said later to Molly. "He's making trouble again."

"At least he enjoys himself."

But when Molly spoke to Daniel that night, she said, "I know he has a good time, but still, I'm glad Mom's not a sex maniac like Duncan. She's so dignified. It does my heart good."

"We're lucky we have such a reasonable, levelheaded mother."

"You've done so much, Daniel, to help her get to this point. Going over there every day and everything."

"Well, so have you. You arranged for Wanda to stay on, you got the Life Alert, you took care of the banking stuff."

They both smiled, thinking of their mother safe, clean, and comfortable in her apartment, her Life Alert wristband securely fastened.

$$— 27 —$$

Joy woke up and, as usual, Aaron was dead.

What was coming was clear to her, and it was a vast emptiness, a blank, much like the winter with its white horizon, dense and low, no distance to the sky at all. The emptiness was everywhere, in every room at every hour. She could feel it draining the life out of her until she, too, would be empty. In the shower, she cried because, there, no one could hear her, though she knew there was no one to hear her anywhere.

Molly had gotten her a medical-alert contraption that came with a wristband with a button on it. Sometimes she pushed the button by accident and a man's voice from the machine asked her if she was all right. It was company.

Wanda stayed on, going home only on the weekends to tend to her alcoholic husband. She made breakfast for Joy. She practically fed it to her with a spoon. Wanda missed Aaron, too. Sometimes they cried together. Sometimes they cleaned drawers.

Walter appeared once to pick up a sweatshirt he'd left behind. He helped her change two burned-out lightbulbs in the kitchen ceiling fixture. He said he would come back and make Foo-foo for her one day. When he left, his absence was acute.

On the weekends, Elvira came at night. Joy would not stay alone. Alone was impossible, it made her shiver, it made her head swim, it made her heart pound, it made her knees buckle, it made her ears ring.

Her children lived in some other world, one that she could see but had left behind, like the wake of a ship. Their lives foamed and splashed while she hurtled forward, away from them, but toward nothing. Well, toward something, and they all knew what that something was.

There wasn't enough money for Elvira or Wanda. She was spending like a drunken sailor, an old decrepit drunken sailor. The children offered to help pay, which was kind but humiliating. And she knew they couldn't afford it. An archaeologist and an environmentalist? They were hanging on by a bourgeois thread. She understood she would have to stay alone eventually. She listened to the wind rattle the windows and knew she was abandoned. She told Molly and Daniel she would not be on the dole.

—— 28 ——

The first night alone was long and she paced from the living room to the bedroom in her nightgown, like a ghost, a skinny, crabby old ghost. The sirens wailed outside, and she paced and wept and took her own pulse and used the toilet and ate crackers and knew she would faint. She paced some more, and the streets became quiet, even the sirens stopped, and she took her pulse again, as if her pulse might account for the silence, and paced some more and waited.

What am I waiting for? she wondered. Whatever it was, it was crucial and elusive. She could hardly breathe. She tripped on the edge of the rug in the hall, but did not fall. She lay on the couch and cried, bitterly and loudly. "I don't care who hears me," she called out to the empty house.

29

In Los Angeles, it was January and it was springtime. Molly saw a hermit thrush. Hummingbirds flitted in and out of white flowers shaped like bells. Pink buds of jasmine hung over the fence ready to burst into bloom. At the beach, surfers slid into the waves with the garish sunset behind them. Finches began to sing. She took one class to Catalina each week to photograph a cave painting and map the area around it. They used a software program that had originally been developed by NASA for the study of photographs of Mars.

"Mars," her mother said when Molly told her about the project. "Well, well. Digital tracing. Isn't that nice."

"I knew you'd be interested."

"Oh, of course."

Molly told her about the bits of ocher the digital tracing had connected, and if her mother sounded less enthusiastic than Molly had expected, Molly attributed that to the weather. The weather was terrible in New York. It snowed and the bitter wind blew, and Joy could not leave her building.

"Well, this will cheer you up, Mom. One of the grad students in engineering built a drone and we attached a 3-D camera and . . ."

Joy drifted from room to room, listening, aimless, trapped.

It wasn't that Joy expected her daughter, and certainly not her son, to come live with her. They had their own lives, just as she had once had her own life. She did expect something from them, though, something they were not providing, she couldn't put her finger on it. Danny was coming once a week for dinner now, Molly planned a trip to New York in the near future, and Joy waited eagerly for their visits. But visits predicted their own end, and an end to a visit meant she would be alone again.

There is a difference between solitude and loneliness, she thought, and wondered what it was.

She should have spent more time with her own mother. She should have moved in with her mother to take care of her, she saw that now. So what if her mother's apartment had been an L-shaped studio? So what if her mother kept it at 102 degrees and could not stand the smell of any food cooking except white rice, and so what if she talked and talked and talked and lived in the past? Now that Joy was older, she understood her mother. It was *cold*, that was why the heat in the apartment was turned up so high. Her mother's ceaseless talking was an *activity*, a way for her to be alive. As for living in the past, the past was all that was real.

Joy would move right in with her mother now, if she could. Daniel and Molly were not old enough, not lonely enough, not cold enough to understand. And what would they do with their wives? And how was it that she had a daughter and a son and they both had wives, anyway?

No one, not even an old lady, wants to live in someone else's house. Both Molly and Daniel had asked her to move in with them, naturally, just as she had asked her own mother to move in with her. They were good, devoted children, just as she had been. They didn't really mean it, just as she had not really meant it.

Rich or poor, her mother used to say, it's better to have money.

Aaron, you were not a prince among men. You were not. You were a weak man. You squandered your fortune like a prince, but you were not a prince. She thought fondly of his affectations of dress, the tweed cap when other men wore brimmed hats, the custom-made English shirts and shoes. How handsome he was, his beard groomed, his hair tousled. It had been so long since she had thought of him as handsome. But now she had trouble picturing him when he hadn't been handsome, when he'd grown bent and stiff and hollow, when his lips were chapped and his teeth dulled, when his eyes went blank, when his clothes devolved into the clothes of a small child, the elastic-waist sweatpants, the hooded sweatshirt that he could not zip himself. Those images were fading. Instead, she could feel her head on his shoulder and his hand running through her hair. She could hear his breath in her ear, feel it, soft and warm. As she tried to fall asleep each night, she saw him as she had first seen him, a young man with no beard, his eyes a watery blue, his jacket handmade in Scotland, she later discovered, his large hand held out as he asked her to dance.

The memories did not comfort her. They made her feel the years that had passed and that, like Aaron, would never return. They made her old. Sometimes, when she got up to go to the bathroom, she caught sight of herself in the mirror and thought it was her grandfather. All she had to do was spit some tobacco. The smell of her grandfather and his chewing tobacco came back to her, and she got back into bed, sleepless and sick to her stomach.

When Danny came to dinner, he always said, "I'll bring a roast chicken from Gourmet Garage so you won't have to cook."

Cook? She could barely recall when she had last cooked. She did make toast. She sometimes boiled an egg. But she would not be cooking Danny a nice dinner like a proper mother, like a proper hostess, she didn't have the strength, he was right about that. She decided she would make the table look pretty. She would use the silver. She would light candles.

She bent down and pulled out the bottom drawer in the kitchen cabinet, where the tablecloths were kept, then stood up holding a fresh bright white embroidered cloth and banged her head on a cabinet door she'd left open. She cried from pain and frustration, but forced herself on, into the dining room, to spread the cloth. But how could she spread the beautiful white cloth? The dining-room table was covered with mail and file folders; there was a tray with an egg-stained plate and a pink jammy crust of bread; large bottles of pills dozed on their sides like sea lions; magazines and catalogues and unread newspapers had slithered out from piles that had then collapsed and fanned across yet another egg-stained plate. A pile of bills, three piles of bills, each topped with a yellow Post-it that said *Urgent*. Joy sat at the table crying and trying to decipher the bills. They made no sense. She began to dial Molly's number to tell her the dining-room table was a mess, as if Molly should fly in from California to straighten it up, then caught herself and hung up.

She choked when Danny came to dinner. A piece of chicken flew out of her throat and landed on her plate, slimy and colorless.

The sounds were hideous, like a crow's, like a gasping dying crow's. KEH-KEH-KEH. She tried to drink water. No air came in, no air went out, her throat was closed and squeezing and pushing, and out came the piece of chicken in a gush of unswallowed liquid. It lay there in a pool of water like a tiny dead baby.

Danny had been pounding her on the back. Now he stood beside her staring at the lump of flesh in its little pond. "Jesus."

Joy patted her mouth with her napkin, then spread it over her plate, covering the chicken.

"Jesus," he said again. He stroked her hair. "Mom, can you talk?"

Joy put her head in her hands. She could talk. But what was there to say?

"So how's Mom?" Molly asked Daniel later that night.

"She says she's okay. She got a piece of chicken stuck in her throat. It was disgusting. And scary."

"But she's okay?"

"Yeah, yeah. You know her. She's a trooper."

"Daniel said you seemed pretty good," Molly said to her mother the next day.

"We had chicken."

"Are you getting out at all? You need to get out, see your friends."

"Oh no. Not in this weather."

"Aren't you going stir-crazy?"

"You know, I'm a very busy person, Molly." Joy gazed at the datebooks splayed in front of her on the dining-room table, one of them so old the cover hung off like an empty sleeve, an amputee's empty sleeve. "Between losing things and looking for things I've lost and going to the bathroom," she said, "well, the day just isn't long enough."

"You're funny."

"I'm not trying to be."

Molly laughed. "You really are funny. Now make a date with a friend. With Natalie. Go to the 92nd Street Y the minute it gets warm enough, okay? I'm so proud of you, Mom! Daniel's right. You really are a trooper."

"She's so strong," Molly and Daniel told each other.

"Of course she misses Dad," they added, "we all do, but what a terrible weight she's been carrying all these years. Now, finally, she can have some time for herself."

"I can talk to her now, really talk to her," they said. "About me."

She seemed to need them more than ever, which was gratifying, but she didn't seem to need them too much, which was more gratifying still.

When the weather warmed up and the ice turned to broad rivers of slush, Joy did try going to the 92nd Street Y, to a poetry reading.

"Count me out," said Natalie. "Poetry is depressing at our age."

"Why at our age particularly?"

"Because everything is depressing at our age."

The Y was dark and frequented by women who did not bother about their hair. The screaming children running in and out, who should have cheered her (that had always been one of her theories, that the generations should mix), were unsettling. She could feel her irregular heart beating more irregularly than usual and she went home.

When Daphne got back from Florida, Joy went out again to meet her at the coffee shop. They had not seen each other since Aaron's funeral.

Joy said, "I miss Aaron. And I don't like being alone."

"The first year is the worst. Then it calms down to a dull roar."

"How's your boyfriend from down there?" Joy asked.

"Dead."

Daphne had two other men she "went to dinner with": one she had picked up at a coffee shop farther downtown near her apartment, the other the widower of an old friend. But it had been a hard winter for them, and for Daphne, too: "All my boyfriends are dead."

Joy felt dizzy. Maybe matzo-ball soup and waffles was a bad idea. "I'm sorry," she said.

"My kids think I should consider going into assisted living."

"*Do* they. Well, what do *you* think?"

"They worry because they're not here. They want me to come

to them in Cincinnati. Well, to a place near them in Cincinnati. I understand. But I can't go to Cincinnati. I told them I'm staying, and it's called 'Aging in Place.' That's what the social workers call it."

"You saw a social worker?"

"No, of course not. In Florida they talk about these things. It's all the rage in the world of gerontology, otherwise known as Florida. Aging in Place."

"Like running in place."

"Going nowhere fast." Daphne laughed.

"Whatever they call it, it's better than a nursing home . . ."

". . . In Cincinnati!"

"I read somewhere that Cincinnati is a very nice city. Or was it Charlotte?"

"The assisted-living place on Eighty-sixth Street is supposed to be beautiful," Daphne said. "Leonard's children sent him there, you know."

"Leonard?" Leonard, their handsome classmate in college, Leonard who had proposed to her all those many years ago. A lot of men had proposed to her. Men did that in those days, proposed. Why? What was their hurry? Oh yes, the Korean War, that was it. She had expected Karl to propose, but he was more sensible than the rest of them, he was waiting until he had a decent job, that's what he said when she told him she was going to marry Aaron. "I saw Leonard about a year ago. He drove past in a red Cadillac convertible with a woman half his age. If that."

"He picked her up in a bar. They went to Bermuda together, and he had a heart attack and wound up in the hospital. His daughter had to fly down, and that, as they say, was the end of that."

"He took her to Bermuda?"

Daphne nodded.

"Who goes to Bermuda?"

Joy got a bad cold after that outing. She stayed in the apartment for a week, ten days, twelve, ordering chicken soup from the coffee shop. The cold turned into bronchitis.

"Whatever you do, *don't* get pneumonia," Molly said.

Joy promised that she would not.

She wondered what her children would do if she did get pneumonia. Put her in a home? Just until you get better, for your own good. What if they decided to leave her there, for her own good? The thought kept her up that night and woke her up many nights after. They had never said anything about sending her off to an assisted-living place. They couldn't send her against her will. They wouldn't send her anywhere against her will! And she didn't even have pneumonia! She told herself these things. But you never know. That was one thing she had learned over the years. You really never know anything.

30

Ruby went to Hebrew school three times a week after school. She babysat for Rabbi Kenny every Thursday night when he and his wife went out to dinner and to the movies. He had five-year-old twin boys.

"The only problem," Daniel told Molly, "is that she wants to change her name to Rachel."

Daniel talked about his daughters incessantly. There had been a time when his fascination with his own offspring had annoyed Molly, but since she'd moved to Los Angeles, Ruby and Cora had become like fantastical figures in a storybook, characters in a book about a magical, faraway place: Home. Now she encouraged Daniel. When he talked about his children, she felt she could safely relax and indulge herself in nostalgia and love for the city she left behind.

"She gave the rabbi's kids all her old Pokémon cards."

"Very generous."

"Well, I guess she kind of outgrew them. And Cora didn't want them. Not that she actually asked Cora."

"I miss everyone so much," Molly said.

"Did you talk to Mom today?"

"I did. She said she was very tired and the doctor told her to use her asthma inhaler thing, and she fell asleep reading the paper and woke up and thought it was morning. She was feeling a little better, so she ordered a turkey burger for dinner and she ate half of it."

They hung up happy in the knowledge that their mother was thriving.

31

Joy began to feel that there was another person in the apartment, a stranger, and it was her. She had to watch over this person, this boring, fearful, sickly person. She had to make sure it took its pills. She had to watch its step so it didn't fall. She made sure it chewed its food so it didn't choke. She worried about the person constantly; the worry was a weight heavy on her shoulders, on her mind, on her heart. It followed her as she followed this person from room to room, this awful, needy person who was herself.

"I don't know what to do with her. *And* she's an *irritating* person. What a responsibility!" she said to Molly.

She had begun timing herself in the morning to see how long it took her to get dressed.

"It feels like two hours, and it is."

Sometimes she didn't bother to get dressed.

"It saves so much time. Some days I don't even want to take a shower, but then I think, Well! I'll do it for my children. I don't want them to have a filthy old mother with fuzzy gray hair."

"You're funny," Molly always said, laughing, relieved—Joy could hear it in her voice. That was another of the responsibilities Joy had, relieving her children of worry. She did not want them to be upset. And she did not want them to send her to an assisted-living facility in Cincinnati. Or anywhere else.

32

Joy looked out her window and felt an affinity for the ugly March street and the ugly March sky. Even her heart felt ugly, especially her heart, dusty and empty except for the shaky memories scattered around like sticks of broken furniture. She was physically ugly, too, listless skin sagging at her jaw, red-rimmed eyes—she examined her face in the mirror and took a certain satisfaction in its fall from beauty. It was the only power she seemed to have anymore—the power to deteriorate. Her hair was too long, too thin, scraggly and white like a witch's hair, and there was a long white hair on her chin. Her clothes, which had once charmed and fascinated her, now sulked in the closet, a closet that had no light. She tried a flashlight. It was too heavy for her, twisting her wrist so painfully she grabbed at the doorframe to keep her balance. Everything was too heavy for her these days, even the clothes themselves. Those she extracted were random and old, decades old. Excellent quality, she could still appreciate that. Pity they didn't fit, pity about the moth holes, pity about so many things. She lost weight, something that automatically pleased her, until she remembered that she'd lost the weight because of illness, stress, old age. Her good Italian knit pants fell right down to her feet, like a clown's pants in the circus, like Aaron's pants, a thought that made her sit on the edge of the bed, that made the room spin. Usually she ended up wearing the same gray sweatshirt, the one Aaron had worn, and a pair of black jersey pants she'd gotten at the Gap, although the drawstring was tied in an inextricable knot.

She sat at the table not even bothering to look at the car lights outside. Lou Barney, Lou Barney, who the hell was Lou Barney? The iPad only wanted to play Lou Barney, flashing his name on the screen. Joy had never heard of him. Why did Molly and Danny ever get her this thing? It was very generous of them, but it always wanted to play Lou Barney, and then wouldn't even play him, whoever he was. Joy shook the iPad. She was just about to call Molly when she decided to try one more time. She changed glasses and tapped the screen.

It wasn't Lou Barney. It was Low Battery.

I really cannot take much more of the modern world, she thought. I really cannot.

Soon after Lou Barney, Molly came for a week, by herself. Joy was still coughing, but the bronchitis was mostly gone. She had not gotten pneumonia.

"That's wonderful, Mom. You look so much better than I expected. You're so independent."

Joy said, Yes, I am. She did not say, Thank god you're here, Molly, I could not have taken one more minute on my own, I'm so weak I can hardly lift my toothbrush.

She took a walk with Molly and tried not to lean on her arm.

"Mom? Are you okay? You look a little pale."

"It's the weather," Joy said.

Molly took her arm gently. "I'm glad you've taken such good care of yourself."

"Danny did what he could," Joy said. "And now you're here."

She felt Molly stiffen, for just a split second. Then Molly stopped and wrapped her arms around her. Joy's face was pressed uncomfortably against the zipper of her daughter's coat.

"I don't want to be a burden," Joy said.

Molly laughed. "I should hope not."

It was about a month later that Joy was finally able to force herself to go back to work. She took a cane. Her bags seemed heavier than ever, but the weather was better, no snow, no rain, just a vicious wind. Gregor got her a cab. She immediately began to worry about whether she'd be able to get a cab home. It would be too windy to wait for the bus even with the cane. The cane had four little feet and a dirty white stripe where someone had torn off the adhesive tape on which the name Aaron Bergman had been scrawled in black Sharpie. I should have gotten him a nicer cane, she thought. How could I have let him walk around with this?

She typed some figures into the computer. The screen shuddered and suddenly there was something different on it. What had she done?

What had she done? What was she doing? Why was she here? These were vast questions that had become horribly small and specific to her. It was hard to remember exactly what she had done earlier in the day. It was hard to focus on what she was doing at that moment. It was hard to understand why she was in this windowless, airless closet.

She tried to concentrate on the report on the air quality necessary for new display cases. She pulled a bottle of water from one of her bags, but she could not unscrew the cap. She glanced at a study of formaldehyde in enclosed environments. She wondered if she was breathing formaldehyde in the enclosed environment that was her office.

She leaned back and looked up. There were several missing ceiling tiles near the light, as well as some wires left hanging from a wall socket. She had filled out all the forms for maintenance, but then she'd been told it would take weeks for anyone to get to it. "Volatile Organic Compounds," she typed, a term for hydrocarbon gases.

When a workman passed she went to the door and hailed him like a cab. He was a lovely man, happy to help her, very sympathetic, even when he had to go and get a ladder. The room had such high ceilings—it was higher than it was wide, higher than it was long. He came back and set up his ladder and fixed everything just like that, one, two, three. He had a daughter in high school. They chatted about the cost of college as he hung her posters.

Then Miss Georgia whisked by the open doorway and, like a character in a cartoon, backed up, demanding to know what was going on. The workman, whose name was Marlon, winked at Joy and slid out the door. Miss Georgia watched him go with a disapproving look, then turned to Joy. "Chop-chop," she said. "We have work to do."

"Excuse me?"

Miss Georgia clapped her hands together like a kindergarten teacher. "Chop-chop."

"Chop-chop?" Joy said, thinking of all the years she had worked to get her master's degree and then her Ph.D., thinking of her training and all her experience, all the years she had worked at this museum before Miss Georgia even knew how to spell museum. Chop-chop? "I'm sorry, but what is it you think I'm doing if not working?"

It was the slight smirk that appeared on the director's face that pushed Joy over the edge.

"Why don't I just stick a broom up my ass and sweep the floor, too?" she said.

Now she lowered her head to the shiny white top of the drawerless desk and did not move for what seemed like a long time. She pictured the director's face after her outburst: truly shocked. Joy wanted to laugh, but she was too tired. The surface of the table was cool and soothing on her forehead. When she lifted her head, the windowless room spun around her like a merry-go-round and the director seemed to be back in her doorway, a file in her hand.

"I've been knocking for quite a while," Miss Georgia said.

Joy stared at her.

When Joy still did not speak, Miss Georgia added, "Yes. The less said the better." Miss Georgia held up a hand, traffic-cop-like, then dropped a thick manuscript on Joy's desk. "Your recommendations for the photographic collection."

Joy pulled it toward her.

"Because you were ill," Miss Georgia said, "we decided to help you out."

Joy started to ask why they thought she needed help on that particular report, which was, after all, finished.

"No, no, don't thank me," Miss Georgia interrupted. "Not necessary. We got some excellent outside help on the project."

"But I—"

"Say no more." Miss Georgia put her finger to her lips.

Joy flipped through the manuscript, a comprehensive guide to protecting the museum's photographs in their new location that she'd worked on for months before the move.

"We read your report, of course," the director said. "But under the circumstances, we felt it would be prudent to hand the project over to outside sources."

Joy's bags were even heavier going home. The report was hundreds of pages long. She put it in the red bag and clutched it to her side. When she finally got a cab, the thought of going home to her empty apartment was too grim. She got off at the coffee shop wondering if they would force her to sit at one of the sad little tables against the wall where all the old widows and widowers sat. She wanted a booth. She wanted to be near a window. She was breathing heavily. It was from anger, of course. Unless she was having a heart attack.

"Joy!" a voice cried out when she got inside, and it was Karl.

She hadn't seen him since before Aaron died. He had been so kind, sending a lovely note on thick creamy stationery. Beautiful old-fashioned fountain-pen handwriting. It had disturbed her, that familiar handwriting from long ago.

"Joy, I'm so sorry about Aaron. I lost a good friend," he said when his attendant had lurched out of the booth, offered her seat to Joy, and disappeared into the night. When her waffle came, Joy pulled a brown glass bottle out of one of her bags.

"Maple syrup," she said. "*Real* maple syrup. No one serves real maple syrup anymore."

They talked about Aaron, about his reminiscences about the war, about the pigeons. Joy cried, just for a minute, and Karl handed her a large, clean white handkerchief with his initials mono-grammed on it. She hesitated before handing it back and had a flash of memory, another large, clean white handkerchief, no mono-gram in those days, a fit of sneezing, the embarrassment of handing it back. She looked up. Karl was smiling.

"I remember," he said.

"Were we on a sailboat?"

He nodded.

"I thought you were very brave to take it back after all that sneezing."

"I didn't have much choice."

She laughed. "I remember thinking it would be very forward of me to keep it. That was the word. 'Forward.' Why didn't I have my own handkerchief? And why do you still use a handkerchief? They're very unsanitary."

"You can keep that one."

"Oh no," she said. "I couldn't. It's too beautiful." She wrapped it in a paper napkin and gave it back to him. Then she ordered a cup of soup, and suddenly, as if she'd known him all her life, which she very nearly had, she began confiding in him, telling him about going back to work, about how awful Miss Georgia had been. She took the report out of the red bag.

"It's a perfectly good report," she said. She began leafing through it, nodding approval at her own conclusions. "An excellent report, actually."

"Joy?"

She had stopped turning the pages. She was staring, riveted, at one page. Then she grinned. "Oh dear," she said, still grinning. "Oh dearie dear." Surely that was supposed to say CUNY facilities. Surely that was not supposed to say CUNT facilities.

"Something wrong?" Karl said.

"Oh no," Joy said. "Just a little typo."

33

Hi, Grandma," Ben said. "Would you like a visit? I have a week off."

In fact, the bar Ben worked at had gone out of business and he had Airbnb'd his apartment out for the month. He wasn't sure why, but he admitted it to his grandmother as soon as he arrived.

"I won't stay for a month or anything, but I didn't know where else to go. Please don't tell Mom. She'll freak out."

Joy found Ben fascinating. He was so sweet and so difficult in such a sweet way, drifting without bothering anyone, unproductive and undemanding, working at what in Joy's day were considered summer jobs for a college man—construction, bartending, temporary doorman. It was not a philosophical choice, this drifting, not like Dolores's granddaughter, who was a Dumpster diver, god help her. Molly worried too much about him, he was a good boy finding his way.

And now he needed her, Joy. She wondered if Molly had put him up to this, part of her plan to keep her relevant.

"As long as you like," she said.

She wanted to dance, she was so relieved. She would not have to sleep in the apartment alone.

Uncle Daniel's old bedroom, a.k.a. the maid's room, was fusty and weird—childish and elderly at the same time. The carpet was as old as his uncle, the paint had once been a lovely shade of blue, he'd been told, but was now a sad colorless shade of nothing, and the window needed no curtains or blinds because it was darkened by grime. The built-in shelves, once so enviously shipshape (at least according to Ben's mother), were claustrophobic and warped. The sink dripped, not too much, just enough to catch you by surprise.

"Honey, do you want some tea?" his grandmother called out.

Yes, he did want some tea, and how comforting to have his grandma make it, though she made the worst tea he had ever tasted, weak and lukewarm. But just the sound of her voice made the little room feel much nicer, more like home. Ben had always loved coming to her apartment. She'd made him cracker sandwiches: buttery orange Ritz crackers and peanut butter. There were toys she'd kept there just for him and interesting junk retrieved from the museum she worked at. There was a Betty Boop videotape he had always loved, it was so sexy and so peculiar—especially when she told him that Betty Boop was Jewish. Sitting on her bureau in her bedroom, there was still a wooden puzzle box in the shape of a butterfly he had gotten her for Christmas when he was a little boy. He'd bought it at a street fair and thought it was the most beautiful and original object anyone had ever given anyone as a gift. One of his paintings from kindergarten was framed in Lucite and hung in the foyer.

The kitchen was long and narrow, a tunnel, really, and at the end was a window. His grandparents had jammed a small square table there. It had two chairs, and you could not open the oven door all the way even if the second chair was pushed in. He sat there with Joy and looked out the window and drank his tea.

"Grandpa and I used to sit here," she said.

"I can see all the flowering trees. It's really pretty."

"Yes. You're in Grandpa's seat."

Oh god. How awkward. "Oh. Right," he said. "Good seat to be in."

His grandmother smiled. "You're a fine person, Ben."

"Like Grandpa."

"He was all right," said Grandma Joy. "Up to a point."

She continued to smile, reaching behind her to grab a package of Oreos. She funneled several cookies into her hand.

"Enjoy," she said absently, rattling the package at Ben.

She could remember so clearly the first time Ben stayed at her apartment. He had been eighteen months old, jabbering quite coherently, with the bottle hanging from the side of his mouth like a cigar. She and Aaron had set up the old crib, a beautiful, highly decorated wooden crib that had originally been Aaron's, then taken it apart again the minute Molly saw it.

"The spokes are too far apart!" she said. "Are you trying to kill him? He could get his head caught. You put us in this? Unbelievable."

So they had moved the beautiful crib from the 1920s back into the cedar closet and bought an ugly blue nylon playpen that could double as a crib. Ben ended up sleeping in their bed, anyway, whenever he stayed with them. Joy could hear his small, even breath; she could smell the warm, bathed skin; she could see his eyelids flutter, his fingers clutch his bear. When she looked at him now, a skinny young man who needed a shave, he was the same to her, her first grandchild.

In the morning, Joy put some sort of clothes on so she wouldn't scare the horses, then staggered weakly to the kitchen to make Ben his breakfast. Standing over the stove to stir the Cream of Wheat, she eliminated the lumps in the cereal with solemn determination.

She put the two bowls of cereal on the kitchen table with two spoons and two cheerful cloth napkins. She put the kettle on and forgot it until its whistle startled her and woke Ben.

"You're the best," he said.

She could feel him watch as she shoveled sugar into her Cream of Wheat.

"Grandma, are you okay with sugar?" he said the first morning. "I thought . . ."

"Oh yes," she said. And to his credit he dropped the subject. He must have gotten that from his father, discretion. Certainly not from his mother. Joy missed his father. Doug Harkavy was such a nice man. Molly was lucky to have married him. Freddie was wonderful, too, of course. But what was the point? Well, the world was upside down, that's all.

"How is your father, Ben?"

"He's great. He has a grandchild. Well, she does, so he does. It's cute, too."

When Molly had announced she was leaving her husband for Freddie, a woman named Freddie, Joy had not fainted, though her heart was pounding and the room began to darken. She had smiled and said she wanted Molly to be happy, to be herself, and it was true, but she'd been thinking, *What about Ben?* He might be shunned by other children, he might be stunted in some Freudian path to maturity. She had worried, Aaron had worried, and then it turned out there was nothing to worry about, after all. Ben's friends—well, it was a different generation, wasn't it?—seemed to take the situation in stride. Ben was miserable about the divorce, but he didn't seem unduly upset about his mother and Freddie. Of course, he was in college. And this is New York City, anything goes, she had said to Aaron. All that worrying for nothing. It had been a great strain, worrying so much and hiding it from Molly.

"Worrying is inefficient," she said to Ben, smiling at him. "Look at you. You're a fine person, Ben."

Ben looked surprised. "Do you worry about me?"

"Not anymore."

"I worry about me. I wish I knew what I really wanted to do."

"Don't you want to go to law school?"

"Sort of. It seems interesting. But what if I have to get a job doing, like, contract law or something? I wish I were, I don't know, passionate about something."

He gazed at her so confidingly. He was very good-looking, and when his eyes shone with emotion like this, he was irresistible. She thought of saying, Passion is for the bedroom! Get a job! Get a job with health insurance! That's all that matters! Don't be like your grandfather, always looking to be happy in his work, excited, creative (English translation: broke). Independence is overrated. It leads to dependence. Get a job in a nice steady corporation and keep your head down, and do your dreaming on the weekends and pay your bills.

Of course there were no nice steady corporations anymore, not the way there used to be. And Aaron's problem had not been independence, it had been entitlement. And why shouldn't Ben try to find something he loved doing? He was young and bright and earnest.

"You'll find what you want," she said. "It may not be what you think it will, it may find you when you least expect it, it might even be law school. And if you're drifting, you might just drift into the right thing. Or if it's the wrong thing, you'll figure out how to turn it into the right thing. Sometimes you have to create your passion. I have great confidence in you. You're young. You have time. You're a fine person, Ben."

He sighed and finished his Cream of Wheat. Then he said, "Thank you." He smiled and got up and kissed her cheek and put his bowl in the sink. It amused her to see that he did not put it in the dishwasher or even rinse it, that he just left it there. "Thank you, Grandma," he said again. "You've always helped me a lot, you know that?"

No, she didn't, but she was extremely happy to hear it now when she felt she was about as useful as one sock.

"You have time," she said again.

They went for a walk every day and sat on the same bench in Central Park watching the dogs parade by. They ate lunch in the coffee shop, and when Ben wasn't seeing his old friends, they ate dinner there, too. They bumped into Karl twice, but they didn't sit with him.

"He was Grandpa's friend in the park."

"Yeah?"

Ben didn't seem interested and Joy had no desire to tell him more. There was nothing to tell, anyway.

She was none too steady on the walks back and forth to the coffee shop. Sometimes her feet just sort of slid forward instead of lifting up and moving the way feet are meant to do.

"I'm shuffling," she said. "I'm going to shuffle right onto my face if I'm not careful."

"You can lean on me," said Ben.

That made Joy smile. She remembered holding his little hand to cross the street, lifting him onto the bus's high step. He used to wear tiny navy-blue sneakers and overalls.

"Yes," she said. "All right, I will."

His arm was wiry and strong. He slowed his step and shortened his long stride.

Ben stayed for six nights before he heard about another job in New Orleans and decided to sleep on a friend's couch down there until he could get his apartment back. But before he left, he asked his grandmother for a favor.

"It's kind of private," he said.

"Do you need money, sweetheart? Of course you do. Here's a twenty. No, that's not enough. Here, I've got eighty bucks."

Why is my grandmother carrying a purse around her own house? Ben wondered. He knew that if he asked her she would tell him a long complicated story that would make no sense to him, so he didn't ask her. But he put his hand out to stop her rummaging in the big shoulder bag.

"No, Grandma, no. It's not money. And you gave me a really generous Christmas present. Really."

She'd had to be creative at Christmas. So much had been going on. There was no way she could have gotten out to go Christmas shopping. A card with nice crisp bills for Ben had done nicely, five twenty-dollar bills. She thought of the two beautiful teacups (they'd been her mother's, just a small chip on one, and she had three more) she'd given Molly and Freddie, plus an opal and silver ring she'd found that Molly had liked as a child, she told them they could share it, there had to be some advantage to having your daughter marry another woman. But money had been fine for Ben.

"Then what can I do for you, Bennie?"

He blushed and reached into the breast pocket of his shirt. It was a nice shirt. Had she given it to him for his birthday last year?

"Did I give you that shirt?"

"Yeah, I think so." He handed her a crumpled wad of pink paper.

"Ben! A traffic ticket? You don't even have a car."

"Don't tell Mom, okay? It's kind of embarrassing."

He did look embarrassed, that was certain. His cheeks were as rosy as a little English choirboy's. It made him even more appealing. He was such a handsome boy. He was such a good boy, staying with her like this. She felt sick at the thought of him leaving. Maybe it would have been better if he had not come at all, then she wouldn't have minded his departure.

"And the problem is, there's a court date," he was saying. "And I won't be here because I'll be back in New Orleans, and so I was wondering . . ."

Joy nodded and smiled. Ben needed her. This strong young man needed her, and it made her feel a bit strong and a bit young herself. A bit manipulated, too, but that was a grandson's god-given right, to manipulate his grandmother.

"I'll pay you back the money for the fine," he said with the generous confidence that his offer would not be accepted.

"But how did you get a parking ticket without a car, Ben?"

"Oh," and he said something in that soft, barely comprehensible mumble young people so often employed.

"What? I hate it when you people mumble. Even your mother does it sometimes."

"You know, um, public urination."

Joy looked down at the piece of pink paper in her hand, then gingerly dropped it onto a paper napkin she pulled out of her pocketbook. "*What?*" she said. "That is disgusting, Ben. What is the matter with you? Is this what people do in New Orleans? Are you insane? . . ."

She went on and on, making her way to the bathroom sink to wash her hands, Ben following like a shamed dog, which is just what he had behaved like, a dog. On the street. Public urination? There was a ticket for that, that specifically? How much urine was on the public street if they had to maintain a special traffic violation category for it? "Why on earth did you pee in the street? In public?"

"It was really late at night. Everything was closed. And, you know, New York has no public bathrooms. In Paris they have public toilets."

She paused. She said, "Ah." She said, "Well."

He knew the word "Paris" would do it. She had taken him to Paris once, when he was quite young. Just the two of them. She had gone to do some research for the museum, and she brought him along. She made him go to a ridiculous number of museums, but mostly they ate and walked.

"Oh, Ben," she said. "What is to become of us?"

"I didn't pee on the ticket, Grandma."

She picked it up and folded it neatly and zipped it up somewhere in her bag. "Our secret," she said.

34

Molly's department had gotten a request to excavate a race-horse that had been buried in the 1960s at a racecourse that was closing. The owners of the horse wanted him and his memorial moved to another racecourse intact. Molly had never heard of the horse, but Freddie told her he was quite famous in California. Her father had been a fan.

Molly called Ruby in New York and said, "I don't know why, I thought it would interest you."

"Do you think I'm morbid, Aunt Molly?"

"A little."

"Yes, it does interest me. Is the horse in a casket?"

"No. Afraid not. A canvas sack. We may not find much. But the shoes should be intact."

"Can I have one?"

"No."

"Can I come?"

The excavation of the racehorse happened to coincide with Ruby's vacation, and after a relentless campaign of whining, Ruby convinced her parents to allow her to go to Los Angeles to stay with her aunts.

Joy was horrified. "We just buried Daddy," she said when Molly phoned to tell her. "Don't you think it's too upsetting for a little girl to dig up a dead body so soon? It's too upsetting for me, that I can tell you. I'm sorry, Molly, but I do not want to hear any more about horse corpses. Goodbye."

"I didn't even think of my father," Molly told Freddie. "My mother said it's a lack of imagination."

"Well, good. You remember him as he was. I remember my mother as she was. It's more realistic, in a way. We don't live in a horror movie, after all."

"No," Molly said. "Do you think my mother does?"

Freddie chose to say nothing, which Molly seemed to find reassuring, because she smiled as if at her own foolishness and said, "Of course not. Of course she doesn't."

At first, Cora did not want to be left behind.

"Do you really want to watch Aunt Molly dig up an old dead horse?" her father asked.

She thought about it. The horse might smell. It was probably a skeleton, which was bad enough, but it might look like the Mummy or a horse zombie. And the digging was slow, which could be boring. "Joanie and I were going to have a lemonade stand outside the building. It's not very warm yet, but you can do good business that week because of tourists."

"So you'd rather stay home?"

Cora nodded. "You write the *e*'s on the sign backward. To make it look childish. It draws customers."

He was glad at least one of them would be home. Daniel had never understood that you could love anyone as much as he loved Ruby and Cora. This love was new, born when they were born. Now life without that love coursing through him was unimaginable. Their voices were like birdsong, their movements like dance.

"Every morning when I see them my heart sings, it really sings," he said to Molly. "I don't want Ruby to visit you. I'll miss her too much."

Molly felt a pang of longing for Ben. "It never goes away, missing them."

"Like Mom and you."

"Not what I was thinking of."

"I, on the other hand, am the good sibling who stayed home," he said happily.

"The oceans are rising," she replied.

Molly stood with Freddie and Ruby waiting for Ruby's suitcase.

"In Japan they have sushi that goes around just like this, on a conveyor belt, but smaller, obviously," Ruby said.

"You've been to Japan?"

"No. But I like sushi. But Daddy says overfishing is ruining the ocean."

"We'll get you some sushi."

"Thank you, Aunt Freddie. And thank you, Aunt Molly, for inviting me to your dig."

"It's not the walls of Troy," Molly said. "But it's good practice for the students. The horse died of colic very suddenly. They didn't even mark the grave properly, so we'll have a bit of a search."

"Did they shoot him?"

Ruby did not look like a morbid child. She was dressed in pink and sparkles and frayed denim like every other little girl in the airport.

"I don't think so. I think they give them shots or something."

"Cora's scared of dead things. But I don't see why. They're dead. I don't mind them. I like to know that things happened before I came along. I don't know why, but I do."

The purple camouflage suitcase appeared on the belt.

"Maybe it helps you realize that things will come along after you, too."

"I think I'm too young to think that."

They found the rib cage first. Ruby dusted off the dirt with a paintbrush, following the curves that outlined the commanding chest. The mighty horse's legs seemed to be galloping even now. The students were silent when they saw all of him, a bas-relief of bones rising from the sandy soil.

Ruby lit a candle for him when they got back to the house. "*Yitgadal v'yitkadash,*" she said. She shrugged. "That's all I know of that one by heart. You're supposed to have ten people, and I'm sure you're not supposed to say it for a horse, but I don't care. And I say it every night for Grandpa." She looked at them defiantly.

Molly wiped away a few tears. She did not sleep that night. Her mother was right, it was too soon after Aaron's death to dig up a body. Ruby was fine. It was Molly who had nightmares.

"You were crying in your sleep," Freddie said. "I couldn't wake you."

Molly didn't want to talk about it. And she certainly didn't want to talk about her bad dreams to Ruby, who looked as chipper as ever when they went into the kitchen. She had helped herself to a large bowl of the neon-colored cereal her parents forbade her.

"Guess what my father said to his ex-girlfriend," Freddie said. She read aloud from an email sent by Green Garden: " 'Thou wouldst eat thine dead vomit up and howlst to get it.' "

Ruby looked up happily from her cereal bowl. "Dead vomit! Can I meet him?"

They went to Santa Anita. Molly and Ruby sat in the backseat, Freddie and her father in the front. Ruby nudged Molly, then pointed to the back of the father's head and the back of the daughter's head. They were shaped identically.

"Molly and her students and Ruby dug up a racehorse and moved him to Santa Anita, Dad."

"Your friends always were peculiar."

"We didn't move him, actually. Just dug him up. Not too many opportunities to dig things up in Los Angeles. It's great experience for the students."

"Students?" Duncan said. "Students of what? Grave-robbing?" He chuckled. Then, "Don't go digging me up, you girls." Then, "Where are the flowers?"

"What flowers?"

"For your mother. I always bring flowers."

"Dad, we are not going to the cemetery. We're going to the track."

"Yeah? Why didn't you say so?"

They ate pastrami sandwiches and bet ten dollars on a horse named Madeira My Dear, who won.

Freddie's father made Ruby promise to go to the track with him again. "You bring luck."

"I'm not superstitious."

"That's okay," he said. "I am."

35

The thought of an outing excited Joy. The brick buildings glowed, genial and rosy in the sun. What a beautiful day and she'd woken up feeling strong. Oh, this was very nice! She began the search for her wallet, her bags, her sunglasses, her gloves.

She bought a tuna-fish sandwich and a ginger ale at the little deli on the corner and watched the man behind the counter wrap the sandwich in white paper, then cut it diagonally. That was nice, too. She liked her sandwiches cut diagonally. This is what she would do when she retired. Go on outings with tuna-fish sandwiches cut on the bias. You couldn't do that in an assisted-living facility, not like this, spontaneously. You probably had to check out at the desk, sign an attendance sheet, get permission, like the loony bin.

She didn't have to ask anyone for anything.

She carried her brown bag out to the street and the wind nearly knocked her down. It was chillier than she'd thought. The tulips planted on the meridian of Park Avenue were bright orange this year. The cherry trees above them were in full pink bloom. The wind would take care of that, soon enough, she supposed. The petals would blow around like bright pink snow, then settle into colorful drifts, then turn brown and rot like all flesh, even flowered flesh. But for now, they danced gaily against the blue sky.

She turned into Aaron's little park and sat on a bench. The sun was glaring. The bread of her sandwich was dry. The wind was cold. This was a mistake. She was not ready. She felt her heart beat unevenly. Atrial fibrillation. Right now, the blood could be languishing, clotting during a skipped beat, and then, wham, a clot could be thrown up to her brain and she would be dead. Or worse.

Karl came into the park just as she was balling up the wrapper from her sandwich.

"Joy!" He pushed his red wheeled walker aside and sat next to her on the bench. "You're a sight for sore eyes."

"You want coffee?" said his attendant, Wanda's friend Marta.

Karl shook his head. "Go, go," he said. "Enjoy."

Joy and Karl sat silently awhile. Joy pulled her hood up. She stood to dump the remains of the sandwich in the trash can, but Karl took it from her and tossed it like a basketball.

"You have good aim," Joy said. "We never went to a basketball game, did we, you and I?"

"Baseball. You're a dirty rotten Yankees fan. I remember."

Did he remember the ride home on the subway, hand in hand?

"Are you still a dirty rotten Yankees fan?" he asked.

She laughed. "I don't pay much attention to sports."

"My wife was a dirty rotten Yankees fan. She died two years ago. It's terrible, Joy. I know it's terrible."

They looked at each other. Why, his eyes were the same, the same eyes they had been when they were young, hazel eyes specked with green. There were tears in them.

"It's so windy," she said.

"My children want me to move."

"Oh, that," Joy said. "Pay no attention."

But sometimes she did worry about her own situation. She did not want her children to send her away to a home. If she became weak enough . . . well, stranger things had happened. They watched her like hawks to make sure she was okay, and like a field mouse she scuttled and hid. Yes, I'm doing quite well, she would say. Nothing to report. They seemed to believe her. They wanted to believe her. They told her she was a good sport.

But the illusion of good sportsmanship was becoming more and more difficult for her to pull off. She did not want to burden them with her problems. That might push them over the edge. She didn't want assisted living; just, sometimes, a little assistance.

"There's so much paperwork," she said to Karl. "In life."

He nodded sympathetically, but he continued to talk about his son who wanted him to move to Rhode Island and his other son who wanted him to move to Denver. "I can't move. I mean, look at me. I, literally, can't move."

The papers accumulating on Joy's dining-room table had begun to haunt her, zombies from another life, infinite and unfinished though Aaron was finite and gone, as if the magazine subscriptions addressed to him were more important, more vital than he had ever been. He lived only in the gruesome form of debts and appointments, doctors' bills.

"I have enough money, I have a nice apartment, I have Marta, who's a godsend. Why don't they leave me alone?"

"Who would want to live in someone else's city?" Joy said. But she was thinking about the piles of papers waiting for her. The papers oozed across the table, an accusing slop of obligation, neglect, pressure, the pressure of a hostile world to pay attention and to pay, pay, pay. She was old and she was alone, and the papers took no pity.

"They mean well," Karl said.

The papers had begun to take on a mythical quality. They were an angry god of chaos who never stopped reproducing himself, growing bigger and stronger, tentacled, menacing, choking her to death.

"I don't understand how they pile up so fast, the papers," she said.

"Maybe it would be nice to move away, just leave all the mess behind. I never thought of it like that."

"Absolutely not," Joy said. "That mess is your life. Don't ever let 'em tell you any different."

Then she hobbled back to her apartment. There it all was, her mess, waiting, turrets and towers of files and mail, its banners of Post-its and crumpled tissues. It was an eclectic collection. Everything had been or was to be filed, but the names on the files had little to do with their contents and few hints for what should be added. There were multiple files labeled, for example, *Urgent!!*, though some were labeled URGENT, all caps, and a few *Urgent!* with just the one exclamation point. There was a *Pay Today* file and a *Pay Immediately* file, a *Miscellaneous* file and a *Miscellany* file. There were *Medical, Medicine, Health, Health Care, Health Insurance, Doctors, Doctor Bills, Medicare*, and there were files by illness as well: *Diabetes, Cancer/Joy*, and *Cancer/Aaron*. Inside were flyers for Roundabout Theater and YIVO, Time Warner, DirecTV, AT&T, Verizon, and free shingles shots from CVS. There were unopened envelopes with requests for money from starving children, dogs, cats, and abandoned farm animals; newsletters from Israel and Trader Joe's; literature from city council candidates, mayoral candidates, cemeteries, the Neptune Society, and juice fasts. Bills and tax returns, X-rays and lab reports showed up, too, here and there, as well as clippings of art reviews by Adam Gopnik from the 1980s.

She adjusted a stack of unopened envelopes, tilting her head at them, like a curious dog. She opened one envelope and carefully read the marketing materials for a service she would never need or want. She put the torn envelope on the table, placed the glossy marketing pamphlet beside it. She shuffled through the stack of unopened envelopes again. She spread them out like a deck of cards on the table. She touched them, moved them slightly, piled them up again. She sighed. She began to read yesterday's paper, which was on the chair next to her. She reached for her scissors. She intently cut out an article and laid it on the table. A crumpled tissue fell from her sleeve. She carefully removed the cellophane from a lemon drop, which she then popped in her mouth, placing the sticky cellophane between the torn envelope and the tissue. She spread the pile of unopened envelopes out like a deck of cards on the table again.

She finally broke down and called Danny. "I think someone has to help me. But no one can help me. What should I do?"

"Close the door," Danny told her. "And never go in again."

When she called Molly, in tears, Molly said, "That's all? God, you scared me."

To them, it was a pile.

To Joy, it was the past and the future jumbled together.

Someday they would understand. They would feel sad the way she felt sad about her own mother, about all the ways she had not been able to understand until she, too, was old. If only everyone could be old together.

"Natalie!" She called her friend immediately. "I just had the most ghastly thought . . ."

Joy ran into Karl at the coffee shop regularly now. As soon as Marta saw her, she hauled herself up, said, "Errands," and lumbered out of the restaurant. It was pleasant for Joy, having someone to sit with, to confide in, someone her own age. And, she admitted this to herself, it was pleasant to spend time with a man.

She ordered her soup and listened to Karl tell one of his stories. She occasionally had to hold her hand up. "Karl," she would say, "my turn to speak."

"He has so many stories," she told Danny that night on the phone. "Very entertaining."

"You knew him in college? How come I never heard anything about him?"

"Oh, we lost track when I got married. You know how it is."

Molly called Daniel every Wednesday after his weekly dinner with their mother. She told Freddie she wanted to be supportive, but Freddie suggested she was just trying to cling to Daniel's devoted-child shirttails.

"Did you have a good time with Mom tonight?" Molly asked her brother. "Did you have a nice dinner?"

"I didn't go. She said she was too tired."

"She told you *not* to come? That doesn't sound good. Is she sick?"

"No. She said she had lunch with a friend and they walked in the park and she got tired."

"Yeah? Natalie?"

"No."

"Well, who, Daniel? You're being weird and mysterious."

"That guy. That Karl guy."

36

Molly called her mother to tell her the plans she and Daniel had made for Passover. Their first Passover without their father.

"We're all going to come. We'll have a real family Passover."

"At the apartment? Without Daddy?"

"It will give us a chance to be together and honor him," Molly said. "As a family."

Joy tried to picture the family gathered around the table without Aaron.

"No, no," she said. "No. Not this year. Not yet."

"Daniel and I worked it all out. We'll take care of the food, of course. You won't have anything to worry about."

"It will be too sad," Joy said. "I think it will be too sad. Everyone there but your father."

"We'll all be *together*, Mom."

At the coffee shop that night, Joy saw Karl, as she had hoped she would.

"I don't want this seder," she told him. "It's just too soon. Why can't they wait till next year?"

"Who knows if we'll be here next year," Karl said.

"That's cheerful."

"Well."

Joy tried to explain it to him. "Just picture it," she said. "The whole family. Picture the whole family, picture Danny, Molly, the wives, the grandchildren, me. And no Aaron. It's like one of those photographs from Russia where they scratch out Trotsky."

"I guess you could invite more people," he said. "Dilute it a little, like soup. Invite other people."

"Other people," Joy said. It was a brilliant plan. "Other people!"

The brilliant plan required a good deal of work. Just the thought of the preparations tired her. She was still not herself. She wondered if she'd ever be herself again, but no one must realize how tired she was. It was an effort to get her socks on, to tie her shoes. Her mugs were too heavy to lift. She now drank her tea in her mother's remaining china teacups.

She still went to work, however. She could not imagine retiring. If she stopped working, her world would screech to a halt, that's what it felt like to her. And she did enjoy the perplexed expression of Miss Georgia each time Joy plodded into the office, slowly and laboriously, leaning on her ugly cane. Then there was the issue of assisted living. If she had no job, it might seem as though she had no reason to remain in New York, in her apartment. She did not want her children to think it was time to move her. They never would, of course.

Unless they thought it would be better for her. She could hear their concerned voices: She'll have more company, you know how social she is; She'll have all her meals taken care of, no more ordering in from that greasy diner; Someone will change the linens; And if she falls . . .

Joy trudged up the miles of steps at the new building. She unlocked the door of her stunted new office. No, no one would be getting rid of her so easily. There would be no excuse to put her out to pasture. The trip on two buses was far more than she could manage, so she took a taxi to work. The cab fare added up to a good portion of her salary. But every little bit helps, she thought. And it's my every little bit, I earn it, I work for it. I am a working woman.

She pushed open the door.

There was another person sitting at her computer, at her desk.

"There's no drawer," Joy said.

The young woman in Joy's desk chair looked confused.

"For pencils," Joy said.

"Can I help you?" the young woman said. She had the sleepless, unkempt, poorly paid aspect of a graduate student. Joy's heart went out to her.

"I'm Dr. Bergman."

A blank look.

Joy tapped the nameplate on the door.

"Oh!" the young woman said, smiling. "Did you come to get your things?"

The graduate student, borrowed from CUNY's student work program, was under the impression Dr. Bergman had retired. She was terribly sorry. She'd just been told to use this office to do conservation work for the museum, though she was actually studying anthropology.

When confronted about the budding anthropologist in Joy's office, Miss Georgia did not have much to say, other than to assure Joy that the museum was operating with much more efficiency than it ever had before and she knew how loyal Joy was to the institution, which was why she had not hesitated in making these changes for the vitality and energetic future of the conservation department, knowing that Joy would welcome the chance to add to the viability and vigor of the museum.

"By retiring?"

Miss Georgia knew she would understand. She could gather up her boxes and books whenever it was convenient for her.

Joy had the taxi drop her off at the coffee shop. Karl was there, thank god.

Marta jumped up in her lumbering way, patted Joy's arm with what seemed like relief, and disappeared out the door.

"Loves her work," Karl said, laughing.

"I was *retired* from *my* work today. I was fired. Behind my back."

She ordered mashed potatoes and scrambled eggs and a lemon meringue pie. She tried to eat, but could manage only the pie.

"You can sue them for age discrimination."

"I'll be dead before it goes to court."

Karl nodded. "True." He was sympathetic, though. He'd been eased out of his law firm, his own firm, by the younger partners. "Experience? They're not interested."

"It's true I missed a few months when I was so sick."

"Months. What's a month?"

"I was a little fuzzy when I got back. The new building is like a railroad station, it's so big."

"They change things just to change them."

"I don't like change. They say you don't like change when you get old, and they're right."

Karl shrugged. "But some change is good." He smiled at her. "It's good we bumped into each other again, isn't it?"

"That's not change," Joy said. "That's continuity. I like continuity."

Karl did not want a bite of her pie. One more thing in his favor, she thought, finishing it with relish, scraping her fork against the plate to get the last lacquer-yellow traces.

37

Molly watched her mother opening folders, closing them, stroking, piling, opening them again. Each time Molly tried to pick one up, her mother swatted her away. It was hopeless. She headed for the kitchen to make some tea.

"What are you doing, Molly? You came all this way to help me clean up for the seder. Now please help me!"

Molly scooped up some mail from the other end of the table and began to sort it, but the sound of envelopes being torn open drew her mother's attention, the way the flutter of wings draws a cat, and Joy abandoned her files to touch each piece of mail, to finger the envelopes as if they were silken Chanel or velvet brocade beaded with seed pearls.

When Joy finally went to lie down on the couch for a rest, Molly furiously extricated the bills from the slippery towers of junk mail, sorting, filing, labeling the files and sliding them, quickly, quickly, before her mother could wake up, into new blue plastic file boxes she had ordered from Staples. She labeled the file boxes. She stuffed the junk mail into kitchen garbage bags and took them out to the back hall, where her mother would not find them.

Out of breath, gathering up the last bobby pin, the matchbooks, doctors' business cards, the coffee shop delivery receipts, Molly heard a horrified gasp behind her.

"My papers. Oh, my papers . . ."

Joy stared at the table, now empty. She sat down in Aaron's chair, her small frame hidden in a voluminous silk bathrobe she had found deep in the cedar closet, a burgundy paisley bathrobe that had been Molly's grandfather's. Heavy fringe hung from the sash. On the lapels was a braided border. She looked like a diminutive general of the Empire in her exotic silk robe and Oriental chair, her delicate little face pale and weary, relieved to hear that the native rebellion had been put down, though at what cost?

"I think I have to lie down again. Or eat something." Joy leaned her head back and closed her eyes.

"Listen, I have an idea. *I* can take care of all your bills from now on, Mom."

"I'm not senile." Eyes still closed.

"I can get everything on the computer and do it for you from L.A."

"I'm certainly not ready for that, thank you very much." Her voice had become rather severe.

"But I could—"

"Molly." Joy stood up, the hem of the silk robe pooling at her feet.

"What?" Molly said, sulky now.

"Let's face it."

"What? Face what?"

"The buck," Joy said, "stops here."

Karl arrived at the apartment exactly on time. Joy opened the door for him and noticed again his eyes, hazel with flecks of green, slightly protruding. She could remember being young and troubled by how earnest those eyes were. He carried flowers, a burst of tulips in many different colors.

"Look who's here," Joy called out to her family.

"That's not Elijah," Cora said. "Is it?"

"This is a very old friend of mine and a dear friend of Grandpa Aaron's," Joy said. "This is Karl."

Molly pulled her aside. "Mom," she whispered, "this seder is for family. Our family."

"One who locks the doors of his courtyard and eats and drinks together with his children and wife and does not feed and give drink to the poor and embittered—this is not the joy of a mitzvah but the joy of his stomach," Ruby said. "Maimonides."

"Oh Christ," said Molly.

"I read it on Chabad.org."

Molly shook her head and walked away. Joy kissed Ruby and said, "That's very wise. But I don't think Karl is either poor or embittered."

"You never know," Ruby said. "I mean, just in case, right?"

Joy nodded. "Just in case. But, Ruby, promise me, no more Chabad."

"Don't worry. I'm a feminist, Grandma."

Joy hurried away to answer the door and let Natalie in.

"Are you poor or embittered?" she asked.

"Embittered."

"Then you may enter."

"I'm poor, Grandma," said Ben, who stood right behind Natalie.

Joy hugged him and kissed him and thanked him for coming so far.

There were two more, Trevor and Melanie, a young couple from England who had just moved into the building.

This time it was Danny who pulled her aside. "Mom, what are you doing? This is a family thing. How many other people are coming? Hi, Natalie! Welcome!"

"This is so kind of you," Melanie said. "We've never been to a seder."

"Americans are so welcoming," said Trevor.

Joy smiled. She wanted to lock herself in the bathroom and never come out. She wanted to sit by herself and think about Aaron and watch the traffic from the kitchen window. She forced another smile and took a seat beside Ben and grabbed his hand and kissed it. His beard had grown in. "You look like Grandpa." Then she did get up and lock herself in the bathroom for a cry, but just a short one.

Looking down the table, Daniel realized that he, Daniel, was expected to lead the service. He cleared his throat and dinged a spoon against his wineglass. "Ahem," he said, and there was a slight diminution of noise. They got through to the first glass of wine without too much commotion. There was an empty place for Elijah, but it looked like a chair waiting for Aaron. Daniel tried not to stare at it. Ben kept filling up the wineglasses. It was thick, viscous stuff, but Daniel had downed several glasses before they got to the part where you raise your second glass. When they finally did, he made a toast to his father and realized he was singing Bob Dylan's "Forever Young." "May your heart always be joyful . . ."

"Daddy called me Joyful," his mother said. She sniffled. "It was ironic."

"Daddy wasn't ironic," said Molly.

"Well, wrong, then. He was wrong."

Ben had to finish the service. Uncle Daniel was lying on the couch by then, staring at the ceiling. Aunt Coco was handing out sticky flourless baked goods, her mouth set in a hard, furious line. Wine made her angry, especially at those who drank too much wine and lay on the couch.

"When do we sing the goat song?" Cora asked.

Ben led the diminished group through a few verses, the children belting out the chorus.

"What's a *zuzim*?" Cora asked. "A penny? Or a dollar, or what?"

Molly had opened a bottle of decent wine. She and Freddie were well on their way to having to join Daniel on the couch, Ben thought.

"Mom," he said, "easy does it."

His mother leaned back in her chair and put her glass to her lips, defiant, like a child. Freddie said, *"Dayenu!"* and drained her glass.

"Your mother drinks like a goy," Joy said.

"Well, you're supposed to drink wine on Passover," Ben said.

"It's okay for me to criticize her, Bennie. I'm her mother."

"Also, that's kind of a stereotype, Grandma." He smiled when he said it. He had noticed his grandmother had become quite sensitive to criticism.

"I love the word 'dipsomaniac,'" Karl said.

Natalie said, "Other people's families are so much less trouble."

Trevor and Melanie seemed content, turning redder with each glass, gamely crunching matzoh. "Brilliant," Trevor said each time Ben poured.

"Brilliant," Cora repeated.

Ruby began reading the four questions in pig Latin, Cora disappeared under the table, and Joy was eating macaroons dipped in chocolate, one after the other.

"Mom, easy does it," Molly said.

Ben laughed, then saw on his mother's flushed face nothing but earnest concern. You're not ironic either, Mom, he thought, but kept it to himself.

"I'll pay for this later," Joy said, licking her fingers. "Oh boy, will I."

Ben wondered if he could sneak away to watch the ball game. It was opening day. It was then that he felt the stab of absence, the moment that he glanced around to ask his grandfather if he wanted to watch, too, and remembered that his grandfather was gone.

The next morning, Molly woke up with a headache. She and Freddie were on a single blow-up bed wedged between the pullout couch that did not pull out and the bookcase.

"It's morning," she said, but Freddie groaned and did not move.

In the bathroom, the door locked, Molly called her brother.

"What the hell was that all about?" she said.

"Okay, I drank too much. I'm sorry I passed out on the couch. Please don't give me a hard time, Molly. Coco has already done that. Several times. And it's not even nine o'clock yet."

"Not you. *Mom*. What was with all those *people*? What was *Karl* doing here? Who is he, anyway? Some random guy from the park? At our first family gathering without Dad? What was she thinking?"

"She knew him in college. But I never heard her mention him until a few days ago. Do you think he was an old boyfriend?"

"Well, he's sure an old boyfriend now."

They both laughed.

"At least no one ended up in the ER after this holiday dinner," Daniel said. But he had been shocked to see Karl there, and hurt. He couldn't admit it even to Molly, but there was a moment when he walked into the apartment when he'd thought, I am the man of the house now, an unworthy thought that filled him with unworthy pride, until it dissolved into sadness and guilt. And then to have Karl appear—it was all wrong. Still, what was an old geezer like that going to do? Switch walkers with Joy when she wasn't looking? Daniel thought of himself as a calm, thoughtful, and reasonable person and he was determined to behave like one, but really his mother could have shown a little more consideration. And the man had brought his mother flowers.

"At least he didn't try to run the seder," he said, calming himself down. "Although it might have been better if he had. But I'm sorry, there was just something about him being there when Dad wasn't. It's only been a few months, for god's sake."

"Is this what Mommy wants?" Molly was saying, talking over him. "Every holiday dinner at the Mount Sinai emergency room with an old sick man who isn't even Daddy? This guy is bad news, Daniel."

"Bad news."

"The man wants a nurse, a *loving* nurse, not a paid companion. That's what they all want. And we can't let Mommy fall into that trap."

"It's like she's not thinking clearly. She's like in shock."

"Look," Molly said. "We have to face facts. Mommy's got nothing left in her life. Nothing. No job to go to. No sick husband to take care of. Her life is empty. She's very vulnerable."

Daniel said, "It's us she needs now."

"It's up to us to protect her."

38

Daniel pulled his mother's suitcase out of the closet. The sting of mold came with it.

"Oh dear," said Joy, sneezing.

"Yeah, it's pretty bad, Mom."

"It's a little like being in the country, though, that smell and the green. It makes me nostalgic."

The suitcase had been a gift from Daniel and Coco ten years ago. He wondered if she'd ever used it.

"Why don't you ever use this when we go Upstate?"

"Danny, honestly, it's full of mold. How could I possibly use it to go anywhere?" She sat on the bed. "Well," she said, "now that we see how the land lies, mold in the suitcase, very unhealthy, I'll just have to stay put in New York. In my own apartment."

Daniel took the suitcase down to the basement and left it by the garbage cans. That was on Saturday. On Sunday, he returned with a new suitcase. At first he'd gone to look for a cheap one in a crummy shop in Chinatown. He found a flimsy roller bag with zebra stripes for eighteen dollars and was about to buy it, thinking,

It doesn't have to last too long, she won't be making too many more trips at her age, then immediately felt so guilty that he left the zebra stripes behind, took the train up to Bloomingdale's, and got her an expensive roller bag in a respectable shade of blue with wheels that swiveled in all directions.

"You shouldn't have done that," Joy said when he spun the bag in graceful circles to demonstrate.

"You can't go to California with your stuff in garbage bags."

"California is not for me, Danny. I've never been there and there's a reason—it's not for me."

In the airport, Joy dropped her boarding pass, not on purpose, but she was not sorry to have lost it. The man pushing her wheelchair went back to look for it while Danny tapped his foot and forced a smile. She hated being a burden, but since she was, she wished people could shoulder her with more grace.

"I'm sorry to gum up the works," she said.

Danny shrugged, not very gallantly. Could you shrug gallantly, she wondered.

People were rushing past her in every direction. Little children were outfitted like their parents, wearing miniature backpacks, pulling little suitcases. Too many people from too many places traveling to too many other places.

How would she bear it? Two months in L.A.

"When you come back, the kids will be out of school and we'll all go Upstate," Danny said.

She was weary and she had not even gotten into the airport proper, much less the plane. People wheeling luggage the size of coffins rumbled past her. She heard a sparrow chirping high above in the rafters. Poor little bird, lost in a vast edifice, trapped, just like me.

"Let's go home," she said.

Danny pretended not to hear her.

"I don't belong here," she said.

"*No one* belongs here. It's an airport."

The wheelchair man had reappeared, victorious, waving the boarding pass. "Okay then, Madame." He spoke with a lilting Caribbean accent. He was almost as old as she was. Had his children made him leave his comfortable home and come to New York City because they were afraid he'd slip and fall?

"I'm supposed to age in place," she said to Danny.

"It's a vacation, Mom, in a warm place with people who love you."

"I don't really need a wheelchair," she said to the wheelchair man, turning, twisting her neck so she could see him. "My children are overly cautious."

"They love you," the man said.

"I'm going to stay with my daughter. In California." She did not mention Freddie. Perhaps that was wrong, but she could not come up with a way to explain Freddie, not on the spur of the moment to the wheelchair man.

"That's beautiful," said the man.

"Yes, I suppose it is."

Danny set off the beeping alarms as he went through security.

"Hips," he said apologetically to the guard. "And knees."

"I am free of prosthetics," Joy said. "I am also free of most of my large bowel, my gallbladder, my uterus, ovaries, and appendix. I have my tonsils and most of my teeth. Check on your machine. You'll see. Go ahead, check."

— 39 —

When she had been in Los Angeles for three days, she knew two things for certain. One: she could not spend two months with her daughter. Two: she could not spend two months with her daughter in California. The California sun was blinding, much brighter than the friendly East Coast sun. This sun was used to shining on a desert, harsh and unrelenting.

"Isn't it beautiful, Mom? Do you see why I love it here?"

"Very nice," Joy said.

Then there was Molly herself, as bright and unrelenting as the sun. Every time Joy put a glass down, Molly picked it up and put it in the dishwasher. The temperature was constantly shifting, depending on where that sun was and at what angle it was hitting the house, and Joy put on and took off sweaters all day long, but each time she reached for a sweater she had removed, it was gone, gone to its closet, hung up there by Molly. Books, magazines, sandwiches—they disappeared practically from Joy's hand. Her toothbrush, which she left on the side of the sink, immediately hid itself in the medicine cabinet. Sometimes, when Joy lifted her coffee cup, a hand with a sponge swiped the spot where it had been on the table before Joy was able to take a sip.

"This is so relaxing, isn't it, Mom?"

"Very nice."

"Are you comfortable, Mommy? We got you a memory foam pad for the bed."

The two girls were so thoughtful, but the bed was so high Joy had trouble getting into it. It loomed before her at night, a great bulbous affair piled with pillows, six, seven, eight pillows. The box spring and mattress and memory foam mattress pad and the down mattress pad on top of that looked like a big billowy hat that might topple off its head at any moment. It might cushion the fall in an earthquake. Then she thought, Earthquake, and could not sleep.

The jasmine bloomed, and it made her eyes water.

She uttered not a word of complaint. Molly was so happy to have her. Even Freddie seemed happy to have her here. Were they insane, both of them? She was a nuisance. Even at her best these days, she was a nuisance.

"I'm very annoying," she said.

"No, you're not," said Molly.

"No, I am. I really am. I'm annoying. I annoy myself, even."

Molly laughed and hugged her. Joy, hugging her back, felt the sturdy flesh of Molly's back. "You certainly are strong."

Molly rolled up her sleeve and made a muscle, like a man. Joy dutifully touched her daughter's biceps and wondered when it was that muscles on women had become fashionable. "Okay, Popeye," she said.

Molly was heading out for a walk. She walked very fast and very far every day. Stop and smell the roses, Joy had said once, but Molly said the roses in California did not have much smell.

"I'll walk you to the gate." Pretty much all she did. There were no doormen to gossip with, no coffee shop to walk to, no park, no friends to have lunch with, no Karl to bump into. "Just let me find my sunglasses."

She looked first through one bag, then through another bag. As she pushed the packages of Kleenex and lipsticks and tubes of moisturizer aside, she began to panic. Her sunglasses had to be in her pocketbook, in this brown eyeglass case perhaps, but no, the brown one was empty, and this one, the turquoise, held her reading glasses, the old ones that worked better than the new ones, she had been searching for them all day, and another glasses case, a hard case, white, this had to be the one with the sunglasses, but these were a pair of glasses she had never seen before, where on earth had *they* come from?

"Here, Mom. I found them. They were in the pocket of your jacket. In the closet."

"Oh thank god. Now I'll just put my shoes on."

Before she could put her shoes on, she had to put on her special elastic stockings that helped her circulation. The special rubber gloves she needed to put on the special stockings were somewhere in the guest room where she slept, which was also Freddie's home office, poor Freddie. She shuffled into the guest room, fumbled through several drawers until she found the rubber gloves.

"Mom, I don't have that much time before I have to get to work." Molly was pacing up and down the hall, all decked out in her sneakers and Lycra. A uniform to take a walk. Joy smiled. Molly had always liked uniforms. She had taken up skating just to get the skates and the silly skirt, horseback riding just to get the breeches and the ratcatcher shirt and the white stock and the shiny black boots; skiing, tennis—she had been very good at sports, but it was all about the equipment.

"You were such a good little tennis player."

"Mom?"

"Yes, all right, but don't rush me," Joy said. "I get flustered."

"Oh, for god's sake. Why didn't you get ready half an hour ago when I said I was going out?"

Joy looked up from her sneaker, the lace of which she was

trying to untangle. "See?" she said, beaming. "I was right! I *am* annoying!"

Molly and Freddie tried, they did try. They took Joy to the beach to watch the sunset. They took her to dinner. They made her dinner. They walked her up and down the street like a much-loved dog. In the evening they sat outside and had their glass of wine and Joy sat with them, but she was alone in those moments, she was alone in every moment. How could she have explained that to the two girls? That's how she had come to think of them, as the two girls. Not The Girls. The Girls were her friends back in New York. The Two Girls were here, attentive, dutiful, insufficient.

I have no life, Joy thought. I belong nowhere. I am residing in someone else's life, in the Two Girls' life.

The days passed, many days, Joy was sure, though she began to lose track of them.

"Give it a little time, Mom. It's only been a week," Molly said.

"It seems like a year. Fish and guests, you know what they say."

Molly looked crestfallen, a word Joy was sure she had not thought of in years. She could not stand to have her daughter look crestfallen. It broke her heart.

"It's lovely," she said quickly. "You two girls are wonderful to me. But what am I doing here, honey? I don't belong here. I'm in your way and I do have my own home. At home."

"It's a change," Molly said. "A change of scenery."

Joy tried to smile appreciatively. She must stop complaining or she'd end up with yet another change of scenery, she thought, the parking lot out of a nursing home window.

That night in bed, Molly whispered to Freddie, "I think she misses him."

"Of course she does, honey. So do you," Freddie whispered back. "So do I. It's been just a few months."

"No, I mean Karl."

Freddie started to say that was unlikely, but then wondered. "You think she's like my father?"

Molly, obviously offended, said, "She's lonely and vulnerable. That's all."

"It's probably pretty boring for her here."

Molly had tried to interest her mother in gardening. She offered to get raised beds if Joy wanted to grow vegetables. Molly did not like gardening, but she saw no reason that her mother shouldn't, and if that meant fresh Tuscan kale and artichokes on Molly's table, so much the better. "It's very spiritual, Mom," she'd said. "Working with the soil." She wished her mother had shown even a little initiative, if not with vegetables, then with flowers. They had a rosebush out front that was not doing at all well.

"She's always on the phone," she whispered to Freddie. "And she's secretive."

She thought it was usually Daniel, sometimes Natalie or one of the other girls. But it could be Karl, for all she really knew.

"She probably misses her cronies, her routine. Old people like routine. That's what they keep telling me at Dad's place. That's one of the things they can't understand about him. He hates routine."

Molly kissed Freddie. "That's it! You are a genius. We'll take her to visit your father. She'll see her peers and feel less lonely. We'll take her to Green Goddess!"

Joy sat glumly in the backseat. The thin end of the wedge. The way they talked this place up, as if it were a resort in the Caribbean—it had happened to her friends, but she had not really expected this from Molly, her own daughter.

"I plan to go back to work in the fall," she said.

"One day at a time," Molly answered.

The parking lot seemed to be home to a number of cats.

"Pets are allowed," Freddie said, "but the cats are feral."

The building was pink stucco. The rooms had small balconies. In the center of an inner courtyard a fountain bubbled, and there was a front desk like a hotel. The whole place felt like a hotel, actually, a small hotel just a bit down at the heels.

"Not bad, right?" Freddie said.

Joy gave a weak smile.

They had lunch in the dining room. Joy was alarmed by the bibs the residents wore, but the food was quite good. She had never met Freddie's father before this, which struck all of them as odd.

"Where have they been hiding you?" Duncan asked.

"I live in New York City." It felt good just to say that: I live in New York.

"What are you doing here with these two harridans?"

"We thought it would be nice for you two to meet, that's all," Freddie said.

Joy felt something on her knee. A hand.

"Well, it's about time, says I," the owner of the hand said. He gave Joy his handsome smile.

Joy shifted, freeing her knee. "Oh yes."

A woman at a nearby table was glaring at her. Joy took a bite of her tuna-fish sandwich. The hand returned to her knee. She felt her throat closing and thought, What if I choke and die with my daughter's father-in-law's hand on my knee?

"So when did you move into Green Acres?" Duncan said.

"Excuse me?"

"She doesn't live here, Dad. She's staying with us."

"Green Acres? That's a good one," Molly said.

"Remember Zsa Zsa Gabor?" Joy said. "Those were the days."

"That was Eva Gabor."

"Sweet girl, Zsa Zsa," said Duncan. "We worked together. Years ago, years ago."

As Duncan described an obscure movie in which he had an even more obscure part, Joy noticed Freddie raising an eyebrow at Molly. They exchanged just noticeable smirks. Joy kicked Molly under the table, which had the advantage of also dislodging Duncan's hand.

"A little respect," Joy said, first to Molly, then to Freddie's father. "A little respect."

"Nothing will come of nothing," said Duncan in his rich and sonorous voice. He tried his smile again.

"Wasn't that fun, Mom?" Molly asked as they drove home. "Jesus, Freddie, do you actually aim for the potholes?"

Freddie laughed.

Freddie really was good-natured, Joy thought. "Your father is a ball of fire," she said. She would not mention the hand. What would be the point?

"Never underestimate a minor character actor," Freddie said. "It's already been done. Their whole life."

"Who was that woman who tried to trip us with her walker?" said Molly.

Freddie shrugged. "One of his girlfriends?"

"I'm sure that was an accident," said Joy. But Green Garden was even more frightening than she had imagined.

Joy leaned on the grocery cart, weary in body and soul. It was an expensive, trendy grocery store, the kind of grocery store in which half the children were probably not vaccinated against measles. Molly examined a small ugly root vegetable.

"I think you girls deserve some privacy," Joy said. "You've been so hospitable." She had tried this before but gotten nowhere, and this time, too, Molly smiled an abstracted smile and said, "Don't worry about it, Mom."

Joy pushed the cart to the fish counter and waited for Molly to catch up. She missed her apartment, her lonely apartment in which she could roam and mourn at will. She missed the doormen. She missed her friends. She missed the park and Karl.

"I'm homesick, Molly. I keep trying to tell you nicely. I want to go home."

"I understand that you're not completely adjusted—"

"Adjusted? No, I'm not adjusted. I don't want to be adjusted." Joy realized she was speaking loudly and the mothers of unvaccinated children were glancing at her suspiciously. Careful, Joy. Don't rile up the natives, don't rile up Molly, especially. "Sweetheart, you and Freddie have been absolutely wonderful, but put yourself in my position."

"That's just what I was talking to Daniel about, and we decided that even more than the change in scenery, even more than the warm weather, that what you need is to be useful."

"Yes," said Joy, suddenly jubilant. At last her son and daughter understood.

"Everyone needs to be useful."

"That is so true." She would go back to work and insist on getting her projects back. She would call Norman, that fellow on the board, the one who Aaron used to play poker with, why hadn't she thought of it before . . .

"We thought you could do something at the Getty, maybe."

"The Getty?"

"Yeah, you know, like volunteer. Or the Skirball. The training for docents is pretty rigorous, but still . . ."

Molly prattled away about Los Angeles museums and their volunteer programs as they loaded the cart with healthful food that Joy could not digest. Joy searched the shelves for Cream of Wheat and said, now and then in hopeless punctuation of Molly's recitation, "Such good ideas! If only I did not already have a museum. In New York."

One evening when Molly was at a meeting and not coming home until late, Joy and Freddie went out to dinner, just the two of them. It was the first time they had done anything like that, and they were both a little nervous, Joy's discomfort manifesting itself in silence, Freddie's in chatter.

"Molly doesn't like this place, she thinks it's boring, but I love it and I think you might like it, too. The traffic will be impossible on the 10, even in this direction, so I think I'll take Venice, oh my god, look at them trying to get to the 405 . . ."

Joy opened the window and let the cool air in. It smelled like flowers even on this busy street. She braced herself for yet another restaurant with painfully loud music, painfully hard benches, women in painfully high heels and men comfortable in sneakers, all of them eating spicy, fishy fragments of raw things on little saucers. It was the same in New York, she supposed, but she never went to restaurants like that in New York. She was in the mood for spaghetti and meatballs.

It seemed like a long time before they finally pulled into a parking structure, then spiraled down several levels until they found a space. Disoriented, Joy squeezed out of the car and followed Freddie to an elevator that took them back to street level. Freddie was still talking. Something about her department at the university trying to screw someone over in a fourth-year review and a committee that never met. Joy thought of the museum, of Miss Georgia, of all the orphaned artifacts she could no longer tend to. She was grateful to Freddie for talking, for trying. Freddie was a good sport. Joy remembered being a good sport. It required energy and optimism and faith, and it had been quite rewarding. Really, she had spent her entire life being a good sport. But to what end? She had grown old and uncomfortable, just like a bad sport. And now she *was* a bad sport. There was no protection in good behavior. She felt suddenly compassionate toward Freddie, struggling on in a unilateral conversation that would not protect her from the disappointments of old age.

"You're a good sport, Freddie," she said.

Freddie's face lit up, that tan, weathered face, into an almost goofy smile. How charming, that large unconscious grin. Freddie's was not a beautiful, womanly face by any stretch of the imagination, more a wary, taut look to her, but when she smiled, the contrast was overwhelmingly pleasant. It made Joy grin back at her. It was like a happy slap on the back, that smile, an arm thrown joyfully around your shoulder. It was as friendly a smile as Joy could remember seeing. It was irresistible. No wonder Molly fell in love with this person. Joy marveled that she had never noticed the warmth of that smile, of everything about Freddie, really. Then she realized she had never really looked at Freddie's face before. It had been an indistinct oval, an unwelcome blur from the dreaded California.

"This is very nice of you," Joy said.

They walked a quarter of a block, then turned into a small strip mall. There was a sushi restaurant, a Korean barbecue, a nail salon, and an Italian restaurant. Freddie opened the door of the Italian restaurant.

"It's so quiet," Joy said.

"It's so comfortable," she added, sliding into a padded booth.

"Spaghetti and meatballs," she told the waiter happily. "Just what I wanted."

"This place has been here forever," Freddie said. "My father used to take us when I was a kid. I bring him back once in a while, but he doesn't remember it, so it's kind of sad."

Joy reached across the table for Freddie's hand. "It's awful when they don't remember what you remember, even when you're right there with them. It's like nothing exists anymore."

Freddie was crying, just a few tears. Joy had never seen her cry. She was such an odd little thing, ebullient and tough all at once. Poignant tears, not like me, Joy thought, with my weeping and wailing every minute. Not like Molly, either.

"No one really understands this particular abyss," Joy said. "Our abyss."

"No, they don't. But why should they, I suppose."

"We're an exclusive club."

"The Abyss Club," Freddie said, laughing. She took her hand back, wiped her eyes with the big cloth napkin.

They had ricotta cheesecake and cannolis for dessert.

"I'll pay for it later," Joy said. "So I always say. But it never stops me."

Molly and Freddie disappeared the next morning and came home with a very small dog.

"You can walk it," they said.

"Step on it is more likely."

"Listen, it's perfect: Freddie and I went to the pound and rescued this little fellow. Now we have a dog, right?"

"Apparently."

"But we both have jobs, right?"

"Thank god. I don't care what the 'experts' report about the economy, people are suffering, that's all I can say."

"We have a dog, but because of our jobs we don't have time to walk the dog. So, Freddie and I really need you, Mom. We need you to walk our dog."

"It would be a big help to us," Freddie said. She smiled, and Joy of course smiled back and took the new plaid leash attached to the tiny dog.

They were such nice girls, and she appreciated the thought and effort that had gone into the plan. It was creative of the girls, she had to give them that. And she was touched that they cared enough about her mental health to go to such lengths to give her something to do. It was not their fault that the dog refused to cooperate.

The dog was named Gatto, which was amusing. But Gatto did not like to take walks. Gatto hated to take walks. The size of a large rat, he was part Chihuahua, part poodle, part parrot, Joy thought, for he was a very vocal little dog, making his wishes known with a remarkably varied vocabulary of squeaks and yelps, and his wishes were to stay home, curled on Joy's lap.

"Gatto, indeed," she said. Gatto squeaked, snorted, stretched, and balled himself up again. Joy patted his head, the size of a nectarine, and dozed uncomfortably. She was afraid to move. She did not want to disturb him.

The days went by, blue skies and pretty smells. She carried Gatto with her on her strolls, mostly as a way of starting conversations. She was uneasy talking to the girls, noticing their impatience, how they interrupted with unnecessarily big smiles to change the subject. Was she talking too much? Had she become boring? She supposed she was and she had. She became more and more quiet at home. But on her walks all kinds of people stopped her to admire the dog. They laughed when she told them his name.

"My daughter got him for me so I could take him on walks, but he doesn't like to walk," she would say, and they would laugh again.

Aaron, she thought, you would not like it here. There's no normal place to get coffee, no normal barber, just an overpriced coffee place where people sit on uncomfortable, oversized wooden boxes, just hair salons for skinny young men. You would not like it here, but you are gone. She sometimes thought he was there beside her, shaking his head at the young people riding bicycles, no helmets, carrying surfboards under one arm.

"Where are all the old people?" she asked.

"It's gotten sort of gentrified," said Freddie. "A lot of tech companies moved in."

"But where are the old people?"

Molly shrugged. "Assisted living?"

Joy did not ask again.

Because Gatto did not like to walk and Joy had gotten so much stronger, Molly and Freddie revised their plans for Joy to be useful. They got her a tricycle.

"It's red," she said. She did not know what else to say. What is there to say when presented with an adult tricycle? It had a basket for Gatto. It had an old-fashioned bell. It was gigantic. It was a tricycle. It was red.

"You can ride on the boardwalk. It's great exercise."

"You can do errands," Freddie added. "Which are so . . ."

"Useful!"

Molly often finished Freddie's sentences, and vice versa.

"Useful." Joy wanted to be useful. She wanted that almost as much as she did not want to be lonely. But was a tricycle really the road to relevance? Were errands the answer? And she would look like a kook.

"Wear a hat for the sun, Mom."

A kook in a hat.

"We got you a water bottle," Freddie said.

Joy had ridden just such a red tricycle when she was a child. It was not dignified then. It was not dignified now.

"I know they mean well," she said to Natalie one morning when both girls were off at work and she could speak freely on the phone.

"Don't you know how to ride a two-wheeler?"

"Of course I do. They wanted me to ride it to the grocery store to get milk yesterday."

"I thought you were lactose-intolerant."

"I am, but I don't want to hurt their feelings. But luckily, I had a terrible bout of diarrhea and couldn't go. At least it's flat here. But they really are making an effort, they're trying."

"Trying to what? Turn their mother into an errand boy?"

"They think I'll feel useful, that they've given meaning to my life."

"Ridiculous. Just ridiculous. Don't they have a car?"

"I just realized something. People will think I lost my license."

"They'll think you're a drunk, an old, eccentric drunk with a DUI."

They laughed at that.

"Okay," Natalie said. "Time to come home."

Joy poked through the bookcase looking for something to read. Molly and Freddie did not get a newspaper. They read it online. What difference did it make, her eyes were terrible anyway. She could read a little if the light was right and she tilted her head and the print was dark. She picked up an old *New York* magazine from a pile in a basket. Interesting that Molly still got *New York* magazine. She must miss New York. Joy caught her breath. Perhaps that meant she would move back. She could get an apartment nearby. They could see each other for lunch. And dinner.

She spent some time searching for her striped bag, then searched through it for her sunglasses. Maybe they were in the green bag. The dog followed her wherever she went. She wondered if he would follow her outside, if it was the leash that made him refuse to go on a walk.

"That way you could get a little exercise, fatso," she said. He really was getting tubby, and so quickly, too. Molly said it was not healthy for him to be so heavy, that Joy should stop feeding him bits of her own food. "We'll show her," Joy said. "You deserve every bit of food you can get after the life you lived, whatever it was." She imagined him on the street, fighting with the crows for pizza crusts.

She put on her sunglasses, got her cane, opened the door, and called Gatto. He made some inquiring noises, then slunk to the door on his belly. Joy went out and down the steps to the street. She called him again. "Come here, come here, Gatto. Cardiovascular activity! Come on!" He looked at her dubiously, then darted out the door and stood beside her. "Good boy." Now she walked down the street, stopping periodically so he could catch up. He lay down on her feet after each of these sprints, but they made it all the way down the block before Joy turned around to go back.

And then, from nowhere, a giant of a dog galloped around the corner, gave a deep thunderous growl, a deeper more thunderous bark, and Gatto was hanging from the beast's jaws like a rag toy.

Probably she hit the dog with her cane. That would account for the owner pushing her out of the way and screaming. Unless the screaming was Joy's, which it may well have been. She grabbed the animal's jaws and tried to pry them apart, that she was sure of. She was sure she ultimately shoved her cane in its mouth and yanked down until Gatto flopped out onto the ground and the beast's owner dragged it away by its collar.

Joy carried Gatto into the house. He was alive. His heart was beating, fluttering like hummingbird wings. There was blood on his belly. Joy wrapped him in a towel and put him in the basket of the tricycle. She pushed open the back gate and pedaled as furiously as an eighty-six-year-old can pedal a tricycle. There was a main thoroughfare one block away, a street with stores and malls and an animal hospital. She pedaled and pedaled and crossed the street against the light and heard cars honking and screamed an obscenity and pedaled some more until she saw the vet's office and pulled the tricycle onto the sidewalk.

Gatto was stitched up and given some shots. The vet was a young woman with freckles sprinkled across her nose who treated him like a VIP, Joy thought. A VIP, she said to Gatto as she pedaled him home. That's what you are, a VIP.

When Molly came home, she found her mother in bed, Gatto beside her, shaved and stitched, both of them fast asleep. The gate to the alley had been left open, and when she went to close it, she noticed the tricycle, in its basket a bloody towel.

"This is a dangerous city," Joy said when she woke up. "I'm taking Gatto home where it's safe."

40

The sadness was there, waiting for her in the apartment. I'm sorry, Joy said to the sadness. I'm sorry I had to leave you behind for so long. But, believe me, the blue skies never fooled me, you were in my thoughts, in my heart, every minute. She looked out the window at the rain and the wet trees and the bleary spots of red taillights and white headlights. I'm home, she said, with relief, to the emptiness.

She sat at the kitchen table and Gatto leaped onto her lap, his nails scratching her leg. He was a good traveler. He hadn't made a peep, zipped up in his bag beneath the seat. She had forgotten he was there, had almost left him behind, abandoned a dog that had already been abandoned, it would have been terrible, and she wondered who would have found him, a flight attendant or one of the cleaning crew, perhaps, and whether they would have taken him home and given him a good life.

"But I didn't abandon you," she said aloud. She petted his hard little head and wondered why *she* felt abandoned. No one had left her behind under an airline seat, it was she who had insisted on leaving California and Molly, but it had taken only a moment for the abandonment to rise up, like a cold flame; it had taken only the sight of Molly turning her back after she got her settled in her JetBlue wheelchair.

Joy pulled the dog up to her face, letting his warmth muffle the silence. "But we didn't belong there, did we?"

Gatto jumped down and lifted his leg against the leg of the table.

Joy watched him blandly. "You think you can scare me with a little pee? Think again, dog. I've been worked over by an expert. With a colostomy bag."

She wiped up the dog pee. She mourned her husband. She mourned her life, which seemed so far away, lost in time. She longed for her daughter and her son, the sounds of their voices, the strength of their arms, and the loving condescension of their hearts. She longed for Aaron.

She didn't seem to belong anywhere anymore. But it was good to be home just the same.

"Promise you'll call me every day and tell me how you're doing," Molly had said before Joy left.

Joy took her promise to heart. She called every day, eagerly, hesitant to disturb Molly, but not hesitant enough to stop dialing. Sometimes she called twice a day, sometimes more. It was dangerous to call so much, signaling need and helplessness, she knew that. She made sure to sound happy and engaged, made sure to share only what bits of information she believed shed a pleasant light on her and her days. The deliveryman from the coffee shop looked cold, she told Molly, so she gave him one of Aaron's scarves, he was so grateful.

"Mom, it's June. How could he be?"

"The point, Molly, is how nice it is to be able to make a gesture like that and have it mean something to someone."

"Which scarf? I hope not the gray cashmere."

Joy tried to monitor her voice and conversation, to weed out any petulance and grievance of tone, but it was difficult. No matter how hard she listened to herself and monitored herself, what she heard was an indolent, wide-ranging, rolling report of the minutiae of a disgruntled old woman's existence: the chronology of meals, of courses within meals, the digestive consequences of meals; the frequency of sleep and sleeplessness, the details of other phone calls, phone calls with people Molly did not even know. She couldn't change the course of her words, they rushed along like a flooded river. She talked about her grandchildren and their bad colds, but also the grandchildren of friends and neighbors with colds that were even worse. Those grandchildren, the grandchildren of friends and neighbors, had cousins, too, whose troubles and triumphs she found herself confiding to Molly. Her voice droned on and she was mesmerized by it, helpless to stop, unwilling to hang up. Not that long ago she had been lying on Molly and Freddie's couch watching television, her daughter giving her a foot massage, and Joy had been longing to be alone with her loneliness. Now she experienced every phone call to Molly as essential, something she could not let slip away.

"I take the dog out every day."

"Yes, you told me, that's great for you, to get out."

"I still have to carry him. It's good he only weighs a few pounds. I'm not as strong as I once was. But yesterday it was so windy the doorman, that nice Ernie who Daddy liked so much, he wouldn't let me out the door. I called the hardware store, Feldman's, the one with all the tchotchkes, and they suggested Wee-Wee pads, but I had to call a pet store to get them. My neighbor upstairs, the man who was always such a sourpuss until he got his poodle, well, he gave me a number, left it with the doorman, actually, and I called . . ."

"Mom? I'm sorry, but I'm in the middle of cooking dinner. I really should get off the phone."

"Oh! The time difference. And why am I rattling on like this? It's a mild form of senility. Good night, sweetheart."

"I wish Mom would get hearing aids," Daniel told Molly after one of his own conversations with their mother.

But Molly didn't think it would make much difference. Their mother wanted to talk, not to listen. It was an exhalation of words, no intake of breath, no pauses, a stream of consciousness into which no one else could dip a toe, an incompleteness so complete there could be no natural end to a conversation. Molly often found these monologues strangely soothing. She wondered if that was what meditation was all about, that absence of meaning, that sense of eternity. She was almost as helpless in that cocoon of superfluous information as her mother. The truth was, she craved the sound of her mother's voice. It calmed her, reassured her. Ah yes, the twins' First Communion. Whose twins? she would wonder idly. But it didn't matter. They were the twins created by her mother's voice, created by her mother.

There was little chance for Molly to interrupt, and she stopped trying. She did not say, for example, *I miss Daddy at the oddest times.* She missed him whenever the fog came in. He used to quote Carl Sandburg when there was fog, little cat feet, silent haunches. She missed him when she made gravy because he hated giblets, or when she made lima beans because he hated lima beans, or pea soup because he loved pea soup. She missed him when she got an ingrown toenail and cut a V in the nail the way he'd taught her. She rarely had a chance to say any of that to her mother, and the few times she tried, she felt intrusive and loud. She didn't say much and she didn't listen carefully. Her mother's voice washed over her, intoxicating.

"Until I can't stand it anymore."

"Well, an hour on the phone is a lot," Freddie said sympathetically.

"It's no skin off your nose," Molly said. "Why do you care?"

Freddie shook her head and laughed. "You're impossible."

"A hundred years ago we would have had to write letters, which would have taken days to get across the country. And I would not have heard her voice. I love her voice. I love to hear it. Until I can't stand it anymore! And then I hang up, and then I miss her and want to listen to her talk more."

Freddie tried to remember her own mother's voice. She could feel it, in her thoughts and in her body, high and fluty, but she couldn't hear it. That night she dreamed about her mother: her mother had been alive all this time, Freddie was surprised and overjoyed to see her, to hold her hand and kiss her and cry with relief.

"The apartment is a shambles," Daniel told his wife. "And there are Wee-Wee pads all over. And my mother is in her pajamas and bathrobe. She never goes out. It's like she's become a recluse in two weeks. The dog is a fat pig."

Coco asked cautiously if he wanted Joy to stay with them.

"Oh, I don't think we're there yet."

"She's so independent," she said, with obvious relief.

"And California was not exactly a success."

"But we would be less intrusive," Coco said. "We would let her go her own way. Your sister and Freddie, well . . ."

"They can be a little . . ."

"Overbearing."

Daniel laughed. He sat next to Coco on the couch and put his arm around her.

"But I hate to think of her in that big old apartment all by herself," Coco said.

"Big? Not for her. She's covered every surface with papers and clothes. She needs more rooms to clutter. Anyway, she's not alone. She's got the obese dog."

He tried to imagine his mother in their loft. They would have to box her in, the way they had the kids. But the kids' little box rooms had the only windows in the back. They could always give

217

Joy a windowless closet, the way the museum did. He remembered the younger Joy, funny and full of eccentric energy. The first day of moving in, she would have had the whole family out bird-watching or making rubbings of manhole covers. Now, though, she spent most of her time shuffling through her apartment looking for her glasses, the dog shuffling after her, or making toast on which she slathered something yellow and glistening that was not butter.

"Oh god, Coco, why are we even thinking about this?" But he was grateful she had brought it up. He wondered what she would have done if he'd said, Yes, that's a splendid idea, let's move her in as soon as we can.

"But, Daniel, we're so lucky to have Cora and Ruby around, I feel almost selfish. They would make things so much more cheerful for your mother."

Daniel could not argue with that. Both he and Coco considered their children an indisputable addition to any situation. They were always surprised when the girls were not included in wedding invitations or cocktail parties. Again, Daniel tried to picture his mother in the loft. It's so drafty, she would say. The lighting is so harsh. He knew she would say those things because she had already said them when they once had Thanksgiving there. I just feel uncomfortable, in my head, the proportions are off, Danny, but at least they fixed your elevator. "Maybe we could just lend the children to her."

Coco said nothing. She was thinking of her own old age. Would Cora or Ruby want her to come and live with them when the time came? She would have to set a good example. "We could make her feel much more at home than Freddie and Molly did."

Daniel suspected her generosity of spirit was propped up just a bit by her certainty that he would not agree. Even though his mother had been so good to him all his life, especially when he'd been sick, coming to the hospital every day before and after work. In so many ways, Daniel had modeled himself on her, trying to do good, to be generous, to repay the world with some of the care she had shown him. Maybe, it occurred to him, he should be repaying *her*, not the planet. Maybe Coco was right and they should share their lives with her the way she had devoted so much of her life to him.

The girls came running into the living room at that moment and demanded ice cream.

"You girls could share a room if Grandma came to live with us," Coco said.

Share? Horror-stricken faces. Pushing. Kicking. Squeals of aggression, squeals of pain.

"Go to your rooms this minute!"

"Yeah, and stay out of my room, too," Cora said to her sister, delivering one last blow.

"Stay out of my room first," said Ruby.

"I'm already out of your room. I win."

Daniel shepherded them into their rooms and shut their doors.

When he came back with two glasses of Scotch, Coco took hers gratefully and said, "I guess that won't work, sharing a room."

"No."

She determined then and there always to have two extra bedrooms when she was old, one for each of her daughters to move into.

41

Daniel asked his mother if she was depressed. She said, "Naturally."

42

Molly had often wondered, too often to tell anyone, even Freddie, what it would feel like to jump off a building, what your thoughts would be. Would your thoughts be narrowed to a simple unthinking scream? Would you think of all those you would miss? Would you wonder if they would miss you? Would you think, What in the world am I doing, falling, falling, no way to stop, no way to go back? Would you think, Why did I do this? Or would you think, Why didn't I do this long ago? That, all of that, was what she felt her mother must be feeling. Her mother was falling through the air of her life. Molly had tried hard to ignore it, but she could hear it in her mother's voice.

And Molly was doing nothing to help her. Nothing.

She sat in the dappled shade of a small garden, admiring a spider's web that ran from the tea tree branch up to the trunk of the apricot tree, a marvel of fantasy engineering, beautiful in the soft afternoon light, ugly as a weapon, a large beetle imprisoned in its lace. She was sitting, staring at a cruel bit of silver embroidery while her mother floated helplessly in her loneliness, stunned and airborne, not even caught in her fall like the beetle. Molly was watching a hummingbird, listening to the whir of its movement, catching the colors of its throat as they changed, and they were dazzling, and the sound of a finch was musical and a flock of noisy parrots flew high above. The flowers of the succulents were blooming, minuscule, stunted, almost invisible. Everything was soft and green and serene. Molly was comfortable and the neighbor's cat stretched beyond the fence, a calico cat, and—she couldn't help herself—she was filled with joy and a sense of wonder. Her happiness made her sad, because it wasn't fair, it couldn't be fair to be happy when her mother was falling from a building toward the cold gray sidewalk.

—— 43 ——

Joy took Gatto and a sandwich to the park.

"I went all the way to Daddy's park," she told Molly. "I bought a turkey sandwich, low sodium, and ate it on a bench."

"I went to Daddy's little park," she told Danny. "It was very peaceful."

She'd been looking for Karl, but he wasn't there. He wasn't at the coffee shop at his usual time, either. She had missed Karl more than she expected when she was in California. She hoped he wasn't dead. She considered walking to his building to ask the doorman if Karl had died while she was in California, but if he had, she would be devastated, and if he hadn't, she would be embarrassed.

"She's seeing that guy again, I'm sure of it," Daniel told Molly. "She went to Daddy's park. That's like code. She's very vulnerable right now. In more ways than one." Daniel had finally worked out where all her bits and pieces of money had been squirreled away in different bank accounts to confuse Aaron, and there wasn't much left. "The good news is, he's a fool if he's after her money."

"She does *not* want to sell Upstate."

"She's running out of dough, Molly."

"We'll help her."

"What if she gets sick again? We can't afford all those aides. She spent everything on Daddy. She's broke."

Molly said, "She's got the house."

"My point exactly."

And so the argument went, round and round and back again. For Molly, Upstate was a tie to home. For Joy, the house was both her past and what she would give to her children's future. Daniel understood all of it. He felt the same way, really.

"But we have to be realistic, Molly. If she sells Upstate, she'll be able to plan properly, plan how much she can spend each year."

"She can't plan," his sister said slowly, clearly, as if talking to someone else's backward child, "because she doesn't know how long she will live. Why are we pretending she can make plans? Why can't she just live her life?"

"Because," he said, just as slowly and clearly, "she has no money."

Joy knew they spoke to each other about her. She didn't like it, but she didn't want to know what it was about, either, because she already did: it was about what to do with her.

They were always coming up with electronics that were meant to make her life easier but ran out of batteries.

"They mean well," she said to Karl. He had not died, but he had suffered from a long bout of flu. This was his first day out.

"I'm sorry I worried you," he said. "Why didn't you call?"

"No news is good news, Karl." They were sitting in Central Park on a bench facing a noisy playground. "Molly and Daniel want me to be happy, but they're driving me crazy. I think someone of my age and experience should be allowed to feel exactly the way she wants."

"Hear, hear."

"Which is miserable."

"Hear, hear."

It was pleasant to have someone to meet in the park, to meet at the coffee shop, someone who knew her when she was young and beautiful, someone who remembered the things she remembered. Karl began to tell her a story about an uncle who had been a bootlegger but got the flu and missed a meet-up at which everyone else got shot. She'd heard the story before and closed her eyes. Oh, Aaron, she thought, her attention drifting comfortably, I do miss you. You should be here with us. You loved this story.

"Are you married?" she asked Marta as the three of them walked slowly across Fifth Avenue. Joy wondered if men still married their nurses, the way they did in World War I novels. No, now it was just doctors who married their young nurses, married doctors who left the wives who had put them through medical school.

"Don't like," Marta said.

"I think marriage is a fine institution." Karl stopped to catch his breath when they reached the sidewalk.

"Institution" is a funny word, Joy thought, like a mental hospital.

"Why don't like?" she asked Marta.

"Husband drink."

"Well, *I* don't drink," Karl said. "Not excessively."

"*Or*," Marta added pointedly, "husband *old*. Get sick."

Joy repeated the conversation to Danny, laughing, but he seemed quite serious and said, "Well, she's right. Terrible to get stuck with an old invalid. At least Marta gets paid for all she does to take care of him."

"Well, of course she's right, in a way, but it never stops anyone, does it? You should hear what goes on in Florida."

"I think I'd rather not."

"I think it's nice she has a friend," Coco said. "Someone she can talk to."

"She can talk to me."

Coco suggested he might be jealous.

"She doesn't understand," Molly said when he told her. "She doesn't understand us," she said to Freddie.

Freddie understood. The clan was pulling together just as they had when Daniel was in the hospital, when Aaron went bankrupt. The Bergmans against the world. There was no room for an outsider. The emptiness left by Aaron's death was not a space to be filled; it was a bond to be protected.

44

Ruby's bat mitzvah was months away, but Joy began going through her clothes, looking for something suitable to wear. It was a tiring business, trying on clothes. She made sure to do it in the morning before her afternoon fatigue set in. The discarded dresses and trousers and jackets and blouses were strewn around her bedroom, colorful, fluttering like flags when she passed.

"What in god's name happened?" Daniel said when he saw her bedroom.

"I'm looking for an outfit."

He pushed some clothes aside and sat on the edge of the bed. "Where do you sleep?"

"On the couch. In the living room."

The dining-room table was again covered in papers. And now that Walter and Wanda were no longer coming and Elvira was back to once every two weeks, the kitchen was a mess. Daniel washed the dishes in the sink, then opened the refrigerator. It was filled with demitasse saucers, some covered with plastic wrap, some with aluminum foil, some with paper towels, some uncovered. How many demitasse saucers could one person own? There had to be thirty diminutive saucers, and beside them was a jumble of plastic containers used for condiments at coffee shops.

"Hungry?" his mother asked. "I have half a hard-boiled egg somewhere, and a little bit of applesauce. There's a bit of chicken soup . . . Oh no, don't touch that dish, that's food for Gatto . . ."

Daniel said he was not hungry. He sat at the kitchen table, his head in his hands.

"Are you all right, sweetheart?" his mother said. "Tired? You work too hard. You need a vacation. You're the one who should have gone to California, Danny, not me." She came over and rubbed his head. He still had all his hair. Just like his father. "Poor dear."

Daniel stared at the floor, at his own big feet, at his mother's feet in scuffed slippers.

"Mom," he said softly. He did not want to alarm her. "Mom, a mouse just ran across your foot."

His mother laughed. "Oh, him again."

Daniel telephoned Molly from the subway platform. "Do you realize how much an attendant will cost?"

"She doesn't need an attendant."

"Oh, but she will. And soon, believe me."

"How do *you* know?"

"Molly, a mouse was standing on her foot."

That was an alarming development, Molly had to admit. "But I don't see how an attendant would help with mice," she said. "Did you call the super?"

"Of course I called the super. The exterminator is coming to-morrow. But that is not the point and you know it. She has to have some help. Which means she has to spend money. Which means she has to get some money. She won't take it from us, and we don't have enough to cover it, anyway, which means she has to sell the house."

"How would Daniel and Coco like it if I told them to sell their loft," she said to Freddie. "How would they like it, the loft they bought so many years ago when no one wanted to live in their disgusting neighborhood, the loft they so lovingly restored bit by bit until now it's worth millions of dollars, how would they feel about *that*?"

"But the point is to keep your mother in her apartment," Freddie said gently, "to keep her independent and, and . . . mouse-free."

"Yes, but—"

"Daniel's just trying to figure things out, honey."

Molly grunted a thank-you, but no one understood about the house. Freddie thought it was a dump, anyway. It wasn't a dump. It was rustic. If by rustic you mean uncomfortable, Daniel once said. No one understood.

45

Joy thought of asking Karl to dinner. Boeuf bourguignon, a baguette, a salad—she could see the meal, it looked lovely, civilized, and Joy would have given a lot to feel civilized. Instead, she felt lurching and matted, like a wild dog. She hadn't made boeuf bourguignon in twenty years. She'd barely eaten boeuf in twenty years. The thought of it, the fat as it browned in the pan, was sickening. And she was no chef these days, scuffing around the kitchen tugging weakly at the recalcitrant refrigerator door, burning toast.

"We'll order Chinese," Karl said when she told him her problem.

"We'll eat on paper plates!"

"Like young people when they move into their first apartment and haven't unpacked the boxes."

Joy wondered what it would have been like to be young in a first apartment with Karl, no money, boxes of books, and a scratched desk from home. Joy and Aaron had furnished their first apartment with a decorator, Danish modern, she had gotten rid of most of it, uncomfortable stuff, though it was worth a fortune now, judging by *Antiques Roadshow*.

"Where was your first apartment?" she asked Karl. "After college?"

"I lived with my parents for a couple of years. Saved money. Then Joan and I got married and we bought the place I'm in now."

"You were always careful."

"And dull."

"No, I mean it in a good way. You were always not careless."

"You were always glamorous."

"And ditzy."

"I mean it in a good way, too. You were like sunshine, that kind of glamorous. Bright and shining and warm and cheerful. And unattainable."

Maybe I'll put out real plates, Joy thought.

The dining room looked pretty. Joy had stacked all her files in shopping bags that were pushed into one corner of the room. At the florist she bought a petite arrangement of small flowers gathered into an old-fashioned bouquet. There were candles, unlit; she could not find a match.

"I go," Marta said when she had helped Karl off with his coat and settled him into a chair. Gatto jumped in his lap.

Joy said, "Just what I needed, right? A dog."

"I had a dog as a kid. I loved that dog."

"Never got one for your own kids?"

"No. Joan couldn't bear it."

"The mess, the walking, and the kids promise to take it out, but then they have homework . . ."

"No. It was just she loved her childhood dog so much, and when he died she was heartbroken, and well, if we had gotten a dog, they don't live that long, it would certainly have died in her lifetime, and she said it was just too painful. She just didn't want to go through that again."

Joy brought the containers of Chinese food out on gaily patterned trays. It was a picnic, the takeout containers right on the table. She noticed Karl did not bother with chopsticks. Aaron had insisted on them when they had Chinese food, saying forks changed the flavor. But Joy was never very handy with chopsticks.

If Karl got a dog, she thought, they could walk their dogs together, if his dog liked to walk. Otherwise they could carry them together. People would stop them to ask about the little dogs. Karl could get a basket for his walker.

"I can't think that way," he was saying.

"About what?"

"Worrying about getting attached, about the pain of losing someone. I can't live like that. Not anymore. Too old . . ."

Joy did not bring up her idea of a basket for Karl's red walker. He didn't seem to be talking about dogs anymore.

— 46 —

Thank god it's almost time to drive Mom Upstate, away from that man and into the bosom of her loving family in her own little house."

"You're a little prudish about your mother," Freddie said. It just came out.

"I don't want her to be taken advantage of, that's all."

"I'm not sure what you and Daniel think Karl is after. Her virginity? Isn't it possible he just really likes her?"

Molly had assumed her sullen face, an expression so infantile and so obvious that Freddie was always tempted to laugh. Instead, she said, "You just don't like it that your mother has a boyfriend. Admit it."

"He's not her boyfriend."

"Whatever that would mean, anyway." But Freddie was happy to drop the subject. She had her own relatives to worry about. Her brothers and sisters would soon be there, though not for long.

"They'll be in L.A. for three days, that's it, three lousy days. It's probably the last time they'll see my father, the last time we'll all be together, and I can't decide if I wish they'd stay longer or leave after one night or not come at all. I have a fucked-up family."

"He's *not* her boyfriend."

"I'll miss you," Karl said.

He was wearing a cashmere blazer. Joy patted his arm. Aaron had favored hearty tweed. She'd always loved his custom-made jackets and suits. Now they called them bespoke. Aaron had looked like a country gentleman, what country she could not have said, but she would have followed him there, she knew that much. She had followed him there, she supposed. The sleeves of his sweaters and tweeds had always been rather itchy to her touch. She ran her hand along Karl's arm again. "Soft," she said.

Karl was someone you could call dapper and mean it as a compliment, not a suggestion of fussiness. Marta did right by him. He looked marvelous today, Joy thought, in the spring sunshine, his shoes polished, his blue shirt pressed, his tie a deeper blue paisley.

"It's a little too wide to be fashionable," he said when she complimented it. "But I've always loved it, so I just keep on wearing it."

He had admitted to her that he kept most of his clothes for decades, that he had shoes from his college days. He took good care of everything. Shoe trees, cedar closet, sweaters wrapped in tissue. His wife had teased him about it.

"You look very good in blue," Joy said.

"You look good in every color."

Joy laughed. They were walking beneath the trees on Fifth Avenue, beneath the fresh new leaves, beneath the sweetness of the air. "The wreck of the *Hesperus*. That's what I feel like. In every color."

Karl pushed his red wheeled walker and Joy kept one hand on it to hold herself steady. In a few days he would be off to stay with his son in Rhode Island. She would be off to her house Upstate.

"I've been thinking," Karl said.

Joy said, "Stop." She had to catch her breath.

In the park, a group of girls wearing headscarves were playing softball. She watched while the banging in her chest slowed. She took a deep breath. "I don't know if it's pollen or my heart. Who can tell anymore?"

"It's the exciting company you keep."

"I used to love softball," she said. The pitcher was winding up. A strike. "Brava."

Karl laughed. "Is that what they say at Yankee Stadium?"

They started walking again. Joy wished that Marta had stuck around. She was feeling a little strange. She had hung two of her bags on Karl's walker, but the third one, with Gatto peering out of it, was weighing her down.

"So," Karl said, "I was thinking."

"Karl, would you mind if we sat down for a minute? I'm feeling wobbly."

They made their way to a bench, backs to a stone wall that separated them from the park, but Joy could hear the park sounds clearly, the high-pitched pleasure of children, the squeak of swings, dogs barking, the ping of bicycle bells, whoops and cheers and chattering squirrels. Gatto emerged from the bag and stretched out in a patch of sun on the ground. Joy closed her eyes against the glare of the afternoon sun reflected from the apartment windows across the street. Someone with a French accent asked Karl where the Guggenheim was. The smell of spring was everywhere. And the faintest smell of urine.

"Oh my god," Joy said, her eyes open. Urine. "I forgot my court date!"

She began to dig frantically in the bag next to her on the bench. "Oh Christ. Oh, how could I do that?"

"Court date?"

"Nothing, nothing, a ticket, nothing . . ." The dog began barking and scratching at her leg. She pulled the other two bags from the handles of the walker and emptied them onto the bench.

"You're sure? Can I help . . . But how did you get a traffic ticket? You don't have a car."

"Don't ask. Gatto, shoosh, not everything is about you." Joy pulled out lipsticks and applesauce containers. How could she have failed Ben like this?

"Well then, listen, Joy, as I said, I've been thinking—"

"Good. Thinking. Good, good." She was pawing through papers and receipts now, candy wrappers, pamphlets.

"Look, we've known each other a long time." Karl hauled the screeching dog onto his lap and stroked him. "Quiet, Gatto. That's right. Good boy. A long time, Joy. Practically our whole lives, give or take a few decades when we lost touch . . ."

Joy saw a yellow piece of paper that she thought might be it. But Ben's ticket was pink, it was pink. What if she had missed his court date? What would happen to him? Some awful permanent mark on his license or his credit rating. It was not as if they'd throw him in jail. Was it? But a fine, there would be a fine . . . He would never trust her again with something important. He would think she was old, senile, useless.

". . . I think it could be good for both of us, and it just makes sense, don't you think?"

In the inside zipper pocket of the largest bag—a black-and-white-striped bag she had gotten on a trip, which trip? Oh, it didn't matter which trip, Joy, for heaven's sake, all that mattered was the court date—she felt something, paper, wadded-up paper.

"Joy?"

She pulled it out. It was pink. She unfolded it.

"What do you think, Joy?"

"I found it! It's not until September!"

"No, I mean about us moving in together."

Joy folded the summons carefully and put it back in the zippered inner pocket. She put everything back in her bags, the thermos, the flashlight, the pads and adult diapers that were, thank god, in an opaque plastic bag. She was nearly panting. So much excitement.

As she went to put her atomizer back in the smaller bag, she took a few puffs, just in case. And finally the dog, into the striped bag.

Living with Karl. What would that mean? The end of loneliness? The echo of another person's footsteps in the house. Someone to pretend to listen to you as you read out loud from the newspaper, with whom to discuss what to have for dinner, someone with whom to chat about the weather, someone with whom to share a life.

"I've been in love with you for sixty-five years," Karl said. "How corny that sounds. But it's true. It's not that I thought of you every day. I didn't. But there was an impression of you, I suppose you could say that. An impression on my heart."

Tears came to Joy's eyes. She was staring blindly down at the pavement. She could not look at him. She wondered what Aaron would think when she told him. But she could not tell him. Aaron, Aaron, how can I know what I feel without you here?

"I'm sorry," Karl said. "Bad idea."

"No, it's a wonderful idea, Karl."

"But?"

She shook her head.

"Your children? I thought that might be a problem."

"No, no. Not them." Although they might not like it, he was right. In which case, she thought, they could lump it.

"It's too soon," Karl said.

"Well, yes, it is too soon."

Karl made a disgusted sound. "I was afraid of that, I understand, but when you think about it, nothing is too soon when you're our age."

"It's not just that, Karl. Although it is too soon for me, even if I'm old. But there's something else. It's my apartment. I can't leave my apartment. I just can't."

"Too many memories, the place where you raised your children, yes, I see."

"No, not that."

"Well, what then?"

"The apartment is . . . rent-controlled."

They both burst out laughing.

"I can't give it up. I mean I just can't," she said, laughing still.

Then Karl took her hand, kissed it. "We are star-crossed lovers," he said good-naturedly.

Joy took his hand now and squeezed it. "Star-crossed lovers." She liked the sound of that. She liked the idea of being any kind of lover at all. She finally looked at him, his clean-shaven face a little pink in the spring air, his heavy eyelids and serious eyes, his fine silver hair shining. He loved her. He had loved her all along. She wondered if she loved him. A shiver of something that could have been love passed through her. Or it could have been simple pleasure. Or vanity. Or was it gratitude? She tried to remember what she had felt like when she had fallen in love as a girl. She remembered the sunlit giddiness, the dizzy confusion of falling through air without moving, the conviction that roared like an animal inside her. She remembered trembling and touching and knowing. She remembered Aaron scooping her up in his long arms. She remembered Karl, too, pushing the hair from her face before he kissed her. She remembered parties and dancing and being held close, her face against Aaron's cheek. Unless it was Karl's. But, no, it was Aaron's, before he grew his beard, she could hear him singing along to the music, his breath in her ear. She could not remember the song. She wished she could remember the song.

"It was all so long ago," she said. "And it's still too soon."

47

For weeks, thick, heavy invitations had been arriving for Ruby, a glory of colors and raised types and complicated inserts. One had a pop-up basketball net and ball, another a locker opening to reveal "baseball cards" featuring the bar mitzvah boy, a cute little boy disfigured by a wad presumably of gum meant to look like chewing tobacco, at bat and leaping for a fly ball. One was a flat pink satin box that opened to reveal not only the invitation but also a string of fake pearls.

Coco collected the mail each day with increasing dread. What origami of excess would fly from the mailbox next?

"Aren't there any nice little gentile children in your school? This is crazy. I guess we better send out our invitations soon," she said.

"Mommy, it's months from now."

Coco fingered the flowered chiffon of one invitation and marveled at it. She had no idea what kind of invitation Ruby would want. A sparkly corncob pipe in honor of Tom Sawyer? Pop-up Dead Sea scrolls to show her seriousness?

"But you will have to have a party. And you'll need party clothes."

"Yes, Mother, that does follow."

Ruby refused to partake in either the excitement or the dread of the social aspect of her coming-of-age.

"As if it all just happens by itself," Coco said to Daniel one night. "I don't know what to do. I'm not a party planner and I'm not a mind reader." She had gone to Sunday school at a Reform temple. She could not remember a single bar or bat mitzvah growing up. "I'm out of my depth."

"Well, just Google it, I guess."

When she did Google "bat mitzvah," she saw dresses that looked to her like figure-skating costumes on thirty-year-old prostitutes. She saw professionally produced videos of little girls dressed as rainbow-hued rappers lip-synching hip-hop songs.

"Daniel, we are in big trouble."

Whenever Coco tried to get Ruby to discuss plans for the bat mitzvah, Ruby was busy doing her homework or studying Hebrew.

"Can't have a party if I can't do the service, Mother," she would say in her new sarcastic way. Mo-ther: Coco noted how ludicrous a status the word suggested.

Finally, Coco ambushed her as she came in from school. "Ruby, sit down. Now."

Ruby slammed herself down on the couch and crossed her arms. "Hello to you, too, Mo-ther."

"About your bat mitzvah . . ."

"You can't talk me out of it, so don't even try."

"I don't want to talk you out of it. What makes you think I want to talk you out of it?"

In truth, though she would never have admitted it to her mother, Ruby was getting a little worn down by Judaism. There were an awful lot of rules. And poor old God was always so annoyed with his chosen people. Rabbi Kenny explained the historical context of the rules and explained the relationship between

God and his people as a dynamic one. She liked talking to Rabbi Kenny. She was still mesmerized by his physical beauty. His eyes were the color of sapphires. And she liked learning the alphabet, the sounds of the language, ancient and secret. She liked to chant, and she liked to think about Genesis and the big bang. All in all, it had been a satisfying hobby. But it was nearly summer. Her best friend, Alexandra, went to a stable in Riverdale twice a week to go horseback riding. Ruby started to go with her. In August they were going to riding camp together.

"I study my Hebrew," Ruby said. "I go to services. What do you want from my life? I'm very assiduous."

You are very supercilious, Coco thought. Put that in your adolescent vocabulary book. But she took a deep breath, reminded herself of the angst of being twelve, an angst she could still remember all too well, and she looked lovingly at the skinny girl sucking on her braces and said, "The party, honey. The invitations. The, you know, the theme. Like the girls on YouTube . . ."

"Mommy!"

". . . I suppose you could make a Katy Perry video. You like her."

"Mommy, stop! I don't want to be on YouTube. That's, that's . . . suburban."

Relieved, infinitely relieved, Coco silently thanked the heavens above. "No Katy Perry, then?"

"Mommy, Katy Perry is for babies. Honestly, Mother."

"Oh."

"Katy Perry," Ruby was muttering with disdain. "God, Mommy, you should know me better than that."

"You don't want a Tom Sawyer party, I suppose."

Ruby burst out laughing. Her braces sparkled in the lamplight. "You're hilarious," she said, leaning companionably against her mother.

They sat like that for a few minutes, enjoying the contact. Don't grow up, please, Coco thought. Just don't do it. Just don't.

48

Joy checked the gigantic calendar she had gotten for Aaron to help him keep track of passing time. She allowed herself a moment of pathos: Time is no more for Aaron Bergman. Time has passed him by. Then she lay down on the couch and elevated her legs and prayed for time to pass a little more quickly for herself. Only a few days until she could escape to Upstate. She was rattled by Karl's proposition. A temptation, there was no doubt about that.

The pleasure of existing in a man's memory as someone young and beautiful and alluring, and the place Karl held in her own memory, a young man besotted and devoted—those were powerful forces that rose delightfully to the surface whenever she saw him, when she thought about him, too. There was also the physical frisson, it was still there, the few ancient remaining hormones rearing their heads like old warhorses at the sound of a trumpet.

Standing beside Karl beneath an awning on Fifth Avenue during a sudden rain shower, close, their shoulders pressing.

Just the two of them.

And the red walker. And Marta.

Well, a nice diversion from bereavement and lamentation, that's how she put it to herself. And added to that was the thought of not being alone. Solitude is not my thing, she said out loud. But was living with a new old man her thing? She didn't know, and all she wanted to do was to see her house in Upstate New York, her white-shingled house with its wavy asphalt roof and rusting porch swing, her own house, nestled among its trees on top of its hill, the stream running merrily below. Someone like Karl, a man who had made his fortune and kept it, might not think much of a house like hers. But it was hers, her own house, unencumbered; she had fought to keep it safe, and now, she thought, it would keep her safe.

She wished she had named it the way people do in English novels. The Remedy, she could call it.

But they all just called it Upstate, and she loved it whatever its name. Every room looked out at different trees she had watched grow over the years, maple trees and birch trees and a weeping willow. The floors squeaked exactly where she expected them to.

She wanted to be in the house immediately, almost feverishly. She could feel the give of the noisy floorboards beneath her feet. She would yank open the windows and let the breeze in, let in the sound of leaves rustling.

Everything in her life had changed when Aaron died. But not the house. The house was not shaken by Aaron's death, it had been through death already, her father's, then her mother's, and it had survived. Once she got to the house, Joy thought, she would finally feel at home again.

49

For the last decade, ever since Aaron had begun to fade, Joy had hired a car to drive them and their stuff to the house Upstate for the summer, always the same car and driver, an aging Vietnam vet from the town nearest their house. The car, a resplendent used limousine he had gotten from a national limo service when it was a mere six years old, was close to twenty now. The driver, Mr. Bailey, was in his seventies.

"I hope you don't mind that I brought Mother," he said, nodding toward a small white-haired head just showing above the passenger seat. The ancient limousine rocked and swayed. The two heads swung back and forth, rhythmic and synchronized. "But she likes an outing, don't you, Mother?"

Mother did not answer.

"Very thoughtful of you," Joy said. She glared at her children, one on either side of her, both giggling like infants. Daniel hummed the *Psycho* shower music under his breath. In the enormous well of the car were a pile of black garbage bags, like so many lumpy corpses—Joy's luggage.

"Thank you for taking the dog," Joy said.

"Oh, we love dogs, don't we, Mother?"

The traffic was heavy. Where were they all going? Why couldn't they stay home and tend to their business? "This is a disaster, darling," she said to the dog.

Daniel looked at the trees, so green and full. "Traffic or no traffic, the house will still be there."

"You're too complacent, Danny."

"I wonder if anyone can be too complacent. Complacent seems like a good thing to be, Mom. Maybe you're not complacent enough."

"Don't you start with the Prozac. I am not taking any of your pills."

"I didn't say anything about Prozac."

"Well, your sister did."

"No, I didn't. Not today."

"I know it's what you're both thinking. But forget it. I'm in mourning."

"So am I," Daniel said.

His mother said, "Oh, sweetie, of course you are," and gave him a package of peanut-butter crackers.

Daniel wished he could wear a crepe hatband, he wished wearing black meant something these days, meant mourning instead of fashion. His father's death had taken some layer of earth out from beneath his feet. He thought of his father more than he ever had when Aaron was alive. He thought of him when he shaved, remembering watching his father shave the two patches above the beard on each cheek, the neck beneath the beard. Daniel had never wanted a beard, never liked his father's fussy attention to its shape and fullness. Now, all of a sudden, he thought about growing one. He thought of his father when he ate. Dad liked bratwurst, he would think. Dad loved smoked whitefish. Dad hated beets. And yogurt. He thought of his father whenever he paid his credit card bills, too. Daniel always paid them on time, the full amount. Dad ran up huge debt, he would think. And along with the anger that had plagued him for so many years, he would think, Poor Dad, poor Dad, always in debt. Daniel had a strong, easy-to-access financial plan. What would Dad do? he would think, and then he would do the opposite. He was not rich, but he was not gambling his family's life away on one lousy business venture after another. But poor Dad, now that poor Dad was dead. His father had always been hopeful, cheerful, sure his next venture would make him a fortune. There was strength in that, he supposed, and he missed his father's strength.

Joy began to rummage in a shopping bag. She extracted aluminum foil packages. "Want one, anyone?" she asked, pulling the foil off a hard-boiled egg. The smell of hard-boiled eggs filled the rocking car.

"No," Molly said, turning away quickly.

"Protein," Joy said. "Yummy protein." She pinched a piece off for Gatto.

Daniel shoved the rest of the egg, whole, into his mouth.

"Is it okay if I open the window?" Molly asked.

"It's very noisy," said Joy. "And with the dog . . ."

"Just for a minute. I feel kind of sick."

"You should eat something," Joy said. She unwrapped another egg.

"Oh, how your father loved this house," Joy said as they pulled in the driveway.

"No, he didn't," Daniel said.

"Yes, he did," said Molly.

Molly stepped out of the car and took in the familiar trees, the warm summer light, the clean white clouds against the rich blue of the sky. She had been going Upstate every summer since she was born. Her mother had spent summers there before that when she was a child. How many people could say that? How many families were that lucky? It was a wonderful house, a family house, full of family memories and full of family every summer. Molly felt the ground beneath her feet, felt it hold her weight, felt its solid, gentle welcome.

Her mother's little dog flew out of the limousine and began to sniff the ground.

"He's happy," Joy said.

Molly sniffed the air, light with honeysuckle and privet.

The house had a front porch, which was already piled with stuff. Coco and the girls had come earlier, the car packed to the roof with toys, all toys and electronics, as far as Joy could tell. She got out of the car with some difficulty, she got so stiff these days, and walked up the flagstone path to the house. She put her hand on the doorknob and waited to be as happy as the dog. A breeze blew. The smell was there, that mixture of humid earth and humid air, of wet bark and grass. She could hear the children calling to each other, her children, but of course they were Danny's children, her children were no longer children. She opened the door to the slight sting of mildew. The dog rushed past her, brushing against her legs, a butterfly of a dog. He was wet, he was fast, he was gone. She held the doorjamb to steady herself. The girls ran past her. Hi, Grandma, they called. They did not stop. They were gone.

"Mom?"

Joy opened her eyes. She hadn't realized they were closed.

"Mom, sorry, I just have to squeeze in here . . ." Molly pressed against her, trying to get inside. "Mom, come on . . ."

"Okay, okay, sorry."

Molly darted past her to the bathroom.

Coco had already unloaded most of the contents of the station wagon: the bicycles and scooters, the computers and Wii console, the electric piano, the stuffed animals, the toy wheelbarrow, and the puppet stage. The volume of child equipment was incomprehensible to Joy. She remembered Daniel's and Molly's toy box when they were growing up. It was yellowy unfinished wood with a top that crashed down on their fingers if they were not quick enough. It was a good size, or so they all thought at the time, the size of a small steamer trunk. What was in it? A truck, some blocks, a doll, a robot, a stuffed monkey, toy pistols and holsters, boxing gloves, a cowboy hat, maybe. She looked at the mound of possessions on the porch of the house.

"Is this really all yours? All that stuff?"

Danny gave her a look, a warning look, as he dragged her black garbage bags into the house.

"Matching luggage," Joy said to the girls.

They barely acknowledged her. "Gatto! Gatto!" they cried, running out the door, this time followed by the clatter of the dog. They ran in circles around the maple tree, then the girls rolled down the hill, getting themselves dizzy, the dog chasing after them. Joy remembered doing that. Now she got dizzy without any rolling.

"Goodbye!" she called to Mr. Bailey as he backed out of the driveway. "Goodbye, Mother!"

Joy wondered what she had packed in all those bags. They looked so anonymous and lumpy. Each July, she would take the bloated garbage bags to the house, and each September she would drag them back, most of them undisturbed since their arrival.

"Upstate is perfect," she said, running her hand along the back of the sagging sofa. "It never changes."

"Everything changes," Danny began in his environmental voice.

Please don't start with climate change, Joy thought. She felt as if the house had taken her hand and said, Welcome home. "Welcome home," she said. "That doesn't change."

She sat on the porch swing and listened to the stream that ran behind the house. Sunlight floated through the maple leaves above. The sounds of decades of summers surrounded her—the robins, the peepers.

She wondered what her life would have been like if she'd married Karl instead of Aaron. She probably would never have had the career she'd had. It would not have been necessary. That would have been a loss. On the other hand, there would have been enough money for them to survive without her scrabbling for work. What a luxury, not to worry about money. She wondered if anyone really had that luxury.

"I'll miss you," she had said to Karl before leaving. She touched his old hand with her old hand. And when she'd said it, she didn't realize how true it was. She missed him already. She could see his earnest eyes, his face opening up into a smile. She could feel his close-shaved cheek as she gave him a kiss goodbye. His cheek was soft, old, but it was new, too, unfamiliar, exciting. Maybe his poor dead wife was right, maybe it was better to let sleeping dogs, dead dogs, lie. It was enough to lose Aaron, to miss Aaron. She didn't need to miss Karl, too. She was too old. She was too tired.

And now at least she was not alone. She was surrounded by the ones she loved. Although they made so much noise. Coco was already banging pots and pans around. Daniel was bumping suitcases up the stairs. The girls were screaming, and Molly was somehow talking to Freddie on the computer she'd brought with her.

But this was the place Joy knew best. She had grown up in the city and lived her entire adult life in the city, but this was where she belonged. The air was her air, as if it had been made for her, air that revived her and soothed her. The light was her light, changing in ways she knew and anticipated and loved. There was nowhere on earth in which she felt more at home. Even the sounds seemed to welcome her, to know her, to greet her. There had been rain and the stream was high and rushed noisily by. A finch sang its chortling musical song. She listened for the cows from the pasture across the road. She heard something low and rumbling, not cows. A tractor plowing a far-off field.

But it was not a tractor, and it was not far off. The sudden crash of rocks reached her, the beeping of heavy machinery backing up, muffled shouts, a jackhammer.

"What are they doing, Grandma?" Cora asked. She climbed onto the roof of the car and looked across the street. "They're digging up rocks with a steam shovel."

Gatto jumped into Joy's arms.

Molly stormed out of the house. "What the hell is going on?" she said, and stomped down the hill, yelling, "Hey! Hey!"

"Well, we're not building this swimming pool for the cows," the foreman said cheerfully when they had all followed Molly to the field.

Joy heard herself say with what she knew was irrelevant conviction, "I am a widow."

The foreman was named Bill. He reached over to pet Gatto and Joy felt the growl building in the dog's chest, but to her disappointment it quickly shifted into a friendly whimper and he licked the foreman's hand.

"How long will you be doing this?" Molly said.

"And what exactly are you doing?" Daniel asked.

"Well, let's see, building a road, of course, and houses. Nine. So yeah, we'll be here awhile, I guess. Beautiful houses, pretty high-end. Pools, too. Hey, little puppy, what's your name?"

There was an unpleasant discussion that night. Daniel said, "With this development going up, someone might actually want to buy our house."

"This is my ancestral home," Joy said. "And yours."

He explained again that Joy was running out of money. "Anyway, our ancestors lived in shtetls."

Molly told him he was morbid. Joy said perhaps she would die and solve everyone's money worries. All of this had to be conducted in whispers, because the girls were asleep.

"Let it go," Coco said to Daniel in bed that night. "Give your mother a summer off."

"I'm just trying to be responsible."

"Let it go."

"Where's Aunt Freddie, anyway?" Cora asked at breakfast.

Aunt Freddie always slipped her a crisp dollar bill when she saw her.

"You're a miser," Ruby said.

"I'm not."

"It means you love money."

"Oh. Then I am. So what?"

"Why do you love money?" Joy asked.

"I collect it."

Joy nodded. Better than fingernail clippings. Molly had collected fingernail clippings.

Molly grabbed Cora and kissed her. She was touched that Cora thought to ask where Freddie was. Sometimes she wondered if any of them remembered Freddie existed when Freddie wasn't standing directly in front of them. Particularly Joy. Since Molly's divorce, her life had become less and less real to her mother. Molly knew her mother was proud of her, knew Joy liked Freddie, but she knew also that she existed in a different way for her mother now, that the new reality was perceived dimly, as if the lights had gone out when she got divorced and her mother had never turned them back on. Molly plus a husband plus a child to raise had made sense to Joy. That was a discernible unit, that family of three. But Molly and Freddie in California? That was not a unit. It was an absence.

"I wish Aunt Freddie were here," she said to Cora.

"Yeah, why isn't she?"

"Good question. Why isn't she?" Daniel asked, as if this were the first moment he'd noticed her absence.

"Daniel, she's with her father," Coco said. "All her sisters and brothers are coming to L.A., remember?"

"That Freddie is a fine, fine person," said Joy.

Molly looked at her in surprise.

"I could see that when I stayed with you. A fine person."

Molly smiled, a grin really. "Thank you, Mommy."

"Why are you thanking me?" Joy asked fondly. "I didn't say you were a fine person. You're lucky Freddie puts up with you."

50

Freddie let her father open the barbershop door for her, discreetly helping him. It was the third time they had been to that barbershop in three days.

"Mr. Hughes! Good to see you."

"I need a haircut, my good man."

The barber caught Freddie's eye. She nodded slightly.

"Okay, Mr. Hughes! Sit right here."

Ever since Freddie told her father about the impending visit of his four other children, he had been insisting he needed a haircut. The insistence continued, the two haircuts in the last two days notwithstanding.

The barber was a stolid middle-aged man whose father had cut Duncan's hair until his retirement ten years ago.

"How's your father?" said Duncan.

"The same. How are you?"

"Still here."

They'd had the same exchange the day before and the day before that.

"Thanks, Mel. Dad was really eager to come in," Freddie said.

"Oh yeah, we're always happy to see Mr. Hughes."

Duncan hummed a little, then faded away for a moment, then caught his own eye in the mirror. "Hello, handsome."

"You do look sharp, Dad."

He was pleased, and as they drove back to Green Garden, he read the signs they passed out loud as if they were lines in a dramatic play. It had always been one of his car trip games. He seemed like his old self and Freddie said nothing, not wanting to break the spell.

51

Sometimes, Joy almost missed the red tricycle.

"Maybe I'll come with you," she said when Coco and the girls set off to the market.

But the market was about to close and they could not wait for Joy to get herself together to go. No one asked her to do errands at the house Upstate. No one asked her to do anything at all. She could have been another cushion on the old sagging couch, she thought, as everyone came and went, busy with things that had once been the things that had busied her, though even the cushions, covered by her mother's petit point, were more useful than she was. No one leans on me, she thought.

At least she could listen to the radio, now that everyone was out of the house. They hated the scratchy sound of her old portable radio. She turned it on, but it was out of batteries. The extra batteries were not in the drawer where she had always kept them. That drawer was filled with coffee filters for Coco's complicated machine. The days were long for Joy, longer than even a summer day should be.

There was some excitement when Ben showed up. He surprised them, arriving on the same train as Daniel. The girls introduced him to the dog, who leaped in the air and shrieked in uncanny, high-pitched glee. Ben patted Gatto, and Molly patted Ben.

"Dinner!" Coco said, and rang the cowbell outside even though they were all already together.

At the table, Ben said he had an announcement to make. No, Grandma, I'm not pregnant. The little girls laughed and pushed each other. Not pregnant, but moving back to New York for August, a job as a paralegal, enrolled in an LSAT study course at night, signed up to take the exam at the end of the month.

"You can stay in my apartment," Joy said. "Would that be helpful?"

Ben gave a sheepish smile. "Well, as a matter of fact, I knew you wouldn't mind, so I kind of already left my stuff there. The doorman let me in."

"But you won't get to be in so many parades if you leave New Orleans," Cora said. "And wear costumes."

"Maybe that's a good thing," said Molly.

Ben's genial smile disappeared. "Why?"

Because it's infantile, she wanted to say. Because all you ever do down there is drink and play dress-up. "Just time for something new."

"New is overrated," Joy said, but no one responded. It was a noisy table and she thought again about getting hearing aids; perhaps she had spoken too softly. It was sometimes hard for her to gauge these days.

"I'm very proud of Ben," she said in a louder voice. "It's difficult to change anything in this life."

Still no one looked her way. They were lost in their excitement and chatter. But Ben must have heard her, for he kissed her cheek and whispered in her ear, "Thank you."

They were sitting outside at the long picnic table. Daniel took in the scene before him with satisfaction: his wife and children, his sister and his nephew, his mother; the corn on the cob, the first corn of the year, the butterflied leg of lamb he'd grilled perfectly, not gray, not blue.

But Ben then announced he was a vegetarian and refused the perfectly grilled lamb. Ruby asked if the lamb was butchered by a kosher butcher, and Cora, horrified at the thoughts brought on by the word "butcher," said she was vegan as of that moment and refused her plate of lamb, too.

Daniel sat in the gloaming, swatting mosquitoes, morosely chewing the perfect lamb, aggrieved by his family and their vegetables, when his mother cleared her throat and said in an uncharacteristically formal voice, "I'd like to invite Karl to Ruby's bat mitzvah."

"What?" he said. "Why?"

"Why?" said Molly.

"Who's Karl?" Ruby asked.

"You remember, Ruby," Ben said. "Old guy with the red walker like Grandpa's?"

Joy wasn't sure she liked that description, but she nodded. "You met him at Passover," she said. "He was a friend of Grandpa's."

"I'm sorry, but this is not appropriate," Daniel said. "He's practically a stranger. Ruby's met him exactly once. Why would he come to her bat mitzvah?"

"He and Grandpa became good friends," Joy said. "And I would like to invite him. Period." She was a little red in the face. Daniel could see the color rising even in the dusk.

"But why do you want him to come," Ruby said, "if he's Grandpa's friend? He won't be able to see Grandpa."

"Ruby," her mother said sharply.

Joy said, "I thought it would be nice, that's all."

"Oh, okay," Ruby said. "Since Grandpa can't come, like a representative."

"Like *instead* of Grandpa," said Cora.

For a moment there was silence, then Coco boomed, "Salad! I forgot the salad," and dashed inside.

"No one can take the place of Grandpa," Daniel said.

"Yeah," Ruby said, giving Cora a punch in the arm.

Cora began to cry, Ruby called her a crybaby, Joy excused herself with a headache, Ben cleared the table, Ruby punched Cora again and said it was her fault that Grandma had a headache because she was such a crying crybaby, Daniel yelled at them both, Coco yelled at Daniel for yelling at the children, Molly filled her glass with wine and downed it, and dinner was over.

"I really think it's, I don't know, unsuitable," Molly said to Daniel as they sat in the lawn chairs in the dark a few hours and a few bottles of wine later. "It's, it's unseemly." She knew she'd had far too much wine, but when your octogenarian mother announces her intention to betray your recently deceased father with her college boyfriend in public, there's not much choice but to drown your sorrow and humiliation in drink, that's what she told Freddie when Freddie called earlier.

Molly looked up at the stars. They were revolving. Stars did revolve, didn't they? No, they didn't. The earth revolved and it looked like stars revolved, she could almost hear that little pedant Ruby correcting her, but these stars were revolving so fast. "Unseemly," she said again. "It's like she's bringing a date. A *date*. To Ruby's bat mitzvah." Molly closed her eyes, but the stars kept spinning.

"Okay, so she has a new friend, okay, fine, good," Daniel said. "But you don't have to bring him to a family thing, right? I think it's disrespectful. To Dad."

"And us."

"The body isn't even cold yet."

"No boundaries," Molly said. "I mean, she's *our* mother."

There was silence, except for the stream.

Then Daniel said, "Do you think they . . ."

"What? Do I think who what?"

"You know. Mom and Karl."

"Daniel! You're, you're a . . ." She wanted to say pervert, but she was overcome by a wave of nausea.

"Molly, oh god, that's disgusting." He moved out of the way as she retched.

"Thank god Ben didn't see that," she muttered, still leaning over the side of the chair.

The next morning was a Saturday and Coco took Cora to a mall an hour away as compensation for too much nature, Ben and Ruby went out on a bike ride, and Molly and Danny were both still asleep. Joy made herself a soft-boiled egg that was too hard and a piece of toast. The house was unusually quiet, no construction equipment grinding next door, no grandchildren squabbling. Even Gatto was silent, asleep in a patch of sun in the kitchen. Joy drank her tea and thought how serene it was.

Alone at last.

That was meant to refer to a couple, surely. Two lovers, alone at last.

Nevertheless.

She and Aaron had lived together for so long they had barely noticed each other, like two old dogs asleep before the fire. Without him, the room was empty, any room. Yet it was wearing to be around other people. That was something she realized more and more. People you love, they wear on you, too. Molly and Danny and Coco and the girls, she wanted them to be near every minute of every day—it was wearing, that was all. Lovely. And wearing.

She looked for the jam in the refrigerator, but then remembered Coco kept it in the cabinet. But she kept peanut butter in the fridge instead of the cabinet. It was aggravating, all this change. Coco and Danny put knives in the dishwasher, they left the bathroom door closed when no one was in it. There were so many things here, Upstate in *her* house, that were done differently now. The television remote was new and made no sense to her, but then, she was not allowed to watch television, anyway, she made it too loud and disturbed everyone. The toilet paper was the wrong brand, as were the paper towels and the dishwashing liquid. The towels were folded oddly and put in the wrong closet when they were clean or, when they had been used, hung wet and moldering on hooks she had never installed in the bathroom. The place had become almost foreign to her, as if she were a stranger, a stranger in the house her mother gave her, the house she had nurtured and protected for so many years.

She wondered what would happen if she agreed to live with Karl. It was possible he would turn out to be another comfortable old dog, just like Aaron, just like her, but it was more likely he would be wearing. New, unfamiliar, and wearing.

Of course she would bring him to Ruby's bat mitzvah. Her children were behaving like children. They should be happy she had a new friend. She hadn't mentioned Karl's proposal that the two of them live together, but even that should make her children happy. Would they prefer she be sent off to a nursing home, by them? Like Freddie's father? To fend off some senile old goat? Like Freddie's father? Molly and Danny were probably worried about their inheritance, that's what it was. She was doomed to rot on a urine-stained sofa like Mrs. Astor. Except there was no inheritance. Except the house. Which they wanted to sell. Where she no longer belonged.

She tried to shake off this feeling that she was an intruder, the sense that even this timeless place had moved on and left her behind. She went outside and sat in one of the Adirondack chairs. Such an unpleasant smell. The dog must have vomited. She moved to the porch swing and breathed in the wet summer air, so familiar, her summer air. But it felt all wrong, even the air was wrong, heavier than she remembered it, stickier. The fresh smell of grass and soil and the damp living smell of the stream evaded her. She had hoped, she'd been sure, that Upstate was where she would get her bearings again. She would walk along the road and pick wildflowers, wade in the stream to cool off from the summer heat, pick raspberries from the thorny hedges at the bottom of the hill.

But everything had gone awry. The weather had gone wrong first, hotter and rainier than any year Joy could remember, but that was just the beginning. There was the construction on the other side of the road, which got worse and worse, puffing out clouds of dust when it didn't rain, oozing mud when it did. And that rain, forcing the field mice to take refuge in the house, the lightning knocking out the power every week. There was a coyote, too, which prowled the property and howled at night. She worried about Gatto, so small, so urban in his experience of the world. Bad enough he'd been attacked by a brute in Los Angeles. What if he wandered out one night and was attacked by a coyote? She wouldn't be there to save him. She'd be inside, asleep. She had become attached to the dog. He was the only one who didn't tell her what to do.

The swing creaked as she stood up. She could not wade in the stream this summer. It was rushing full speed ahead, carrying fallen branches, no time to wait for an old lady and her poor balance. She could not pick raspberries, either. The bulldozers had ripped the bushes out of the ground. And the wildflowers had been crushed beneath enormous tire treads.

She walked out onto the lawn and looked back at her house. Perhaps she should sell it, after all. It stood on the hill, dim and weather-beaten, her own house, a house she loved and had loved for almost as long as she could remember. But at that moment, in the gray morning heat, this wonderful place, this house that had given itself over to the happiness of so many generations of children, seemed to feel as out of place as Joy did.

The sky was suddenly dark, thunder grumbling in the distance. Poor Ben and Ruby. They'd get soaked. What if they went under a tree to get out of the rain? What if they touched a wire fence? They could be electrocuted. Joy felt herself tilting, listing to one side. The bottom of the earth shot away from her, from beneath her feet, then came back. Vertigo, a new plague, thank you very much. And her eyes, so unreliable. There had been several trips to the ophthalmologist in the city and an emergency repair of a cataract lens that was far from successful. She closed one eye, but the sky still threatened rain.

She wished Ruby was not going off to sleep-away camp. She wished Cora would not be going to day camp every weekday. She wished Danny didn't have to go to the office. She wished Aaron were not dead.

It's your fault, damn you, she thought. All your fault, Aaron.

What was the point of everyone being together if people went away?

If the black clouds above had not spelled certain death for Ruby and Ben, she would have welcomed the darkening sky and thought it beautiful, much more beautiful, certainly, than the dingy clouds of dust, the dun-colored fog, that was usually lurking in the sky from the building site. The digging had done something to the septic tank as well, something obstructive, and there had been over-flowing toilets. The fireflies had given way to houseflies and bees and wasps and, with all the rain, a burgeoning crop of mosqui-toes. Inside, the air conditioners labored noisily and the doors and windows were kept shut.

The girls sometimes sat on her lap, smelling of dirt and child-hood, and she would say, "I'm so lucky to be able to spend so much time with you."

"Yes, you belong here with us, Mom," Danny would say, benevolent, as if the house were his and Joy were his guest.

And Joy would think, I don't belong anywhere. Then: Joy! Are you such a delicate flower? Get a grip.

"Mom!" Danny said, pushing the screen door open, still in his pajamas.

He was angry, Joy realized with surprise. He was so rarely angry about anything that did not have to do with climate change. Maybe another glacier had melted.

"We have to talk," he said. "Right now."

"Don't come out here barefoot, Danny. The deer ticks . . ."

"Come in, then." He gestured impatiently.

As she sat at the kitchen table, Joy allowed herself to feel just how tired she was. Then she sat up straight and smiled at her son. "We'll sell it, that's all," she said.

"Sell what?"

"The house. This. The house, the house."

"No. Karl. We have to talk about this Karl guy."

"This Karl guy? Is that how you think of your father's friend?"

"Oh come on, Mom, let's cut the 'Daddy's friend' crap."

Joy was stunned. Danny never spoke to her like that.

"What is the matter with you?" she said. "Good lord."

Joy went outside again. It was raining now. Good. She would catch pneumonia and die and everyone would have to stop lecturing her.

The raindrops were enormous. She could almost hear them as they hit the ground. They were cold on her arms, on her face, a shock in the steaming heat of the day. Her clothes were soaked through immediately, her pants sticking to her legs.

"Mom, come inside. What are you doing?" It was Molly. She ran outside.

"You're barefoot! You'll get a tick!" Joy said.

Molly pulled her inside and threw a beach towel around her.

"It's only water," Joy said. Her teeth were chattering. She let Molly rub the towel on her hair, her back, her arms. She obediently went into her room and put on dry clothes. When she came out, Molly handed her a mug of coffee.

"I can't drink coffee. My digestion . . ."

Molly snatched it back. "Fine."

"Where's Danny?"

"Sulking in his bedroom."

"He was very rude to me. I'm eighty-six years old and I deserve some respect." Joy felt the tears and willed them back.

Molly sat across from her at the table, bedraggled, her hair wet and matted, dark circles under her eyes. "Yes, let's talk about respect," she was saying. "Respect for your husband, my father, Daniel's father. Let's talk about that. Since we're talking about respect."

"Why did you make such a fuss about the rain? It's about a hundred degrees out."

"Mom, it's disrespectful to Daddy to invite Karl to Ruby's bat mitzvah. That's what Daniel is upset about. And so am I."

"That's ridiculous. Karl was your father's friend."

"He's *your* friend."

"Am I not allowed to have friends now? What is wrong with you two?"

Molly offered her mother a cup of tea, which Joy accepted. She did not want tea. It would make her have to pee. And the kitchen was humid and hot. But she could see Molly trying to be civil. It was important to be civil. She had tried to teach her children that.

"Look, Mom, you can't bring him to the bat mitzvah, okay? You just can't. It wouldn't look right. I mean, it's only been a few months. It might, you know, embarrass Ruby."

"Ruby? You mean it will embarrass you two, although god knows why."

"You think he can take Dad's place?" Molly said, all pretense at civility gone. "Well, he can't. Ever."

She was shouting now, and Daniel stomped down the stairs to join in: "The body is not even cold. How can you do this to us?"

Joy looked away from them, her two beloved children, yelling and stamping their feet like toddlers. Graying toddlers. She tilted her head back and looked at the ceiling and wondered if it might fall in and shut them up.

"What has Karl ever done to you?" she said softly.

There was silence, just the thunder, closer now, and the rain on the roof.

"Did you know that Karl asked me to live with him?"

"See?" Daniel said to Molly. "See? I told you."

"Mommy! You can't. You'll turn into a caretaker."

"Your father liked Karl. Your father would have wanted me to have some companionship. Your father would be ashamed of you both."

They shifted uneasily.

"Yeah, well, still, it's just . . ." Daniel's words trailed off.

"And whether I choose to live with Karl or not," Joy continued, "one thing I can see clearly now. I cannot stay in this house one day longer. I am not welcome. I do not belong."

And she marched out, slammed her door, and began packing.

52

Duncan smiled and smiled, but he did not say much. If he was overwhelmed, he could hardly be blamed. His family had gathered around him from the four corners of the earth, as Gordon put it. There were grandchildren, too, Gordon's kids, now quite grown up: one of them, the daughter, in college; the son engaged and holding the hand of his fiancée. Freddie was overwhelmed, so why shouldn't her father be? None of it seemed quite real. Laurel and Pamela wore colorful sundresses, not identical in pattern, but complementary, and identical enough: four spaghetti straps cutting into four plump white shoulders. Freddie, who was wiry and always had been, who wore gray and always had, knew she looked a little dreary beside them, a caterpillar beside two butterflies. Her brothers were somewhat more soberly attired, but still in vacation costumes—and they did seem like costumes to Freddie, the golf shirt and white pleated Bermuda shorts of her brother Gordon, a similar golf outfit on his wife; the jeans and big silver belt buckle, the chestnut-colored cowboy boots Alan wore. But they probably thought she was in costume, the same costume she'd worn since the age of six. Jeans and a T-shirt. Only the grandchild generation looked right. Perhaps because they were at the Third Street Promenade in a pedestrian mall filled with other young people.

Freddie wearily followed the group into another shop. They seemed to be drawn to chain stores that also had outlets in their own countries. Duncan was a bit pale, but he shambled along behind them.

"Are you okay, Dad?"

He did not answer, but smiled, grabbed her arm to steady himself.

"Well, *I'm* exhausted," Freddie said. "Maybe we should go sit down somewhere," she said to her siblings, all of whom were trying on sunglasses.

They wanted to sit outside. It was winter where they lived. Wasn't the sun beautiful and warm here in Los Angeles?

The beautiful warm Los Angeles sun beat down upon them. Freddie never sat in the sun as a rule, and certainly not in July. The air, even in Santa Monica, so near the beach, was blazing hot, dry as dust, and still. But her siblings were ecstatic. What a good time of year they had picked. What a perfect vacation. They began to trade tales of vacations that had gone wrong. Food poisoning, sharks, terrorism, cyclones, earthquakes.

They did not mention heart attacks. But that's what Duncan had. The paramedics came and hustled him away in an ambulance. Freddie sat next to him, holding his hand. The rest of the family followed in a caravan of rented cars.

53

Joy was dressed and packed. The garbage bags, undisturbed since their arrival, could stay and rot for all she cared. She had stuffed her clothes and pills and creams into her California roller bag. She had called Mr. Bailey and he said he and Mother would be right over to drive her to the station.

She waited on the porch swing and pictured her apartment, dim, stuffy, mail piled high, Ben's dirty dishes in the sink, though he had not even stayed there yet. It didn't matter. It had to be better than staying here, where no one wanted her, where no one made room for her, and where, she now realized, no one trusted her.

"This is ridiculous, Joy," Coco said. "You don't have to go, and you certainly don't have to take a car service. If you insist on leaving, let me drive you. I'm driving Molly to the station anyway."

Molly was going back to California to be with Freddie, whose father was in pretty bad shape in the hospital.

"That's quite all right."

Coco stood in the doorway. Danny appeared behind her.

"Mom, come on. You're acting crazy."

Joy narrowed her eyes. "Don't you dare call me crazy. The first step to sending the elderly to a home is saying they're crazy. Well, just forget it. I'm not going to a home. I'm going to *my* home in New York. Since you've taken over this one."

"Now you're being paranoid."

"Me? You're the one who is paranoid, all this fuss about a simple invitation to a bat mitzvah."

"She has a point," Coco said. "What is the big deal?"

Danny stormed back inside, followed by Coco saying, "Well, really, Daniel, you're being silly . . ."

"I have choices," Joy yelled after them.

"She's moving in with him," Danny was shouting inside. "You didn't believe me, but you hear her."

"Oh, so what?" Coco said.

Joy dreaded the arrival of Mr. Bailey and his car. Her heart was hammering and her vertigo was sweeping in like nauseous fog. She was arguing with Danny, her dear sweet Danny. Why? Over Karl? I don't want to live with him, she wanted to call out. I just want to invite him to my granddaughter's celebration. I want someone there I can lean on, literally lean on the red walker that is just like Daddy's walker; I want to smile at someone and be proud and have him see how proud I am instead of seeing a problem who has to be taken to the ladies' room, who has to be helped down the stairs to the street, who has to be transported the three blocks from the synagogue to the restaurant.

Cora and Ruby came outside and settled themselves on the swing, one on either side.

"You can invite whoever you want," Ruby said.

"I'm inviting a friend," Cora said, "so I don't see why you shouldn't."

"Yeah, Daddy's being silly." Ruby sounded like Coco, dismissive; even her gesture, hands held up in mock surrender, reminded Joy of Coco. Without thinking, Joy said, "He is not."

Molly was the next to perch on the swing to try to talk her out of going back to the city.

"You're one to talk," Joy said. "*You're* leaving. I don't see why. You're not a doctor. It's not as if you can do anything for the old goat."

Molly gave her a baleful look.

"Oh, I didn't mean that. Of course you have to go back to be with Freddie. I'm selfish, I admit it, but I look forward *all year* to spending this time with you, Molly."

"But if you're not even going to be here, what difference does it make if I go home to L.A.?"

"I have to be honest," Joy said.

Ben climbed into Mr. Bailey's old limo next to his grandmother and Gatto.

"Stay here, Bennie. You have a whole day before you have to be back. I don't want to cut your time in the country short."

He shrugged. "Mom's leaving, you're leaving, it's awkward now anyway. Everyone is so upset."

He carried her bag up the steps to the platform.

"You're a good boy," she said, but she might have been talking to the dog.

She was silent then, until they were on the train. "I was having a temper tantrum," she said. "That's all."

"So was Uncle Daniel. And Mom, too."

Ben thought back to his own temper tantrums.

"Do you see red when you get angry?" he asked.

"I think that expression has to do with bulls and the red cape the toreador swishes around."

"But I see red. I always saw red when I had temper tantrums when I was little." A soft dark red screen, behind it the grown-ups above him talking and talking, hollering, but no sound coming through, just the rush of blood in his ears, red blood—that's how he remembered his childhood tantrums. And he'd had quite a few of them.

"At least your father and I don't kick," his grandmother was saying. "You were a kicker."

He sensed that she had started to cry and he turned away, staring out the window at the weedy cliffs rushing by. Then he turned back and wrapped her in his arms and let her weep against his chest. He wondered if this was what it meant to be an adult, to be on the other side of the tantrum.

54

Joy decided she was not speaking to either Danny or Molly.

"I have never played favorites," she told Natalie proudly when she got back to New York. "I'm not going to start now."

Natalie was the only one of the girls in town. She never left New York City, nor could she understand those who did. But since neither Joy nor Natalie wanted to venture out in the heat, they might as well have been in different countries. They were speaking on the phone, each in her air-conditioned bedroom.

"I'm surprised they didn't follow you into town. As chaperones."

"First they want me to stop grieving. Then they think I'm not grieving enough."

Joy was angry, but the silent treatment was difficult for her to maintain. She wondered how Freddie's father was. And she wanted to tell Molly about the deliveryman (the turkey burger she ordered was too dry, but she put sliced tomatoes on it and microwaved it and it was delicious), the same deliveryman she'd given the scarf to. She'd asked if he was cold and wanted another scarf, and they had laughed and laughed. Then, too, she wanted to call Danny to tell him about the letter Ruby had written her and stuffed in her suitcase begging her to send candy to camp immediately, it was an emergency, this way it would be there when Ruby arrived, and it should be flat and hidden inside a magazine or book. Danny had done the same thing when he went to camp. Some things never changed.

Joy gave the telephone a poisonous glance. Never mind. Let them stew.

"She needs space?" Molly said when Ben answered the phone. "What does that mean? She's not my boyfriend. We're not twenty."

"Mom," Ben said, "she needs some time on her own."

"*You're* there."

"Just give her some time. It's hard to be an old Jew, remember?"

Daniel called a few minutes later.

"She's so sensitive. Honestly," he said when Ben said she could not speak to him because she was too upset, and he hung up, his feelings hurt.

Joy was relieved that Karl was still in Rhode Island with his son. She could not imagine speaking to him, either. She was happy when Ben went out. She spent the day quietly, adjusting the air conditioners, looking for her glasses, reading the newspaper, petting the dog. The coffee shop delivered her meals. In the late evening, when it was less hot, she took a short, careful walk, Gatto under her arm. She could not remember the last time she had spent a summer day in the city. She could see the sunset between the buildings.

Coco called to try to make peace. Joy told Ben to tell her she would let her know if and when she was ready to negotiate.

When Freddie called, though, Joy got on the phone.

"I'm so sorry, dear. I hope your father recovers very quickly. It must be a nightmare for you. All that family. Family is a nightmare, isn't it?"

She pictured Freddie surrounded by all her brothers and sisters.

And nieces and nephews. And Molly. Was Molly standing right beside her?

"Is Molly there?"

"Yes. Do you want to talk to her? She's very ashamed of herself. Aren't you, Molly?"

Joy heard a mumbled assent.

"Very," Freddie added.

"Well, then."

"And she misses you. She can't stand it that she hasn't spoken to you."

"She just got off the plane."

"True. We're going straight from the airport to the hospital to see my father."

Joy sat down in the kitchen. There were so few cars on the street. No sirens. She thought of Freddie's father in the hospital, in a coma, unable to speak to his daughters or his sons. And Freddie and Molly going to see him, to stand silently at his silent bedside.

"That's good," Joy said. "Good girls."

And the feud was finished.

55

In the weeks that followed, Duncan's grandchildren and sons and daughters-in-law all returned home, but Pamela and Laurel stayed on. Their father lay unconscious in a hospital bed, and they sat every day, one on either side of him, discussing the disposition of his property. Freddie explained to them that he had no property to speak of, but they spoke of it anyway. There was the jewelry, their mother's jewelry, which had never been distributed. It was costume jewelry, but you never knew. And there were Duncan's watches, vintage watches that had become valuable. Not to mention his life insurance, which was all paid up years ago, and his car.

"He sold the car after his last accident," Freddie said.

"Well, then, the proceeds . . ."

"For scrap. He sold it for scrap. Can we discuss this somewhere else? Or not at all?"

"Oh, he can't hear a thing, can you, Dad?" said Pamela. "And if you could, you wouldn't mind, would you? He certainly can't take care of all these details himself, Freddie."

"We're being practical," Laurel said. "Someone has to."

Freddie went to the hospital every day, too, but one day slid seamlessly into the next, her father the same, his chest moving up with great effort and, then, with equal effort, down. His cheeks had sunk into his skull, he got no better, he got no worse. Her sisters had moved out of their hotel room into his room at Green Garden.

"I know they're going through his things," Freddie told Molly. "It's ghoulish."

Molly was kind and distracted, the distraction perhaps making her kinder than she would ordinarily be. The argument with her mother had shaken her.

"It was only a day, only a little quarrel, I know, but it was almost as if she had died. I don't want her to die. I don't want your father to die. It's a very messed-up system, death. I don't like it at all."

She was gone a lot of the time, too, taking her summer field session students to Catalina Island to drag sensors behind kayaks, measuring the temperature, looking for fresh water feeding into the ocean. The first year she taught this class, one of the students had asked her which ocean it was. This year the group was smart and dedicated, although when she pointed out the bay where Natalie Wood drowned, they asked who Natalie Wood was.

"It made me feel so old," she said.

But she and Freddie both knew that until their parents died, they would still be the children.

56

Joy discovered that she rather liked Manhattan in August. She could see the lightning and hear the thunder and not worry that her power would go out. She could watch the raindrops stain the pavement from six stories above and not wonder if the basement would flood. The early mornings were bearable, and she took Gatto in her bag in one hand, the other bags hooked on Aaron's walker, just to be safe, you never knew, and made her way to Aaron's park to mourn him and, now and then, to silently rail at him as the pigeons cooed and the sparrows chirped. No other people were there, in the park, or on the streets. The city was as quiet as a small town.

The invitations to the bat mitzvah had been sent out last month, but Danny made sure to tell her that one had now been sent to Karl, too. "My response was a little out of proportion" was his way of apologizing. Joy said, "We all mourn in our own ways, Danny. Some of us regress, that's all."

Karl had called her from his son's house. They did not stay on the phone. Men so rarely did. He asked her if she had thought any more about what they talked about. She said she had, and that was true. She had thought about it a great deal. And the more she thought about living with Karl, the more she enjoyed living with Ben. Ben was never there. He went to work during the day and to class in the evening. At night, he was out until the wee hours. Joy saw traces of him, reassuring traces. A mug in the sink. An empty carton of milk put back in the refrigerator.

So when he arrived at the apartment unexpectedly early one afternoon, Joy was surprised but delighted.

"Did you get the afternoon off? We can go out to the early-bird special!"

"My life is ruined," he said, flinging himself onto the couch. He thrashed around a bit, then said, "They want a urine sample."

"For DNA? But they saw you, Ben. The police know it was you. What a waste of city resources."

"No, Grandma, not the city. The law firm. They want a urine sample."

"You and your urine, Ben. Really."

"I have to give it to them today, and you know, I was out last night and so there might be, you know, traces. Of stuff. They'll fire me and I'll never get into law school."

"Stuff? Like drugs? You take drugs? Bennie, Bennie . . ."

"Just weed, Grandma. But it's against their policy and . . ." He took an empty plastic specimen jar from his pocket and looked at it sorrowfully. "I'll have to be a bartender forever."

"Oh, for heaven's sake," his grandmother said. "Give me that." She went in the bathroom and filled it up.

"Here, take this." She was really angry. "Marijuana! As if it's any business of theirs."

57

n the baking, desiccated air of September, Duncan sat up. He demanded to see all his children just once more before he died.

"Die? You just woke up. Slow down, Dad." Freddie was so happy she felt almost sick. She had not expected to hear her father's deep, smooth voice ever again.

The doctors were stunned. He's a tough nut, they kept saying. A tough nut.

"Do this for me so I can die in peace."

Freddie had already called her sisters, still encamped in Duncan's room at Green Garden, and they were on their way.

"They're coming, Dad. Laurel and Pamela are coming from Green Garden."

"The traffic," he muttered, looking at the clock on the wall. "I could be gone before they get here."

As for her brothers, the best Freddie could do was FaceTime them.

Duncan sat up in his hospital bed when they all assembled. He stretched out one pallid skinny arm, tubes dangling from it.

" 'Howl, howl, howl, howl! O! you are men of stones.' "

Someone, one of the brothers on FaceTime, muttered, "This really cannot be happening."

" 'Had I your tongues and eyes,' " Duncan continued, his voice low now, " 'I'd use them so that heaven's vaults should crack.' "

"It's his last performance," Pamela whispered. Laurel nodded, eyes wide.

" 'A plague upon you, murderers, traitors all!' " Duncan roared.

It was a disjointed piece of theater, he spoke only Lear's lines, but it was moving nonetheless. Freddie was tempted to fill in the missing dialogue, but stopped herself. She saw that this was her father's show, and a show it was, Duncan's voice rising and falling with emotion, his arms flung out, then pulled back to his heaving chest.

" 'No, no, no life!' " he cried, turning first to Pamela, then Laurel, to each son's face, one on Freddie's phone screen, one on Molly's. At last he turned to Freddie herself. " 'Why should a dog, a horse, a rat, have life, and thou no breath at all?' "

"I'm breathing, Daddy," she reassured him softly.

But suddenly, it appeared, Daddy was not breathing. He dropped back on his pillows, his mouth agape, his arms hanging from either side of the bed.

There was a hush.

Then Lear opened an eye.

Lauren gasped. "He's not dead."

"Rotten trick, Dad," said Gordon's FaceTime voice. "You scared the living daylights out of us."

Duncan, though pale, trembling, and clearly exhausted, smiled through the fatigue, sat up, and bowed from the waist, first to the left side of the room, then the right, then straight ahead.

Freddie began to clap. What else was there to do? It had been a brilliant performance.

58

The great day arrived. Ruby sat nervously waiting to be called to read her Torah portion. It was a portion full of curses cast on the people, but she could not really blame God—the Israelites were always straying. She had recently seen an old black-and-white movie in which Lassie, actually Lassie's son Bill, a perfect and brilliant collie sheepdog belonging to a young Elizabeth Taylor, accidentally goes off to World War II and comes home with Post Traumatic Stress Disorder, growling at and biting anyone who comes near him, raiding chicken coops, until at last he is reunited with Elizabeth Taylor and regains his calm and loving nature. Ruby had, in the last few days of frantically practicing her Haftorah, begun to confuse the behavior of God and of Bill, both of them essentially good, both of them driven to violence by the misbehavior of human beings. She sensed this must be sacrilegious, the comparison of a dog, however regal, and the god of the Israelites, but the thought was hard to get out of her head once it had planted itself there.

Her sister had wanted to wear a matching dress. Ruby had not had to throw a fit, though she was prepared to do so. Their mother had pointed Cora to a frilly dress she knew Ruby would never have worn, and Cora had fallen for the bait. Ruby was content in a dress her grandmother called elegant. Her mother had been willing to spend quite a bit of money on it, she was so relieved it was not a bejeweled ice-skating costume. "Sophisticated" was the word Ruby used to describe it, and herself, to herself.

She looked down at her grandmother, in the first row, who was rather violently slapping her legs together, then moving them apart, then slapping them together again, staring meaningfully at Ruby. Maybe Grandma Joy had to go to the bathroom. But it was very distracting.

"Why won't Ruby put her legs together?" Joy whispered to Danny. She slapped her own closed again, instructively. "She looks like Sharon Stone, for heaven's sake."

Ruby could not remember much of the actual ceremony. She was aware of the rabbi, her wonderful rabbi, right beside her, a strong and comforting presence. The cantor was wearing perfume, which made Ruby sneeze once. She had no love for the cantor, a cold, shrill taskmaster in soft feminine sheep's clothing. The Hebrew letters of the sacred yellowed scroll came in and out of focus, but the words were there, in her head, in her soul, she realized, and she chanted a little louder, her voice firm and high and only occasionally off pitch.

Karl sat on Joy's other side, murmuring along with the prayers. Danny had insisted Karl sit there, right in front, and that was nice, but Joy's escort was someone else, someone not there; she felt Aaron's absence as if it were a physical presence beside her. She wore sunglasses and cried freely. Aaron, she thought, you would be so proud. Aaron had not been religious, not at all; he had not been brought up with any Jewish education and he claimed to think all religion was superstition. He did not in the least mind singing about Jesus Christ when Purcell or Handel wrote about him, he was as comfortable in a church as in a synagogue, but he would have been happiest now, proud of his granddaughter up there, so brave, so learned. Joy pressed the damp Kleenex to her cheek. Danny was grinning and crying, too. Cora was kicking her feet, but they were in the front row, so she wasn't bothering anyone. Joy wished she believed she would see Aaron again in heaven, but since she did not, she was grateful to think of him here in this place, at this moment, when he would have been so gloriously happy.

The party had no theme. It was a party, a celebration, pure and simple. There were about sixty of them in the restaurant, an old neighborhood Italian place that Ruby had loved since she was a small child. They filled the restaurant. Ruby made sure to thank Manuel, the owner of the corner store she had defaced, for coming. She introduced him and his wife to her Aunt Molly and Aunt Freddie. "I introduced Ruby to the rabbi," Manuel said. He grinned and looked proud, and Ruby made her retreat before he said any more. She took a sip from her mother's glass of champagne and was brushed gently away. Then Ben grabbed her and she was placed on a chair and lifted high in the air, waving regally. It wasn't a horse, and she had been assured by both parents that she would never be getting a horse, but, she thought, up there on the wobbling chair, it was an awfully good ride.

In the car that was driving them back to the Upper East Side, Joy and Karl sat quietly side by side.

"You have a wonderful family," he said.

"I do." She gazed out the window. The Pepsi sign was cursive and bright, the river sparkled with the reflection of the city. Queens. Even Queens was no longer affordable, that's what the young people at the party had been saying.

"I told my sons about you, Joy."

She looked at him in surprise. "Really? What did you say? They were not too pleased, if my children are anything to go by."

"I said I wanted to marry you."

"Oh boy. I bet they didn't like that."

"No, they didn't. They think I've lost my marbles. They were furious." He started laughing. "It was worth it just to hear them sputtering, trying to come up with reasons it would be a bad idea. I told them we would have a prenup of course, and that calmed them down."

"But, Karl honey, did you tell them that I don't want to marry you?"

He shifted, took out his handkerchief, blew his nose, shifted some more. "No."

"Oh."

"Joy, I know it's too soon, and we'll probably both drop dead before it's not too soon . . ."

". . . carried to the altar feetfirst."

Karl laughed and said, "But you never know. In this life you never know."

Outside, on the river, a tugboat pushed a barge. "You know certain things," she said.

"It was very satisfying, at any rate, telling the kids," Karl said. "Put the fear of god into them."

Joy nodded. "Good. That's good. Poor things."

Then she had an idea.

She didn't want to marry him, and she didn't want to live with him, it was true. They were both too old and set in their ways, and her apartment turned out to be just big enough for her and all her mail, and now that she had the dog, she didn't mind staying there alone. But, well, she had feelings for Karl. She did. Strong feelings. She loved being with him, having dinner or sitting beside him in the park. She missed him when they were not together. Karl bracketed her long love for Aaron—on the one side hovered the youthful, passionate Karl and the foggy memories of a college beau, on the other this new foggy tolerant affection for a man in old age.

Marriage, however, even living with him—that was a time together they had missed, a time that could not be recovered.

"No wedding," she said. "No oldies shacking up."

"I know, I know."

But their children, they'd gotten her back up. Who did they think they were, those sons of his, telling Karl he shouldn't marry someone if he wanted to? As for Molly and Daniel, had Karl's presence at the bat mitzvah hurt anyone?

"The children mean well," she said. "But it can be a bit much."

He said, "Amen."

"Well, here's my idea," she said. "We'll get engaged. Just engaged. Nothing decided, nothing certain, no plans, but always that possibility. It's very existential. *And* it'll keep those kids all on their toes."

Karl laughed. He lifted her hand and kissed it. "Joy," he said, "you take my breath away."

A ticket window and a growl from the female functionary. The paint was thick and tired on the walls. The trip down to 2 Washington Street had been a tiring fuss of bumps and jerks, horns, the sputtering of the taxi TV that would not turn off, the smell of the driver's lunch, which he ate as he swore automatically and without passion in his second language. The fare was a shock, and Joy tried to put it out of her mind as she waited for the elevator, waited and waited, then forgot what floor she was going to and guessed the fifth. She was right, there was a sign, and she turned and stood before a counter that had obviously emigrated from Eastern Europe well before the Velvet Revolution. Joy gave Ben's name and handed over the rumpled pink traffic ticket.

"Is this where I belong?" she asked the clerk.

The woman nodded, and Joy said, "But I don't really. I'm here for my grandson. He's back in New Orleans tending bar while he applies to law school. He did very well on the LSATs. So he's not here. But I am his emissary."

The clerk handed her a card with a number and name scribbled on it.

"Where do I go?" Joy asked.

The clerk pointed to a hallway.

In the courtroom, Joy walked down the center aisle. On either side were long benches crowded with people, like a well-attended church, although a round-shouldered resentment permeated the space, a communal almost penal resentment and resignation. Joy found a space far in the back and settled on the hard bench. She was out of breath. She was out of her element. She was out of her mind. She could have been married to a nice old man who loved her and had enough money to keep her safe and warm and fed and to hire someone to wipe the drool from her chin. Aaron, she thought, don't you think I should have said yes? I still could, though it would be so undignified. What do you think, Aaron? But Aaron had no answers for her. Why should he? He was safely out of this vale of tears. Well, enjoy, she said to him. Don't worry about me, left behind in this place where I have no place. Enjoy.

There was a judge in the room, though he was not seated high above them on an elaborate wooden platform as Joy had expected. The bench in this case appeared to be a metal folding chair. In front of the judge, a lawyer stood and seemed to interview each defendant, reading out their names and crimes in a loud ringing voice, asking them questions, then repeating it all to the judge, who sat not more than two feet away.

Joy had dressed for a civic appointment. Her outfit did not fit her as well as she would have liked, that's how much weight she had lost since Aaron's death, but it was respectable, and with her silk scarf, it was quite elegant, she thought. The other traffic offenders had been somewhat less exacting about their clothing. Most of the men were wearing tank-top undershirts, and it was hot for a September day, Joy had to admit. There weren't too many women present, but the ones who were there were also, for the most part, wearing tank tops, though theirs were brightly colored. So many young people had tattooed their arms and shoulders and necks. Joy could see tigers and winking eyes and dragons and flags and long-tailed birds. She was wearing a long-sleeved shirt. She had not a single tattoo. She could not imagine what tattoo she would wear if she chose to wear a tattoo. Her grandchildren's initials? Betty Boop, perhaps.

She was overcome with self-consciousness. I do not belong here. I have no tattoo. I am out of place. My clothing is wrong. No, their clothing is wrong. How dare people come to a public hearing dressed for the beach? But that's how it's done these days, that must be how it's done. I have lost touch with normal social behavior. I no longer know what is expected. And when I find out what is expected, undershirts and tattoos, I do not like it.

I do not belong here. I do not belong anywhere.

A gust of the place's generalized resentment wafted over her for a moment, becoming her own resentment, resentment toward Ben for peeing in the street, resentment toward New York City for giving him no alternative, resentment toward the courtroom full of sweating people in shorts and flip-flops. Then the resentment eased into resignation, the room's other mood, heavier, oppressive. Here I am, she thought, where I don't belong. One more place in which I do not belong. A great spinning globe of places revolved beneath her feet, and not one patch of it was the right patch for her, Joy Bergman.

She thought of the museum, of her job, of Molly and Freddie and their house in California, of her own house Upstate, of her apartment with the windows looking over the white headlights and the red taillights and no one to sit beside to watch them.

The judge, who may or may not have been listening to the lawyer hollering information in his direction, perhaps he was deaf like Joy and all her friends, spoke softly into the lawyer's ear, leaning forward, his hand cuffed over his mouth. He was no spring chicken. There were young men and middle-aged men in the pews, young women and middle-aged women, but there was no one, neither man nor woman, who approached Joy's age, not even the elderly judge.

The big clock on the wall behind the judge proclaimed the time was now 3:39. Three thirty-nine p.m., Eastern Standard Time, Joy thought. Or was it Eastern Daylight Time? When young people said, "This is my time," they meant it was the portion of their lives to treasure and to live fully. When old people said, "This is my time," they meant it was their time to die.

Joy took a juice box from one of her bags, but a guard in a brown uniform shook his head and she put it back. She had already inserted the straw. It would leak.

She waited and watched the tattoos that went by. Some were so elaborate and colorful. She wondered if Ben had a tattoo, a hidden tattoo. So much about a young person's life is hidden. So much about anyone's life. That was a blessing. Other people's secrets were so often tawdry and so rarely surprising, even the most extravagant gossip. Gossip was not what it used to be, which was to say, shocking.

Nothing was shocking anymore because everything was shocking. Public urination. Public urination certainly existed when Joy was young. It must have. But no one knew about it, or talked about it, or asked their grandmothers to go to court about it.

The room was hot and the air was stale. Joy noticed it blurring, first the heads of the people in front of her, then the walls. There was a golden light. Fluorescent light, yellow walls. A blurry room. Oh, a blurry room was never a good sign.

The man next to her said, "You okay, Mommy?" He smiled and fanned her with his *New York Post*.

For a moment she thought he was Danny. Who else would call her Mommy? But he was short and thickset and had a perspiring bald head, and the hand that held the newspaper was hairy and loaded with chunky gold rings. How beautiful that hand looked to her, bringing the gentle breeze.

"You are so kind," she said. "Oh, thank you."

The man on the other side of her offered her a Life Saver. Mint. Perfect. "You feel better, Mommy?" he asked.

"Yes, I do," she said. "You are such gentlemen. Old-fashioned gentlemen."

The room straightened itself out slowly.

Joy sucked on the Life Saver, felt the rim of the circle sharpen, sucked on it until it was a paper-thin sliver.

A man in front of her was called up for a broken taillight. A woman was called for no signal lights.

Oh, Ben, Joy thought. Public urination? Was that really necessary?

A missing muffler.

Bennie, Bennie, Bennie.

The nice man who had given her the mint Life Saver was called up. He squeezed apologetically past her. A missing headlight.

A missing headlight, Ben. A missing headlight. But Ben had always been a difficult child. Sweet. But difficult.

"I'm here for my grandson," she whispered to the gentleman with the *New York Post*.

He smiled.

And then she heard a name. Bea Harkavy. Harkavy was Ben's last name. Bea Harkavy, the clerk said again, even louder. Joy looked at the card the Cold War clerk had given her. There it was. Bea Harkavy.

"No, it's Ben," she said, standing up.

"Bea Harkavy," the clerk called again.

Joy made her way to the center aisle.

"Public urination," the clerk called out loudly.

"It's not me," Joy was saying. "It's my grandson . . ."

And then she looked around at all the men and women whose cars did not have taillights or headlights or side-view mirrors, all the men and women who had made mistakes on their registration papers or had read a form wrong or who had forgotten to mail some paper or who'd just never gotten around to going to the garage to get the muffler fixed, and she thought, This is humanity, all these people with shining sweaty bare shoulders and Life Savers and *New York Posts* folded into fans and excuses and worries and troubles and fines, and here they were all together. Everyone was so kind. Everyone was so helpful. It was really very cosmopolitan. Here she was surrounded by her fellow citizens, part of them, one of them.

"Bea Harkavy," the voice boomed. "Public urination."

"Is that correct?" the lawyer asked Joy.

"Oh yes," said Joy. "This is exactly where I belong."

Acknowledgments

I would like to thank Lynn Swartz Dodd and the USC Wrigley Marine Science Center for sharing Catalina with me; my friend Elizabeth Strout; my editor, Sarah Crichton; my agent, Molly Friedrich; my dearest Janet; and my entire endlessly indulgent and good-humored family.

A Note About the Author

Cathleen Schine is the author of *The Three Weissmanns of West-port*, *The Love Letter*, and *The New Yorkers*, among other novels. She has contributed to *The New Yorker*, *The New York Review of Books*, *The New York Times Magazine*, and *The New York Times Book Review*. She lives in Los Angeles.